PRAISE FOR
PARRIS AFTON BONDS:

"Parris Afton Bonds will satisfy your need for adventurous romance!" —*Romantic Times*

"Parris Afton Bonds has an innate ability to spin a good yarn!" —*Love Lines*

"Ms. Bonds has a knack for creating feisty, headstrong heroines who adore becoming involved in dangerous situations!" —*Romantic Times*

"One of the three bestselling romance authors in the nation today." —*Nightline,* ABC

RELUCTANT LOVERS

Mad Dog turned Modesty to face him. "Thou art a virgin?"

"Find out."

"I mean to." He had really shot himself in the foot this time.

Modesty chewed on her bottom lip. "I suppose, as long as we are married, we might as well make the best of it. I suggest we get this business over with."

"Will you shut up?" He pulled her against him. His fingertips traced both sides of her jaw; then he tilted her head up and kissed her lightly. "'Twill be easier next time."

"That will be a comfort."

Her truculent tone annoyed him. A tough little wench, she was.

"Wot is yewr given name? 'Tis difficult to call yew Mad Dog in bed."

"You may call me any name you desire. I only require that you come when *I* call *you.*"

Parris Afton Bonds
The Savage

LEISURE BOOKS **NEW YORK CITY**

For Lena Pacheco and Keith Yutzy—
you turned drudgery into delight.

And with special thanks to
Scott Hollingsworth, Master Magician

A LEISURE BOOK®

May 1995

Published by

Dorchester Publishing Co., Inc.
276 Fifth Avenue
New York, NY 10001

Cover Art by John Ennis

Printed in the United States of America.

Chapter One

The Virginia Company of London seeks one hundred willing maids for marriage to bachelor planters of James Cittie Colony. Maids must be young, handsome, and honestly educated.

Gingerly, Modesty nudged aside the still-wet blue snuffbox she'd painted so that she could better view the advertisement beneath it. After hours of tedious work, her eyes ached. They were her bane. Needed glasses, she did. And a pair of eyes the same color would be wonderful. One green and one brown was an occasional cause for consternation.

Her stepfather had been ought to say, "'Tis a sure sign of the devil." And her cleft chin a sign of lewdness.

Little wonder her mother died early. If the

7

plague hadn't killed her, her husband's sanctimonious carping would have.

Modesty leaned closer to the broadside. Her nose, which she considered too large for her face, was a thimble's length from the print. Her finger, its nail crusted with blue paint, followed the words. Posted notices for available sailor berths shared space with names of ships in port and a list of merchants' goods that included Moorish slaves and Oriental spices.

Paint fumes blurred her vision, and she pushed away the jar of cobalt blue. She squinted at the broadside's date. March 9, 1620. The announcement was only three days old.

She read further. James Cittie was described as a "thriving towne amidst faire meddowes and goodly tall trees."

The broadside stated that the Virginia Company of London had elected to invest in the importation of the females for the purpose of selling them off to the enormous number of bachelors who could afford to buy a wife.

She made a sound that was half snort and half chuckle. "Young, handsome, and honestly educated," she mused.

Well, at twenty-six, she wasn't young.

If an hourglass figure and fair features were prerequisites for being considered handsome, then she didn't qualify in that category either.

Her nocturnal activities would certainly discredit her claim to honesty.

That left the attribute of "educated." Aha. Now that was a quality to which her stepfather could attest, bless his shriveled soul.

Thomas Fanshaw had been a harsh taskmaster. Her fingers and her shoulders had smarted enough under his razor strap when her penmanship went awry or her scribbled sum was not the correct total. Thanks to his pious and exacting nature, she could recite the books of the Bible and quote its scripture. He had been a chorister in the Canterbury cathedral, a fact that hardly determined her life path. Or just mayhap it did.

When Thomas Fanshaw had allowed the village vicar, an Anglican with a strong puritan bent, to order an awl driven through the tongue of her brother Robby for swearing, she forsook both society's God and its religion.

She sighed. To dwell with regret on the past was foolish. The hour was late, nearly four in the morning. At this rate, she would get less than four hours sleep before she exchanged her painter's smock for an alehouse maid's apron.

She picked up the paintbrush, dipped it in the jar, and went back to work on her latest masterpiece: transforming Lord Pemberton's black snuffbox, embossed with his gold seal, into a blue one festooned with a fairy ring.

With a goodly measure of pride, Modesty considered herself one of the best of London's craftsmen in the art of camouflaging or altering watches, seals, rings, and other valuable stolen items.

* * *

Located between Fleet Street and the Thames, Modesty's derelict, run-down neighborhood, the Bridewell Dock area, with its narrow courts and alleyways, was the haunt of all manner of thieves, strumpets, and cutthroats who disposed of their victims' bodies in the stinking River Fleet at night. Every day Modesty saw these lowlifes pass through the Bridewell Dock Grog Shop's battered door. Even at this time of morning, nearing the tenth hour, the alehouse—the remains of a portion of an old Saxon castle—reeked of cheap drink, stale vomit, and piss.

Few heads turned when Modesty spotted the rakishly dressed Handsome Jack Holloway stroll in. Most of the alehouse occupants, as well as Modesty, knew Jack for what he was— a skilled pickpocket and a fencer of stolen goods.

In spite of rewards offered for information of his whereabouts, Jack swaggered around in flamboyant finery. Wearing a ruffled white silk shirt, red velvet suit, silver-hilted sword, diamond rings on every finger, and a gold watch dangling from his waistcoat, he cut a dashing figure.

Through the white haze of pipe smoke, his bright blue eyes found Modesty. She set the tin cup of ale before one sour-faced patron and waited for Jack to wend his way to her through the maze of God's neglected souls.

Jack employed a team of artists to alter stolen valuables and owned several warehouses for the storage of these goods. She sincerely liked her nocturnal employer. He might cheat, steal, and lie, but he was the gentlest of souls. Wouldn't harm a cockroach. She was lucky to work for him.

Yes, between the alehouse and her artistry, she was most fortunate. She had a roof over her head and food in her belly. Security was hers.

Jack wasn't smiling, and she suspected her news wouldn't cheer him any. He might find her repartee entertaining, but she sensed that now was not the time for salty byplay. Bluntly, she told him, "The snuffbox isn't finished."

"We are." His mouth, as mobile as his hands, was set in grim lines. "We've been fingered. I'm just one step ahead of the bailiffs."

Fear robbed her of her breath. She had no desire to be shackled in leg irons.

Jack grabbed her shoulders and shook her lightly. "Modesty! You're gawking like a simpleton. We've got to do something! Quick!"

She focused on his face, where a roguish mouth warred for dominance with a deceptive angel-innocent gaze. Was it genuine concern that showed this time in those thick-lashed eyes? "I am. I'm getting married."

"My felicitations," he said without missing a beat, which was so like Jack. He was adaptable, a mark of their profession.

Gallant even in the face of calamity, he made a leg, then began to saunter back past the noisy tables of clothed primates. When the alehouse door swung open once more to reveal two burly men, he pivoted in the opposite direction. "Hide me!" he mouthed at her.

"The taproom." She nodded toward the rear of the alehouse. If luck was with him, and it usually was, he might appropriate an empty cask for temporary living quarters.

As Jack beat a retreat for the taproom, Lemuel, the slovenly alehouse keeper, sidled up to her and said, "High Sheriff's officials from the looks of them."

"No doubt here to monitor yewr ale." The publican was an adept at watering down the ale with lime.

But one of the Crown's two ruffians was pointing her out to his partner. Casually, she removed her stained apron and tossed it on a counter slick with sludge and littered with flat-sided bottles. "I'm on me way to the Virginia Colony, Lemuel."

He stared at the two, now weaving through the alehouse's patrons toward her. "I'd say ye be on 'oor way to Newgate."

"No time for fond faretheewells then." She sprinted to the taproom, saw that the only available cask was occupied, and sped on toward the back door, which opened onto an alley that was home to rats, vagabonds, and odorous garbage. Negotiating the narrow way speedily could be tricky. Slime, rotten food, and raw sewage threatened to impede her flying feet.

In back of her, she heard shouts for her to halt.

Incarceration in Newgate Prison, where the

vice, drunkenness, immorality and filth far exceeded her present circumstances and where prisoners died off like flies from jail fever—well, the images spurred her even faster.

She picked up her skirts, hopped over a derelict drunk, and dodged a chamber pot being emptied from a second-story window. The alley abutted the Fleet Ditch, a tributary of the Thames. Twenty thousand boats, from heavy barges and scuttling river ferries to the towering fortresses of the East Indian Company, blocked her view—and her escape.

With nothing to lose, she jumped into a skiff moored in the ditch. The skiff lurched dangerously. From the skiff, she bounded onto a barge. Then she gathered every ounce of her might to vault to the opposite bank—a span that not even a chimney sweep would attempt. And she made it!

"Ta da!" she called to her two pursuers, waved a grimy hand, and hurried on toward Guildhall.

Opposite the Quarter Moon Grog Shop and a row of shops, Guildhall was thronged with the unemployed who were often subject to imprisonment.

After a few questions, she found the room designated as the Board of Trade and Plantations. "I am here to apply for the position of bride, as advertised by the Virginia Company of London," she breathlessly told the magistrate, who stared at her over his bulbous nose.

Her hair had come loose from her pins during her mad dash, and tangled wisps straggled from beneath her dingy white cap to her shoulders. Her red, cheap satinet skirts were splashed with muck. She and the satinet had both seen better days.

"You meet the qualifications?" he inquired, his brows arched in skepticism.

"As God is me witness, yewr lordship."

She might not be young, handsome, or honest but she was shrewd—and desperate. So the opportunity to marry a planter who lived at the edge of the world was God-sent.

Not that she believed in God, of course.

Chapter Two

Hardly had the *God Sent* begun its voyage before a storm lashed the Atlantic. With such a name for a vessel on which she was a passenger, Modesty reckoned she should have expected the foul weather. The wind shrieked and the storm was so violent that the vessel tossed helplessly like a piece of driftwood upon the ocean. In the hold, Modesty felt the ship roll over to its gunwales, then rise up only to pitch forward again in a steep dive.

Conditions in the hold deteriorated rapidly. The galley fires remained washed out, and hot meals were out of the question. Cold, dampness, and putrid air pervaded 'tween decks. Water seeped below to add to the misery. The bilge water stagnated, and the stench was indescribable. In addition, the lack of privacy equaled that of the animals on the Ark.

The one hundred maids confined in between decks with Modesty no longer had the strength to brace themselves to meet each roll and pitch of the *God Sent*. They were crowded into the chill, dark, and bleak spaces to lay out their bedding wherever they could find room. Undernourished and far too seasick even to look at cold food, they lay uncaring in their wet and soiled bedding.

All but Modesty, who was wedged between Rose Crackston and Annie Brewster. They moaned. She hummed. A ditty whose stanza came unbidden to her lips.

> "In the sprightly month of May,
> When all smells sweet and looks so gay,
> There tripp'd along a buxom lass,
> With a milk-pail o'er—"

"Me ass!"

Modesty smiled serenely at the tall, gaunt, and big-boned Annie. The recent widow from a remote East Devon village looked a ghastly green. Beneath a dirty and wilted coif, the eighteen-year-old's hennaed locks were a matted mess. "No, Annie. Not yewr ass. The grass. 'With a milk-pail o'er the grass.' "

Annie let out a rumbling, good-natured laugh.

The ship's bell marked the hour of the watch. Modesty counted six strokes before being interrupted by Rose's groan.

"Oh, me stomach!"

Hastily, Modesty rolled onto her left side, away from the tiny, swarthy, and plain brunette. Rose was a wool carder from the Middlesex countryside who wanted to better her lot.

As did most of the maids aboard the ship. All but the delicate-featured Clarissa Lockridge. She had a wonderful oval face, remarkable for its harmony of lines. Beneath an embroidered coronet, her hair, the shade of a gold florin, was brushed smoothly back at her nape, where it was gathered into a lovelock that draped over one shoulder. Her bertha was of the finest lace, her gown of blue silk fastened fashionably down the front with silver ribbon bows. All of which told Modesty that the Lady Clarissa could not better her lot by much.

Modesty counted herself lucky that the Company kept no registry of people going to the colony. In fact, she was happy just to be alive, which was doubtlessly more than she could say for Handsome Jack Holloway.

If jail fever didn't get him first, the gallows would. Last she had heard of him, after his capture at the Bridewell Dock Grog Shop he had been slapped in leg irons and handcuffs for trial at Old Bailey.

She considered her present plight. Since running away from home at twelve, after the deaths of her mother and brother, she had managed to survive many a scrape. In London, she had taken lodgings with an old Irish woman, who introduced her to a group of cutpurses and pickpockets, who in turn introduced her to Jack of the short yellow locks.

Many a lass had her head turned by Jack Holloway. But not she. She wanted something more solid, something of more substance than a mere angel. Like shillings and silver candlesticks and soft beds and sumptuous meals. Security, they were.

If the stories were true, that the lonely and homesick men of Jamestown Colony outnumbered the women fifteen to one, then her hodgepodge looks of a too-wide mouth, mismatched eyes, stringent jaw, high-bridged nose, thick brows, and, of course, the cleft chin would be of little consequence.

Having been blown off course, the *God Sent* took four months to arrive at its destination, and Modesty smelled land before she saw it. A smell of sweet perfume.

Yet her first look at the Virginia shoreline was not very promising: gray skies, rain, heavy breakers pounding the beach. But once the ship reached the wide mouth of the James River, the rain ceased and the water quieted. Everything quieted.

August's heavy scents lay over the alien land. Despite the faint breeze, perspiration broke out on her face and under her arms, where sweat stains already ringed her gray lutestring dress. She swatted absently at tiny, stinging pests that attacked her exposed flesh. The ship's crew said these vermin were called *muskeetos* by the Indians.

The utter isolation of the landscape made her uneasy. Great oaks, junipers, and pines shadowed the shoreline. What savages lurked there? Rumors aboard ship were that more than 12,000 Indians roamed the primeval forests.

Vaguely, she recalled tales of the visit of the Indian princess, Pocahontas, to London four years earlier. Ironically, the poor girl, barely twenty or so, had grown up in an uncivilized state only to die in London of smallpox.

As the ship sailed up the silent and deep tidewater river, Modesty noted that the flat shoreland was bordered by virgin forests. At one point, a slothful river channel meandered into a swamp with bleached skeletons of long-dead trees. A shiver rippled up her spine. What had she gotten herself into?

Occasional clearings that exposed one-room frame cottages with steep thatched roofs were more reassuring. The sight of a two-story, brick-and-timber home indicated a prosperous plantation and gave her and the other maidens hope. Crowded against the main deck and half deck railing, she and her companions speculated about the plantation's crops, although tobacco seemed to be the general guess and was confirmed and pointed out to them by one of the crew. The maidens speculated more so on its owner. Would they be among the fortunate to land one of the wealthier bachelors?

"As long as he isn't some ignorant lout," Clarissa said, stifling a yawn with a porcelaneous hand. "I would that I had a husband who will not bore me."

If Modesty had to marry, it seemed to her that her best course of action would be to marry an old gent. An old rich gent. One not long for earthly pleasures. One she could manage with a sweet smile, a soothing hand, and soft words. A few months in a pastoral exile, then back to glorious London it would be. By that time and with a little luck, the furor over her would have been long forgotten.

At last, late in the afternoon, the sea-weary vessel rounded a peninsula and a turf fort came into view. By squinting, she could make out the steeple of a church rising reassuringly among the backdrop of trees. Civilization!

Immediately, the maids began primping. With wry amusement, Modesty watched them tuck in errant curls, pinch their pallid cheeks to elicit a becoming flush, and smooth down wrinkled but clean skirts.

Like the other maids, she had been provided with two changes of clothing by the Virginia Company of London when she signed a contract agreeing to marry a colonist. Once the colonist purchased the marriage contract, which paid the Virginia Company's representative for the cost of a maid's clothing, food, and transportation, then a wedding service would be performed.

Modesty thought the bridal convoy the most woebegone of women as she had learned much about them during the long voyage. She looked at Rose whose small body now showed she was with child. If she didn't wed before the child's birth, Church law prescribed that she be publicly whipped. That the father went unpunished, Modesty considered justification for her disgust with the Church.

Then there was Annie who had been in Ludgate Prison, supposedly for murdering her husband. Another female was feebleminded, taken straight from Bedlam Hospital. Most of the young women were like herself, hard women who had known hard lives. Mayhap, Modesty thought, they were perfect for this outpost of the English empire, after all.

She had learned from the crew that Jamestown's prime attractions were that it was far enough inland to be safe from attack by the Spanish and its deep-water shoreline serviced the largest of sea-going vessels. Unfortunately, the colonial capital had been established in a swampy area, and the wells were contaminated with salt at high tide.

The number of dugouts, barges, shallops, scows, and ships of sail anchored before the waterfront town was both reassuring and a cause for concern. Virginia was notorious in England for her thirst for liquor, and the barks and brigs were said to be moving taverns. Modesty had been told that women were scarcer even than liquor and fetched a higher price.

Ships' crews and their captains, indentured servants wearing pothook iron collars welded around their necks, traders, soldiers with pike-staffs, and other ordinary-looking men congregated on the wharf or before the warehouses outside the triangular fort's timbered gates.

The broadside that Modesty had read the night she'd worked on the snuffbox had reported a population of almost 1,300 people spread over the Virginia Colony. To the east of the fort was a community of cottages, which had outgrown the fort's fifteen-foot-high palisades. Some of these new homes were two-storied timbered houses, and the governor's residence was said to be there.

She saw few females, which may have explained why the men stopped to stare as she and the other women were welcomed ashore by one of the Lord Commissioners of Trade and Plantations.

Dressed in a silver-buttoned coat with skirts that flared to the thighs, he had eyes like red coals. They seemed to inventory each maid as a personal investment, a commodity.

Modesty knew she had met this man before. Those eyes, the way they instantly filed away a person's shortcomings reminded her of a specific incident. But what?

When he removed his feathered hat with its cocked brim to fan himself against the heat, she saw the crest of prematurely white hair and recognized Richard Ratcliff. In her opinion even the most ill-informed Londoner knew that Ratcliff had been a formidable member of the Star Chamber, an infamous branch of the judiciary

22

answerable only to the king. A dissolute heir of the former comptroller general of finances, the highly intelligent Ratcliff was accustomed to debauchery and could not do without it. From personal experience, she knew this gossip to be well-founded.

Licentious, he was given to all sorts of vices, gambling being one of his fancies. He was gifted at cards. Too gifted. His cardsharping had won for him priceless paintings that he had collected with discrimination, rare tapestries, and even a London townhouse.

She recalled encountering Ratcliff at the Duke of Lauderdale's Ham House the year before. Jack had insinuated her in as a serving maid for the duke's garden party. Jack had employees trained to steal from churches, others to attend at court on birthdays and balls, and others who specialized in thieving from both Houses of Parliament.

At Ham House, she had seen Ratcliff openly fondling the Duke of Lauderdale's helpless link-boy. When later she had spotted Ratcliff, who was gambling at piquet, palm a card—a technique Jack had taught her—she had decided that an act of God was called for.

Playing the country bumpkin, she had instantly blurted, "Oh, sire, yew picked up two cards by mistake, didn't yew now, Master Ratcliff?"

Exposed for a cheat, he faced the wrath of the duke and was banished from polite society as well as relieved of his privileged position in the Star Chamber.

As for herself, she had made sure that she had avoided the fashionable areas of London for a while; and now she averted her face as she passed by the depraved Ratcliff.

She and the other brides-to-be, portmanteaus and small chests in hand, entered the palisaded fort. It enclosed forty or fifty thatched houses as well as a few two-story framed timber houses.

After all those months at sea, the first thing Modesty noticed was odors. She sniffed freshly baked bread and ginger cookies, bayberry wax melting for candle dipping, sawdust from the new buildings under construction, and an apothecary's herbs.

Beneath a huge Flanders tent were vegetables or fruits, she wasn't sure which, mounded or stacked on blankets. Strange-looking foods. But food! Fresh food! Few people milled about to examine the wildly colored foods or make their purchases. Almost everyone's attention was centered on the women's arrival.

"A naked man!" gasped Polly, a carter's plump daughter with stringy mouse-brown hair.

Amidst the outbreak of feminine giggles, Modesty glanced in the direction the girl pointed. There were, in fact, several partially naked men. Their swarthy skin and half-shaven heads with a single plait of hair proclaimed them Indians. Some kind of hide girded their loins and shod their feet. Some were obviously drunk. Others squatted sullenly and stared at the procession.

Rapidly, more and more male colonists gathered to watch and cheer. The currier put aside his moon knife and pincers to stand at his doorway. A man in a blood-speckled apron raised his butcher's cleaver in a jolly salute. A pot-helmeted soldier wearing a sweltering shirt of mail waved a gauntleted hand. Two bowlers on the green deserted their game to follow the women.

"Damn me, if they don't think this is a public show," Annie remarked at Modesty's side.

The ogling glances and whistling and cheering didn't bother Modesty. What she saw did. Or rather, what she did not see. No soaring spires of lead and wood such as adorned St. Paul's Cathedral, no graceful arches that braced London Bridge with its row of shops, no rounded columns that supported pleasant balconies.

Not counting a blockhouse, a powder house, and a munitions house, she saw only numerous grog shops and stick-and-straw houses. Street after street of them, wherever tobacco wasn't planted. Pigs and chickens ran wild across the grounds.

She stared stupidly at her surroundings and at the men who one by one followed the stream of flustered young women along one of the narrow streets filled with pungent odors of frying fish, boiling cabbage, and melting lard.

The procession halted at a long, wooden

building set on a broad green which appeared to Modesty to be a council hall. "The State Building," a stocky male volunteered eagerly to one inquiring maid. Built of timber on brick and cobble foundation, it was more substantial than the others within the fort and was flanked by tall yaupons.

When they entered, Modesty saw that benches occupied most of the room, with several tables flanking a desk at the front of the room. Behind the desk, the official great seal of the Virginia Company of London was affixed to the wall.

She followed the other women as they filled the benches, and the male colonists, hats in hands, crowded two and three deep along the walls. They were romantics, these Virginians, Modesty thought. They were treating the women like priceless objects. No Englishman did.

In place of padded breeches, knee-length coats, and waistcoats, most of the colonists wore more serviceable clothing the color of the forest's natural dull shades of brown and green: doublets, jerkins, surcoats, and tabards. All were armed with dirks, broadswords, blunderbusses, and flintlock pistols.

Attempts made at keeping their hair short, as was the style back in England, had resulted in some hacked and chopped cuts. To Modesty, their faces mirrored yearning and open hunger at the mere sight of the white women. She wondered how many men were left of the original

105 males who had first cleared the somber forests in 1607, thirteen years earlier.

Feverish murmurings of the king's English, Irish, and Gaelic, which Modesty had occasionally overheard in London, as well as the guttural-sounding Indian language, crescendoed to babbling confusion.

Modesty eyed the scurvy lot of men. The Indians she had glimpsed looked healthier than they did. She searched for some tottering old geezer but found mostly young, lean faces. Apparently, only the hardiest survived the harshness of wilderness life.

A foppish man in two-inch heels adjusted his red waistcoat as he hurried down the center aisle. Once behind the desk, he cleared his throat and identified himself as the colonial governor, Sir George Yeardley. He had a little pointed beard and a waxed mustache that curled up at the ends.

"On behalf of our men, I warmly welcome our new arrivals. We realize you are hungry and weary. Tonight, you will be quartered here, at the inn, and in our church, and tomorrow—"

"Tomorrow begins the courtships!" a lusty male voice called out from the back and was followed by further cheers from the men.

Their excitement was interrupted by the London Company representative, who rose from behind the table to the left of the governor and gave a perfunctory smile. Ratcliff's long teeth betokened his name. Modesty kept her head down as he spoke. "I remind you of the Company rules: that a female has the right of choice, has three days in which to comply with her contract, and can choose only one groom."

A titter of nervous laughter erupted as the women were assigned their sleeping quarters. Modesty was not one of the sixteen brides-to-be selected to sleep at the large half-completed inn on Back Street but was shepherded to the log church. Fortunately, it was a more substantial shelter, though austere didn't do full justice to the description of its interior. At least the small wavy-glass panes mounted in the leaded lattice windows permitted daylight.

A hot meal of maize, squash, and stewed tomatoes, food new to Modesty and the other women, was provided by the few Company wives. "Prithee, do try my bread pudding," urged a little guinea hen of a woman who identified herself as Mistress Priscilla.

Modesty needed no urging. Just the smell of the hickory-smoked ham made her mouth water.

Clarissa's table manners were refined, but she was finicky about what she ate from the shared wooden trenchers.

Rose ate little, Polly licked her fingers with a sigh of ecstasy, and Annie kept up a running stream of talk while she ate.

Her mouth full, she said, "The Company has paid for our transportation, and ye can bet your bones it's going to demand its pound of flesh."

Modesty quenched her thirst from a leather

28

noggin of ale shared by all of them. "As long as 'tis not me own flesh."

Another Company wife, Mistress Pierce, was a wiry woman who appeared to be forty or more with hair as white as her widow's cap. She claimed she had married a captain in the military and had lived at Jamestown over ten years now. Her husband had died, but she had over sixty acres to sustain her.

"Planted with corn, wheat, and peas, they be. None of this tobacco that offers nought for the belly.

"Ye must ask your suitor how many acres he has cleared. Does his house have a floor? And how many rooms? Any livestock? Cattle? Swine? A man with a horse—aye, even a slow-footed saddle horse—well, he will be a goodly catch."

"Unless he be a drunkard," the raw-boned Annie retorted to Mistress Pierce's advice. "Had meself a lout of a husband who took delight in his cups. Then he would get mean."

Modesty closed a prison door on the memory of her stepfather and his penchant for taking the strap to her. Yes, better she find an old man too helpless to lift a cup—or a strap.

"Ye mean ye're already married?" the moon-faced Polly asked.

With a deep-throated chuckle, Annie cast the circle of women a broad wink. "Me husband died of a fall, he did. Courts didn't believe me story, though."

At last, the goodwives retired to their own

homes, and Modesty and her companions settled down to sleep on their pallets spread on the white pine flooring. Modesty was restless. A solitary candle burned low on the church altar, but it wasn't the flickering light that disturbed her. At first it was the utter quiet, broken only by the acrid sputtering of the tallow candle.

Then it was the noisy night sounds of birds, of giant frogs that Mistress Pierce had called bullfrogs, crickets clicking, and a caterwauling that the old goodwife had attributed to pumas.

Rose touched her shoulder. "Modesty, are ye awake?"

"No. Of course I am."

"I'm scared. About the morrow. I would that I 'ad a man court me out of love. Not necessity."

"Love is for fools. Get yewrself an unambitious soldier, Rose. He has a pension. If yew be lucky, he'll get killed, and yew can collect it and return to lovely London to marry a man who isn't a pauper and raise yewr child civilized-like."

"Oh, ye can't mean that about marrying a soldier in 'opes 'e'll die," the olive-skinned woman said. "Ye sound so serious when ye joke, Modesty."

" 'Tis a Rose of Sharon ye are," she muttered and rolled over onto her side, hoping to fall asleep.

Clarissa's mellow voice intervened. "What if a maid does not find someone pleasing to her? What then?"

"Out of several hundred men ye could not find

30

a single man to please ye? Ye must be daft," Annie scoffed.

Modesty rolled onto on her back, her hands clasped behind her head, as she stared up into the darkened rafters. "The trick is to find a husband who will dance to yewr tune."

Clarissa sat erect, her arms wrapped around her drawn-up knees. "There has to be a way out!" Her smoky contralto voice had the plaintive cry of a caged bird.

Modesty studied Clarissa's profile. The young woman of quality had violet eyes that immediately attracted one's attention. Modesty's dealings with London's seamier underside had taught her to read people. The hint of willfulness about Clarissa's mouth suggested that she was accustomed to having her way. Of all the women only she had come with a trunk of the finest clothes and accessories, like those of a trousseau.

"Yew are escaping a marriage not to yewr liking, aren't yew?" Modesty asked, hazarding a guess. Doubtless to a tottering rich old gent, just the kind of marriage she herself sought.

Clarissa's small, oval chin nodded in affirmation.

Too bad she couldn't change places with Clarissa, Modesty thought. But not even a silk dress and fine manners would make her into what she was not.

She was a child of the streets who had been robbed of all illusions. In a society where only the strongest survived, she had only her mediocre talent of art and her worldly knowledge of human nature to barter—

"That's it!" she said, springing to a sitting position.

"What's it?" Rose asked.

"We need someone to barter the best marriage arrangement for ourselves. A marriage broker!"

She hurried on, her words spilling out barely ahead of her thoughts. "Think about it. 'Tis *yewr* choice. Why not make the best arrangement possible—accept only the proposals of those bachelors who can offer yew something in exchange besides years of hard work?" She thought of the independent Mistress Pierce with her own sixty acres. "Land, animals, conditions to yewr liking—all these can be arranged for yew."

"What if . . . what if I want a marriage that doesn't require . . . " Clarissa tried again, her expression set in determined lines. "I love someone else. A poet. I couldn't imagine giving my maidenhead to any but Nigel Jarvis. Especially not to the old Duke of Clarence."

Modesty's mouth crimped in exasperation. "Surely yew knew what would be expected of yew once yew signed that marriage contract."

"I didn't think. I had no time to make other plans."

"And I wager yew relied on the two things that had always helped yew out of uncomfortable situations before—yewr wealth and beauty. Well, they're useless here." She was feeling irritated with Clarissa and slightly sorry for herself. Wasn't she in the same tight spot?

"I only knew that I had to find a way to stall," Clarissa explained. "My father arranged to have Nigel sent to Marshalsea for two years."

Modesty knew that the prison was used mainly for pirates and debtors. "Obviously, yewr poet is no pirate."

"He was imprisoned for penning pagan sonnets."

Modesty rubbed her chin, then snapped her fingers. "That's it! It could be stipulated in the marriage arrangement that no"—she searched for the biblical word—"no connubial relations with yewr husband would be required."

"Three acres," Annie said. "That's what I want for meself. Like Mistress Pierce."

"But we already have contracts," Rose pointed out with a yawn and blinked her eyes sleepily.

"Contracts to marry the men of **our** choice. Nothing was said against our making the terms of our marriage."

Clarissa pushed her tumbled doubloon-colored curls back from her face. "Who would we find among the rabble of this godforsaken outpost to act as a marriage broker?"

Modesty's smile was barely modest. "Why, meself."

On the morrow, more men streamed into the fort. Modesty estimated there had to be at least 600 men, as thick as the mosquitoes, swarming after the women in Market Square, the scene of the courting.

The day had dawned hot and humid and grew only more so as Modesty and a score of other young women clustered beneath a palmetto-roofed shed used to cure tobacco. Like most Londoners, Modesty knew that up until now Jamestown had served as a market for the sale of white Englishmen and Irishmen into servitude. But today it was marriage contracts being sold.

She saw the maids coyly eye the swains and whisper among themselves in frivolity. She had instructed the women with whom she had billeted the night before to look and ask questions to their hearts' content but to give no pledge today. That evening, they would discuss whom they were attracted to and what requirements they desired in exchange for marriage. Then, the following day she would begin negotiations.

Modesty watched as, their hats doffed, some of the men bashfully drew near enough to talk, then drifted away to the shade of long-beaned catalpa trees. From their gestures and the occasional words she overheard, they were discoursing among themselves about the merits of the maids. Other bachelors scrapped like dogs over a bone.

"Good teeth and skin," Modesty heard remarked about herself. Then another in a baggy brown tradesman suit replied, "But flat as a bed slat. Give me a pair of strong hands—"

"—and a pair of melons to match," another

34

man finished with a bawdy gesture and a purely masculine snort.

Modesty knew she had not Polly's ample bosom, and as for strong hands . . . she glanced down at her slender hands, hands that had done little besides wash an ale tankard or wield a paintbrush.

For her part, she measured the men who passed by and found them wanting. Never would there be one as handsome as Jack. Nor as fascinating. Nor as much a scoundrel.

If she had calculated correctly, she figured that with a commission from each arranged marriage she could buy back her marriage contract from the Virginia Company. An acre here, a couple of swine there—why, in time she could return to London to live out the rest of her life in security.

However, it was not for herself she needed to study the men but for the women for whom she had agreed to negotiate marriage contracts. She felt obligated to obtain the best terms for each of them.

She surveyed young men, middle-aged ones, tall ones and short ones. Spindly ones and squat ones. Here was a man who bore the mark of childhood smallpox upon his cheeks; there was one who limped.

But it was the expressions and gestures she studied closely. The man who punched the palm of one hand with the fist of the other—a browbeater. The one with a thin mouth—definitely a stingy soul.

The man in a simple snuff-brown suit who rubbed his palms—here was an opportunistic sort. A young man with his head ducked could be timorous . . . or hiding something maybe even he didn't want to face. The downturned lines around one man's mouth indicated a cantankerous spirit.

Lechery glinted in another's eyes. One man's eyebrows that curved upward bespoke possible humor.

She interviewed a bumptious shipwright, an impertinent glassblower, and a cooper who wiped his nose on his sleeve.

Then a man who had a face like a cliff, the somber gaze of an ascetic, and a libertine's sensuous mouth introduced himself as Reverend Patrick Dartmouth from the tiny upriver settlement of Henrico. His rangy frame was clothed in black broadcloth with a puritan's white bibbed collar, and a black hat with a high crown topped his head.

At the sight of the gold buckle that adorned his hat, she had to repress a smirk. For all their piety, these Anglican parsons with their puritan streak lived with gusto. She shuddered, thinking that the exacting hand of the Anglican Church stretched across even 3,000 miles of water.

"Greetings, mistress." He removed his hat, and sandy hair fell across his forehead. "I hope thou finds Jamestown to thy liking."

She shrugged. "Neither Jamestown nor its men."

His full mouth curved gently. "Ahh, then. I shall have to seek a wife elsewhere."

She regretted her harsh words. She had not thought a man of the cloth would be buying a wife. "Come to me on the morrow, good sir. I shall have a perfect wife for yew."

Plenty of men yet thronged the marketplace. The day was only half gone, and another day was left to make selections. The determined males were like rutting bucks and were beginning to press Modesty and the still-unattached women for answers.

"Modesty!"

She turned. It couldn't be. Jack Holloway. A scraggly beard hid his handsome face. He started toward her in a shuffle and came up short. She noticed then the chains that bound his ankles—and bound him to the man-beast next to him.

Jack managed to make a jaunty bow and flash her that familiar droll smile. "Modesty, my dear, let me present you to the gentleman whose fluid eloquence convinced the rabid governor of Jamestown that I shouldn't be broken on the wheel for the theft of his purse—Mad Dog Jones, my master."

Modesty's gaze shifted to the long-haired savage who could have been anywhere between thirty and forty years of age. His great mane of tawny-brown hair fell well below his massive shoulders.

He was wearing clothing right off the backs of animals. After only a short time in the colony, she had learned to identify the wierd wilderness clothing to which the Indians and a few settlers resorted. This man's fringed hunting shirt of supple deerhide hung halfway down his thighs and was confined by a cincture tied behind his waist. Suspended from the cincture on his right was a flintlock pistol of large bore, a knife on his left, a bullet bag in front. At his right side was a big pouch hanging from a shoulder strap. Tied to the same strap above the pouch was a powder horn.

Her startled gaze dropped lower. He wore only knee-high leather moccasins and an Indian breechclout. His bare thighs had the girth of bronze cannons.

His imposing size, his leonine head, his fierce visage—she might not believe in God, but at that moment she believed in the devil.

Chapter Three

"A confederate of yours?" Mad Dog Jones asked his newly purchased indentured servant. The woman in question had been sharply summoned back to the palmetto shed by an irate Ratcliff.

There were ladies of quality and there were ladies of the street. This woman with her too-bold manner obviously belonged to the latter category, an uncommon sort who was part of the Virginia Company's enterprise on behalf of Hymen. Of the women from the *God Sent* that Mad Dog had glimpsed, few would inspire sonnets of rapture. Discounting, perhaps, the fair maiden known as Clarissa.

"Modesty Brown is an . . . acquaintance," his bondsman said. The man's eyes, the clear blue shade of Santo Domingo's baywaters, managed a twinkle, which was one of the reasons Mad Dog had pled for the scrawny felon's life and then bought his indenture papers. The other was the man's will to live. Mad Dog had seen it in the felon's eyes like a falling star flashing through the night sky, and he thought Jack Holloway might just defy the odds of surviving in Jamestown.

Mad Dog was aware that the London Company calculated that six people out of every seven who came to the colony died within the first year of their arrival.

He knew from his own experience that before the emigrants boarded the ships at London, Southampton, or Bristol, many of them already suffered from malnutrition, jail fever, and other communicable diseases. And conditions on the ships didn't contribute to their health.

Few adjusted well to the colony's torpid climate. Furthermore, Jamestown's small port was located in the midst of marshlands and swamps. The plague of mosquitoes, innumerable rats, brackish water, lack of nutritional crops, and, of course, the ever-present menace of the Indians didn't help.

Arriving during the sickly season, June through August, was as bad as a death sentence. People came down with what the colonists called the sleeping sickness, the desire to sleep all the time. Mad Dog thought it more a disease of the mind than of the body. The colony was overpraised in England. Upon seeing it, most immigrants went into a decline of spirit. Being predominantly male, the immigrants had no family life; nearly all of them were lonely if not homesick. The will to live was not strong in such defeated men. Or women.

He studied the woman, in spirited discussion with Ratcliff. Some sort of arguing was afoot. She looked to be as rapscallion as they came, but she was no match for the cloven-hoofed Ratcliff. River gossip of Ratcliff's arrival in the colony two years before had reached Mad Dog at his homestead, but he had not seen the man until today. Now all the old rage Mad Dog thought he had left behind in another country, another world, came flooding back. He battled back his emotions and refocused on the woman. "Well, your friend Mistress Brown will be most fortunate if she survives the Year of Seasoning."

"The woman is the most skilled of artists," Holloway said.

"A pickpocket artist, most likely." He caught Holloway eyeing him with wary regard and said, "I've seen it all."

"How did you get the nickname Mad Dog?"

He narrowed his gaze on the felon and decided it would better serve his purpose to tell the man the truth. "I'm quite mad."

"I am a man of detail," Richard Ratcliff said, taking a pinch of snuff from its box and sniffing it up one nostril. "I am certain I remember your face from somewhere."

Modesty dipped a hasty curtsy, and kept her

head bowed. "I don't think the likes of me would mingle in yewr high circle, me lord."

"Those bizarre eyes." His gauntleted hand rested suggestively on the ruby hilt of his sheathed rapier. "Something I would not be likely to forget."

She was tempted to tell him that his own eyes looked like broken glass filled in with red dye but prudently held her tongue. "I'm just a simple farm girl, yewr lordship. From Hertfordshire."

He didn't look convinced. "Regardless, you go through with this mutinous scheme of marriage brokering, and I shall see that you pay dearly!"

Modesty watched the London Company representative stalk away, the spurs of his buff leather boots ringing ominously. Somehow, word had gotten out about her venture.

It was obvious to Modesty that Ratcliff was taking no chances that her machinations might upset his applecart. He likely feared that the London Company might withdraw his representative's license.

She had overheard a colonist's wife say that a company representative was the most important permanent office, since governors, normally appointed to two-year tenures, came and went.

Therefore, as the Company's representative, Ratcliff held a position of political and commercial importance. It was said he had the power to seize all newly arriving bondservants, sources of labor for his plantation.

In addition, the colonial wife gossiped that he sold imported Company-manufactured goods at two or three times the prices set by the Company investors. Between importing human flesh and exporting tobacco, Modesty figured he must have made himself quite wealthy.

She was already discovering that there were only two social categories in this far-flung outpost: a person was either free or servant, either an exploiter or a resource. She didn't intend to become a resource. Since she hadn't come as a bondservant, she reckoned that as long as the Company got its money for the cost of her contract, Ratcliff could do nothing to her.

Her thoughts flew to Jack. She had barely gotten to speak with him before Ratcliff had interrupted. As a bondservant, Jack's free spirit would wither, especially with a master like that savage, Mad Dog Jones. God help the poor woman that man ever took to wife. Word had it that he lived beyond the colony's furthermost settlement, that he was a hermit, preferring seclusion.

That evening, Modesty sat on the church's oak floor with the other women, who were in various states of undress. Some were still in their petticoats and smocks, while others were already in their night rails. She scanned the circle of expectant faces. Their number had now grown to almost twenty maidens interested in her proposition as a way to better their future.

They talked among themselves about the colonial men.

"They are none too happy," Annie said. With her hennaed hair, she was slatternly-looking, but Modesty determined her to be stout of heart in her unflagging spirit and stout of lungs with her deep-chested laugh.

Rose's ebony curls bobbed. "Aye, I've heard grumbling aplenty. They want an answer."

"So what do we do?" Polly asked. Despite the poor food aboard ship, she had debarked on Virginian soil with rounded arms and a buxom bosom and an easygoing nature. "I would have me own house." Her full face dimpled with her smile. "And me own man."

Modesty held up her palms. "I'm coming to that. Yesterday I spied a Scotsman. They call him Duncan Kilbride."

The young woman with considerable charms to match her considerable girth nodded enthusiastically. "Aye, he be a shopkeeper. Do ye think ye could bargain for a looking glass?"

"Yew're bargaining with the devil himself when yew bargain with a Scotsman, but I'll haggle a looking glass for yew."

Modesty switched her attention to Clarissa, who clasped and unclasped her aristocratic hands. Her whole person breathed seduction. "Did yew find a man to suit yew?"

Clarissa shook her head, her chin tilted haughtily. "I can't go through with this."

"Yew'd rather marry the old fart yewr parents have arranged for yewr husband?"

She shook her head again, this time more vigorously, and her golden lovelocks tumbled about her shoulders. "No," she said in a frayed voice. "No, never."

Modesty thought for a minute, then said what had been on her mind. "Since marry yew must, methinks that the Reverend Dartmouth would make a right goodly husband."

"We talked briefly this morning. The Church sent him over as a missionary last year. But he seems so"—she rolled her violet eyes—"so colorless."

"True, the parson has a puritan streak. Still, I think he'd be the most willing of the men to abide by an agreement between yew to . . . uh . . . forgo carnal knowledge."

Clarissa's brows, like her lashes, darker than her hair, rose in outright skepticism. "Forever? I doubt that."

Modesty's wide mouth expanded into a big grin. "Who said anything about forever? Dartmouth's a man of the cloth, isn't he? Isn't a divorce granted if the faith of one partner lapses? Should down the road he discover he has a pagan for a wife, he will grant yew a divorce quicker than this," she said with a snap of her fingers.

All sorts of conflicting thoughts had to be going on behind those violet eyes, but at last Clarissa acceded to her suggestion. "Should he call on me tomorrow with an offer—"

"Oh, he'll call upon yew." It was inconceivable to Modesty that any man wouldn't want Clarissa. If she had to, she would put a bug in the good reverend's ear. "Send him round to me anon."

Modesty then glanced at Rose. "Yew found someone?"

"Aye, Walter Bannock, the sawyer from a settlement upriver. He's balding and he stutters, but he has two children who need a mother. They're adorable little mites."

"But what about *him?*" Annie asked. "What does he have to offer yew?"

Rose looked abashed. "Well, he's been here ten years now, so he seems the solid sort. And"—her swarthy skin actually flushed—"he has agreed to take me as . . . as I am, with child and all."

How generous of him, Modesty wanted to say. Through discreet inquiry, she had learned that for each person a colonist brought to Virginia, whether it be indentured servant or freeman, the colonist received fifty acres headright. For Rose, the widower Bannock would received one hundred acres, double his due. "Wot do yew want me to ask in exchange for yewr hand, then?"

Rose wrinkled her tiny, upturned nose. "Well . . . a spinning wheel. With me experience in carding, I could bring in an extra tuppence here and there."

"Oh, how jolly!" Clarissa said with a cynical twist to her rosebud lips. "More work."

"Methinks a milk cow would serve me well," Annie said. "And the three acres."

46

"Yew've picked yewrself a husband?" Modesty asked.

Annie screwed up her mouth in consideration. "He would have to be an elf of a man who would not be lifting his hand to me or else I shall box his ears."

"Then tomorrow I shall send yew a man I think will be to yewr liking. James Harwell."

Modesty listened and made mental notes as the priggish Elizabeth, Jane who bit her nails to the quick, and the other remaining women put forth their requests.

Aye, it looked to Modesty that she was setting out on a profitable venture. She could not remember feeling so much optimism.

By the ninth hour of the next morning, Jamestown was bursting with men at its fort's gates. Barges and canoes slapped against each other's sides at the wharf or were drawn upon the narrow banks to make a boardwalk of the tree-lined shores as far as the eye could see in either direction. Horses, of which Modesty had spied few, now were so numerous that they threatened to trample the tobacco planted in every plot not occupied by a building or a street.

Tobacco was a commodity as good as gold, which she duly noted. Take her commission in barter, and she would have enough to buy back her contract and more. Then she could buy a plot of land and plant a better staple—parsnips, turnips, carrots, and onions, as well as parsley, thyme, and marjoram.

Why, she could make her fortune here—honestly! In a couple of years, she could return to London a financially secure woman of means.

The sober Scotsman, Duncan Kilbride, was the first male to approach her with an offer for a bride-to-be. A brawny man of twenty-five or so and with cheeks as red as her poor satinet dress, Duncan would be man enough for Polly.

"'Tis unfair advantage ye are takin', mistress," he grumbled. "We lads are a puir lot. With no lass to—"

"My lady Polly would make yew a wonderful wife. Any man for that matter. 'Tis but a small thing, she asks, Master Kilbride. A looking glass."

His arms crossed over his chest, he tried blustering. "Now listen to me, mistress. Ye aren't talkin' to a fool. I be a Leith man. A shopkeeper by trade. What is in this for ye?"

The skinflint. She flashed a smile, revealing her best asset, perfect teeth. "A Leith man are yew? Why, me aunt married an Edinburgh bookkeeper."

A small fib, but if it served to ease the dour man's spirit . . .

"Her husband, me dear uncle, always told me, 'Lass, make people happy, and people will make yew happy.' Now, Duncan, I know that Mistress Polly will make yew a verry happy man." Rolling her r's should certainly help. "As for meself, why, I'd be content with a wee show of gratitude. Say thirty pounds of tobacco?"

48

"I be a shopkeeper," he growled, "not a tobacco planter."

She judged him to be one of those enterprising and intrepid Scots, so she continued to haggle. She spread her hands. "But 'twould be so little trouble to take some leaves in trade. Wot think yew?"

He rubbed his lanternlike jaw. "A shipment of rum has come in from Bermuda."

"Three kegs, then."

"One and no more."

"Two—oh, and do not be forgetting the looking glass for the Mistress Polly."

"'Tis a bargain, but ye are taking advantage of a puir mon, and I like it not."

Clarissa's minister was not much more amenable. Tall and shy, he moved in a loose-jointed way. "What she's asking—'tis near sacrilege." He removed his sugarloaf hat, his slender fingers absently tracing its gold buckle. Beneath sandy-haired eyebrows, his hazel eyes evidenced exasperation. "The Bible teaches us that it is the duty of man to procreate!"

The Madonna could not have smiled as sweetly as Modesty. "Me lady Clarissa wants children, Reverend Dartmouth." That the lovelorn beauty would prefer an immaculate conception need not be stated. "Give her a little time. As for me services, I ask little."

His gaze grew milder. "But this is too much— to barter with you for the Lady Clarissa Lockridge. I might remind you, Mistress Brown, that our Lord Jesus of Nazareth turned over the money changers' tables in the temple."

"Are yew not yewrself exchanging money with the London Company for a wife? Are yew not buying a marriage contract? I ask only for a small recompense, friend."

His somber features gave way to reluctant admiration. "You twist words like the Devil himself."

She managed a sagacious nod. "Verily, the Devil is a male, is he not? Godspeed, friend."

James Harwell came calling, his flat cap in hand. The milner was a plump little pumpkin of a man with a red-veined nose and round eyes that grew rounder when Modesty suggested that Annie was interested in him. Then his eyes grew nigh the size of saucers when she told him what her own fee would be.

"Why, I won't pay it. This is highway robbery. We were told we only had to pay for the females' contracts. I shall report ye to the Board of Trade!"

"But, sirrah, by that time the lovely maiden will have chosen another husband. In faith, a husband who values Annie enough to give her the three acres and the milk cow she desires and render the small fee I require, a milk cow for meself."

James Harwell's lips opened as wide as the bell-mouth pistol tucked into his belt. After a moment of concentrated thinking, he conceded. "So done."

She curtseyed. "Enjoy the day full well, sirrah."

The honorable Walter Bannock, Rose's selection, was a tall, balding scarecrow of a man. Of slow and halting speech, he had an unimpressive mustache. No wonder Modesty had not taken note of the sawyer before. He was singularly unappealing. But his brown eyes were warm. That was promising. "The lady Rose fancies thee, Master Bannock."

"I—'tis true, I find her fair—fair of face—the lady has not given her pledge—your commission she spoke of—"

"Wot ails thee, Master Bannock?"

He spread his hands, one missing a forefinger. "I have no spinning wheel to give the lady, nor the fee—fee—you demand."

Stalwart, Modesty judged him, most likely good for Rose, but his wits should be as sharp as his dirk strapped at his waist. "Yew are a sawyer, are yew not? Build her a spinning wheel. Nay, build two. I will take the second in trade for tobacco."

"But, but—'twas not me understand—standing—that a man would have to—to pay twice for a maid."

"Thou doth play the fool, Master Bannock, if thou wouldst haggle over a spinning wheel." A man would need more than a spoonful of brains to deal with her.

He was wringing his hands like a papist would rosary beads. "Well, I sup—suppose. All right, I pledge to build two spinning wheels."

It was all Modesty could do to keep from dancing a little jig. Aye, after all these years of dreaming and scheming, by the morrow security such as she had never known would be hers at last.

The morrow brought the continuing arrival in the churchyard of her commissions: hogsheads of green tobacco leaves, a looking glass, a keg of rum, and much more. Enough for Modesty to start up a business as a shopkeeper herself, should she so desire. That the milk cow died was but a small loss.

At noon, the bridal procession marched to the commons for the wedding ceremonies. Each of the women wore one of their two dresses provided by the Company. Except for Clarissa.

Her gown was of white silk, its scooped neckline and cuffs trimmed in tambour lace. The gown retained the Spanish sense of formality but with a more pronounced decolletage that gave a view of her white breasts.

The commons was even more crowded than on the day of Modesty's arrival, if that were possible. Children were engaged in the rough-and-tumble rural English pleasures of running or wrestling. Men were sampling dippersful of hard cider or peach brandy.

Every woman had selected a groom from among the surfeit of men. All but Modesty, of course.

Ratcliff stood just beyond the bowling green with the town officials, and when she passed by, he grabbed her arm. Beneath his white shock of hair, his bloodshot eyes glittered. "I remember now." His narrow lips drew back to reveal canine teeth. "You cost me dearly!"

"I don't know wot yew're talking about, yewr worship."

"I think you do."

She felt her blood ripple with disquiet. London gossip had said that after fraud accusations had been leveled against Ratcliff's father involving the sale of black-market wheat during a famine, his mother had been forcibly removed from her box in the royal theater. Gossip further related that he had never forgiven this insult, and that his insatiability for pleasure and power was only surpassed by his drive for revenge.

Without looking at him, she shook off his arm and continued on toward the church.

One of the Colonial wives had told Modesty that the publication of the banns, which had sufficed at home to alert a village of an impending marriage, had failed to work among the dispersed settlements of the New World colony. In order to spread the word to all of the intended event, the marriage license had been created.

When her turn in line came for signing the license, she said, "Prithee, inform Sir Yeardley that I shall be buying back me marriage contract."

The old reverend, outgoing chaplain to the governor, raised his white brows, then glanced uncertainly at Ratcliff and the colonial governor, who had just entered the church and were deep in conversation. With no help evidenced from that quarter, the reverend told her, "As you wish."

With the Book of Common Prayer open, he solemnized each ceremony with few words and posthaste.

"John Rogers, do ye take this maid to be your wife?"

"Aye, I do."

"And Mary Mullins, do you take this man to be your husband?"

"Indeed, I do."

"Then by the laws of God and the Company, I pronounce you man and wife."

After the minister completed the ceremonies, a round of cheers went up and hats were tossed in the air. Now the festivities began. Mistress Pierce had informed Modesty and the other women that there would be dancing at the council chambers, followed by an elegant supper that evening and then more dancing, card playing, spiced drink, and convivial song and conversation. Modesty kept an attentive ear for the latter as she threaded her way through the crowd.

When she stopped at one of the tables to get a drink, she overheard the men standing there.

"Heard tell Wolstoneholme Town has a licensed distiller," a ship's chandler said, winking at his drinking partner.

"They say the price of tobacco is dropping in London," a paunchy man was telling a fellow planter.

"Everyone's raising it," said another, his

pipestem almost as long as his nose. "The market is flooded."

Now that the brides had been married off, tobacco, the economic mainstay of the colony, was once again the main subject of conversation among the men.

When she moved to the other side of the room, Modesty listened as the score or so of town wives discussed the more frightening subject of Indians. "Dashed the poor babe against a tree and splattered his brains, the Powhattans did," one woman said, shuddering with revulsion.

Modesty gleaned from the wives that thirty-two tribes were united under the Powhattan chief, Itopatin, though his younger brother, Opechancanough, controlled the tribes from behind the scenes. Though insisting that his people desired peace, Itopatin felt that the white population was infringing on tribal lands and threatening the entire Indian society. He asserted that the random killings of colonists were the acts of renegade Indians.

"How many more of these indiscriminate murderings will Yeardley tolerate before he and the council order a reprisal?" one settler's wife demanded in a low voice.

Modesty didn't have the chance to hear more about the Indians, however, as she was a sought-after partner for reels and another type of folk dancing which often tripped her untutored steps. The fiddle music was energetic if not elegant, and the bachelors likewise. Their eager attention would turn the head of a less experienced maiden than Modesty.

Roger Martin, the town cordwainer, promised her a pair of red Spanish cordovan leather shoes if she would but agree to a single dance. Dan Warwick, the tallow-chandler, begged her to give him the opportunity to set her heart afire.

Captain Dick Heffernan, so gallant in his leather buff coat, boots, and riding spurs, swore that his heart wouldn't survive the season without her. His eyes burned bright as the candle-light. But Modesty knew that candles, like passion, were easily lit and easily extinguished. Still, she enjoyed all the attention—which was blighted by the approach of the governor and his chaplain.

"Mistress," Yeardley began, his bushy white brows beetling down, "the parson informs me that you have not honored your marriage contract with the Company."

She dipped her deepest curtsey. "Yewr lord-ship, I desire to buy back me contract. The Company will be lacking not a farthing for me transportation costs."

"But Jamestown is lacking a bride."

"Would Jamestown want a bride who is a witch?" Ratcliff drawled from behind the governor.

"What?" Yeardley asked.

"Wot?" she echoed.

As the dancing ceased and the merrymakers grew quiet, Ratcliff paused to inhale a pinch of snuff, doubtless for dramatic effect, then said, "Mistress Brown has been accepting possessions from the bachelors. 'Tis obvious she seeks to cast spells on all the males of Jamestown."

The circle of revelers seemed to shrink away from her and her accusers. " 'Tis true," Ethan Wheeler said. "She took a beaver hat from me."

"Wanted a pair of Spanish leather shoes from me," Roger Martin put in.

"Are yew all daft?" she demanded. "Meself a witch?"

Ratcliff glanced around the room, his expression one of stark concern. "Did not good neighbor Harwell's milk cow die this morning? I ask you, neighbors, look upon this wicked woman if you dare and behold—she has eyes of different colors. One green, one brown. She has the power of the Evil Eye. The Devil's accomplice, if ever there was one among us. Burn her, I say."

"Burn me?" Her voice was little more than a croak.

"Burn the witch!" an old harpy cried out.

A chorus of terror-filled voices reverberated around the room. "Burn her! Burn her!"

Without realizing it, she was backing away from menacing faces that seemed to crowd suddenly in on her. Among the faces, Ratcliff's satisfied smile crackled like flame. She could already feel herself sweating from its heat.

Yeardley raised placating palms to the crowd. "Now wait! There'll be no rioting here. Tomorrow I shall call a meeting of the General Assembly a fortnight hence to determine the maid's guilt. Until that time, she'll be placed in the pillory for twenty-four hours for failing to comply with her contract and then remanded to the gaol."

Shame vied with anger inside her. She struggled as two summoned soldiers bearing unwieldy blunderbusses seized her by her arms to escort her out. Now the spectators backed away from her as if she were a leper.

"Consorted with the Devil, I wager," the glassblower said.

"I knew her for a witch when first I laid sight on those oddly colored eyes," Mistress Pierce said.

Why, the Company widow had even offered advice on how to select a husband according to his possessions!

"A pox on yew all!" Modesty shouted over her shoulder before being ushered out into the darkness.

The soldiers half dragged, half propelled her toward the commons. After the din inside, the sudden silence of the night was terrifying. Her heart was fair to bursting with her terror. To be burned at the stake . . . she beat back the image of such suffering. Still, her fear only crept away like a cat and crouched somewhere beyond.

Across from the commons, a lantern hanging by the mortar-and-pestle sign of an apothecary shop cast a ghostly light on the pillory and stocks.

A female colonist dozed in a sitting position, her bony ankles thrust through the stocks' wooden framework. At the approach of Modesty and her captors, the woman awoke with a start. "Got charged for being a scold, eh?" she cackled.

"Nay. For being a witch."

With an alarmed outcry, the old hag drew back as far as the stocks would allow. Modesty ignored the woman. One of the soldiers hefted the pillory's upper framework, and the other thrust her head and wrists in its slots. At this point, struggling was useless. She envied the other woman's mode of punishment. At least the hag didn't have to stand.

After the solders departed, the poor old woman was too petrified to utter another word, which was just as well with Modesty. She needed to think. Her wits had always gotten her through precarious times before. Did she not have a fortnight to assess her situation? Surely she could contrive some way to save her hide.

One thing she did know: Joan of Arc she was not.

Chapter Four

Wild vines and begonias intertwined at the base of large trees, climbed the trunks, and crept along the branches to link with other trees. In the wanderings from tree to tree, the creepers sometimes crossed the arm of a river over which they threw a bridge of flowers.

The land seemed too intoxicating for a puritan. Even the bears became intoxicated on the wild grapes. As for Patrick Dartmouth, he was intoxicated by the frivolous young woman he had taken to wife, the arrogant lady who now rode pillion on his nag, her arms wrapped securely around his middle.

He must be seven kinds of a fool. He had not even intended to buy himself a wife. Fleeing the smoke and smell and noise of daily living in a cramped and oppressively close London, he had arrived in the colony a year ago, just after the first meeting of its self-governing body—a radical deviation from English law.

This year, he had journeyed from upriver Henrico to Jamestown out of curiosity about this General Assembly of representatives called by the governor. He had found himself appointed the chaplain to next year's incoming governor, Sir Francis Wyatt.

After the General Assembly was over, Patrick had stayed on a few days in order to be there when the *God Sent* arrived with its cargo of brides for sale, and so he'd been there to watch this vision of Aphrodite descend the gangplank.

She had worn an Italian gown, black laced, with a standing band collar and ribbon girdle belt. Like a dunce, he had agreed with the terms set down by Mistress Modesty Brown and obligated himself to a trappist monk's lifelong chastity. Anger perched on his shoulder like a deriding demon, but he had only himself to blame.

If he was going to purchase a wife, why had he not selected that gentle and biddable but plain Rose Crankston?

How was he to support a titled lady who was more accustomed to monogrammed silver plate and well-crafted carriages? Even her heavy ornate chest of medieval design, which he had sent on ahead by barge, was filled with silks, furs, and satins.

The gold buckle on his hat was the closest he came to owning anything ornate. That and a handsome chalice of silver, a Communion set valued at fifty pounds, and four divinity books.

Of course, as many ministers did, he could add to his income by being a tutor. With the granting of 10,000 acres for a university at Henrico, he could supplement his income teaching once the construction of the university was finished.

However, that could take years. Henrico consisted of little more than frame houses lining three streets, a storehouse, watchtowers, and huts, not to mention the two most important establishments in the community—the alehouse and his church.

His newly purchased wife interrupted his introspection. "What will become of Modesty Brown? You can't really believe that she is a witch, can you?"

He pitied the lively, saucy woman. "Witch or not, she has apparently made an implacable enemy of the London Company's representative by her bartering with the marriage contracts, and that does not help her cause."

"Richard Ratcliff—the man who denounced her as a witch?"

"Aye."

"The man is a profiteer," Clarissa said. "I've heard his name bandied about in London. Can't you do something? She has only ten days more before the General Assembly re-meets."

There it was again, his Maker forcing him to confront injustice. "I informed the council that neither I nor my church would have ought to do with this persecution."

His old buckskin slogged around a fallen tree that blocked the path. It was an ancient Indian road that was sufficiently inland from the James to facilitate the crossing of the many little creeks. In the spring, spawning shad clogged these tidal streams.

At the noisy approach of Patrick's saddleback horse, a land turtle plodded off the trail and plowed beneath a paper mulberry's dead leaves of last autumn.

In response, the Lady Clarissa's arms tightened around him. "Indians?" she whispered.

He savored the heady sensation of both her embrace and her throaty voice. "No, mistress. Only one of God's more gentle creatures, a land turtle."

"What if Indians attack us?" she persisted in a perturbed voice. "You carry no weapon to defend us."

"I do not believe in killing, mistress."

"You may be fearless, but what good is your courage while the Indians are taking our scalps?"

Fearless? If the young woman, his wife he reminded himself, but realized the coward who hid in his skin.

His pugnacious father, a captain under Queen Elizabeth, had been created the first Earl of Bridgeshore as a reward for his successful raid of Ruthven. His three eldest sons also followed in his martial footsteps: Percy, who fought in the Dutch wars; Reginald, who sailed with the 1596 Cadiz expedition; and Robert, who led an Italian army into Hungary to thwart the infidel Turk.

As the youngest of four warfaring brothers, Patrick had developed an aversion to the violence of military life. Instead, he had hid in books as an escape. He had pursued an education at Gloucester Hall, earned a master of arts from Oxford, and then enrolled at the Middle Temple.

But when fellow students had gleefully tortured a Jewish mendicant, Patrick's fear of becoming a victim of their violence had kept him from intervening. So he had donned the pious vestments of the clergy to hide his eternal shame and perpetual fear.

"The Powhattans have made an alliance with Sir Yeardley," he said, hoping to put his bride at ease.

She gave a dainty little snort. "Mistress Pierce said that there are still wandering bands of Algonquins who don't believe in a peace treaty. A weapon might at least scare them away."

"A single weapon?" He had to smile. " 'The world's mine oyster, which I with sword will open.' "

"A minister who speaks lines penned for the theater?" she scoffed, her breath warming the back of his neck.

"Ahh, but Shakespeare wrote so well, did he not? A verse for every situation and every personality. Even thine own, mistress: 'Your accent is something finer than you purchase in so removed a dwelling,' he quoted.

She said nothing, but he felt her stiffen.

"Which brings me to question how thee, an aristocrat, came to be bagged with the other maidens of the *God Sent?*"

Silence. The wind quickened and sucked down the forest-banked shore. At last she replied. "I was born bored. Mine was the ennui of a jaded princess. So for diversion I took up writing pornography." She paused, evidently waiting for his response.

He was shocked. He fought to control his judgmental feelings. "And for that thee was forced to flee England?"

"Oh, not for that," she said airily. "My writings left nothing sacred. Orgies, licentious ministers, saturnalias. It was when I wrote an archbishop into a ménage à trois role that I was forced to flee."

Oh God, help him. He had let his carnal side gain control of his spiritual nature. Now he must make the best of his situation. He felt like a man on spring ice. He managed to say nonchalantly, "I would be most interested in reading your work."

She was silent again. He could almost hear her ruminating. Woodpeckers, cardinals, and mockingbirds warbled while he waited for her next revelation.

"Since you brought up the matter of work," she said, "I think you should know that I don't. Work, that is. I cannot cook, weave, spin, rend lard, dip candles, make butter, scour—"

His mouth carved out a rueful smile. "There is no doubt but that I have bought a wife in name only."

"After a couple of years, you may decide you have erred. You may even choose to divorce me."

"Mistress," he said grimly, keeping his eye on the trail ahead, "I have erred in many things. I have succumbed to the allure of lechery, the protection of falsehood, the relief of profanity. But if I have any virtue, it is this—I am steadfast. I am committed to our marriage."

Persimmons, a fruit new to Rose, grew like ropes of onions. The countless streams, the limitless land, the abundance of game—she found it difficult to believe there had ever been starvation. But Walter Bannock swore that in the winter of 1609, the colonists had fed on corpses.

"Land, water, wood," Walter was saying as he flicked the whip over the ox that pulled their cart. "Everything that England is lack—lacking. Its forests have vanished into pl—planks for ships. That's why I chose Henrico as a site for my sawmill. While all of England is still saw—sawing wood by hand, I can build one driven by waterpower! What with the university being built there—"

"The boys?" she asked. She was more concerned with how his sons would accept her. She truly hoped she could make them understand she wasn't trying to take their mother's place.

"They're staying with John Rolfe's wi—wife.

You'll like Falling Brook. The house isn't much. Abandoned by an iron—ironworker who returned to England. But close enough to Henrico to get supplies. Only a mile or so away."

"But how far is Ant Hill from Falling Brook?"

Her husband's mustache dipped at either end with his grimace. "Jones's place is four—four miles farther, just before the falls."

"You don't approve of Master Jones?"

"I don't know him that well. He went native. Keeps to himself. 'Tis your mi—mission I don't approve of."

Lightly, timidly, she touched Walter's knee. "Modesty Brown meant well, husband. I can't let her down. All that I need do is deliver her message to Master Jones."

He glanced down at her hand, and she quickly withdrew it. There she went again, always trying to please. As a child, it had been her father. She had felt sorry for him, the way her mother was always nagging him about how unambitious he was. Her mother had been born high enough to climb higher—and hadn't.

Then Rose had wanted to please Henry, a yeoman's son, who had seemed to be interested in her. Her hand drifted to her rounding stomach. When out of gratitude she had given herself to Henry, he had lost interest.

"Of course, owning a sawmill can be risky," Walter said, reverting to his passion. "An iced-over stream could cl—close it down in winter, the easiest time to haul logs from the for—forest."

She listened dutifully.

"A spring freshet might wash out the retaining dam and wreck the water—waterwheel. A summer drought could keep the machinery idle. And then there's the ri—ripsaw blade and the up-and-down steel-edged saw to con—contend with."

Her glance took in his missing finger. "I had not thought about how dangerous operating a sawmill could be, Walter."

His words might twist in his mouth when he grew excited. Some might find him dull. But that was because they could not see his stalwart spirit. Hadn't he proved it by marrying her?

Yet would he ever come to love her?

"Yew filthy old bawd," Modesty screeched at one woman who was trying to constrain her twisting, turning, and dodging. Jamestown's goodwives were escorting her back across the green to the pillory.

The Jamestown gaol had been a loathsome cell. For two weeks Modesty had been chained to an Indian woman imprisoned for prostitution for the third time. The two women had not had privacy to do what nature required, nor fresh air in the windowless gaol to relieve the stench of their own excrement. Their legs had been in one bolt and they had been bound to a post with an ox chain.

In the past fortnight, Modesty had had plenty of time to learn Algonquin phrases from the Chesapeake Indian woman, whose name was

Palantochas. *Ka ka torawincs yowo*—what call you this?; *Pokatawer*—fire; *mockasins*—shoes; *tomahacks*—axes; and *Casacunnakack, peya quagh acquintan uttasantasough*—In how many days will there come hither any more English ships?

The arrival of which would mean more customers for the industrious Palantochas.

In turn, the squat but chipper Indian maiden had learned some English phrases from Modesty, mostly ones of profanity that she had picked up along the Thames docks. "Yew arse rug! Yew bloody meat monger! Yew puck fist!"

Even now, Modesty was making liberal use of her English swear words, because her two female captors were shoving her along faster than she could walk, what with the irons.

Left on long enough the irons would rot the flesh. Of course, that wasn't going to happen to her. Surely the irons would be removed by the time she was brought before the General Assembly. Already, she could see the councilmen and the burgesses arriving from the outlying areas, even though, according to Palantochas, it wasn't yet the noon hour.

Two soldiers in quilted coats and with baldrics worn over their shoulders to support their swords took over for the Company women. Quickly and efficiently, they installed Modesty in the pillory, her head and hands poking through its wooden slots. By now a crowd was gathering to watch.

Then a stout woman approached the pillory

with a razor's long, glinting blade. Great fear stole the breath out of Modesty. What had she ever done to these people to be so punished?

One of the soldiers jerked loose the strings of Modesty's coif, and out spilled her hair. Then she realized what was intended. "Yew lousy slut!" she screeched at the old dame who was shearing her like a sheep.

The more she thrashed, the more nicks her scalp suffered. Her humiliation was more painful than the razor cuts. She swallowed back the acrid bile in her mouth.

Suddenly she went still. Not because she had given up resisting the shearing, but because of the activity that had started up in the center of the green. Men were dragging in brush, faggots, and logs. They were piling them around a center stake.

She knew then not to expect justice from the General Assembly. What she could expect was to be burned alive.

Chapter Five

Mad Dog stood at the back of the Council Hall, his straw hat tugged low. People eyed him askance, but they were there for the witch trial, and soon their gazes turned from him toward the front of the hall.

The large room overflowed with spectators, who spilled out into the narrow dusty street. As Mad Dog surveyed the crowd, he recognized pioneers from settlements scattered as far west as the fall line of the James, as well as the twenty-two members of the House of Burgesses. Two men were appointed by each of the eleven boroughs' settlements to represent them, and even though the burgesses had adjourned from their annual assembly only a little more than a fortnight before, they had returned today. Only death was accepted as a valid excuse for absence.

Like the burgesses, here was Mad Dog back for the second time in less than a month. However, more than three years had passed since his last visit to the colonial capital.

Yeardley was presiding behind the desk at the front of the room when the female prisoner was brought in. Spitting like a scalded cat, she scuffled and grappled with her two gaolers. Mad Dog was shocked by her appearance. Since he had last seen her a fortnight earlier, her head had been shaven.

She had not been comely to look upon to begin with. Of medium height and bony, she had mismatched eyes and a nose that overpowered her fawnlike face. True, the eyes were lively and inquisitive, noting everything, and her nose was of strong and pure line.

Pure, however, was not a word one would ascribe to Mistress Modesty Brown. She was obviously woven from the seamier side of London's fabric. Mad Dog supposed he should feel compassion. After all, she had been someone's infant daughter. Who was he to question what life had sculpted from that infant lump of Thames clay?

The idea that she might be a witch he found preposterous. He put no faith in what he could not see. Demons, witches, warlocks—the only power those concepts held was the power that one gave them.

Crafty, the wench was. He had to give her

that, as evidenced by the bargain she had offered him.

Goodwife Rose Bannock, one of the recently married maids, had brought Mistress Brown's request to him. Or rather, the goodwife's husband had brought her by cart all the way to his place upriver from Henrico.

With a curtsey for him at his door and a blush that brought the color of her given name to her cheeks, Goodwife Bannock had relayed by rote the wench's message: "Plead me innocence before the General Assembly, as you did your bondservant Jack Holloway. If I go free, I will marry you. In exchange, you receive fifty acres of additional headright land, a pair of willing hands, and a faithful heart."

Willing? Faithful? He doubted that the woman possessed those attributes.

Something inside him had advised it wasn't safe to come to the General Assembly, but he had come anyway. It was like that for him, that ungovernable anger that made him reckless. I am here, his mind shouted to his faceless foes, so come on.

"Take yewr bloody hands off me!" the wench screamed at her guards.

The two soldiers were quite ready to oblige her. A witch, especially an uncooperative witch as she, was not to their liking.

A disturbing creature she was. Her hands bound, she stood erect, her cleft chin outthrust. Her eyes, which seemed abnormally large due to her shorn skull, blazed. They searched the spectators and found him. He did not acknowledge the question in those cat-slanted eyes.

The members of the House of Burgesses sat apart from the ordinary folk. They listened as Yeardley opened the hastily convened session with a grave expression. "The Honorable Ratcliff has brought before the assembly charges against one Mistress Modesty Brown of witchcraft. Of sucking the milk dry from Neighbor Harwell's cow until it died. Of cursing our colonists with the pox. Of tricking the bachelors of the Virginia colony into giving her certain possessions of theirs upon which she intended to cast spells."

He paused and peered down his long nose at her. "Mistress Brown, thou hast forsworn the right to counsel. How dost thou plead to the charges?"

"Yew jackanapes, has smoking the stinking weed clouded yewr senses? I didn't touch the milk cow. Have any townsfolk succumbed to the pox, I ask yew? Nor have—"

The governor interrupted with a thud of his mallet. "How dost thou plead, mistress?"

Her mouth set itself in a mutinous line.

Clay pipes ceased to puff. Their owners leaned forward, all ears. She stared down the room's avid faces. Her silence was doing her plight no good.

Mad Dog heaved a sigh and shouldered his way through the press of people.

Yeardley was saying, "Then I hereby recommend the burgesses and the council recess to deliberate the charges against Mistress Brown and, if the woman be found guilty of such charges, I recommend the administering of the commandment in the good book of Exodus, 22: 18, that states, 'Thou shalt not suffer a witch to live.' "

"I stand to defend the good"—the word almost stuck in Mad Dog's throat—"woman of the charges of witchcraft."

The burgesses and council members, many of whom had half risen from their seats, jerked around to stare at him.

Mad Dog turned to the assembled colonists. Like wild sunflowers, their faces were trained on him intently. He, who had once been insatiable for pleasure, knowledge, and glory, summoned long-forgotten skills to do what he had once done so well.

What an oddity he must present. A wild man in long hair, looking for all the world like John the Baptist preaching in the wilderness of the New World, dressed in animal skins, his food locusts and wild honey. But Mad Dog found the deerhide easy to repair, and it dried quickly over a fire after being wrung out. "I beseech the council to allow me to represent Mistress Brown."

"What?" Yeardley asked, his white brows climbing above his wrinkled forehead. "By whose authority?"

"Her own."

"Your credentials?" Ratcliff drawled.

So the man still didn't recognize him. As be-

77

fitting his position of representative for the London Company, Ratcliff sat indolently at the table to the right of the governor.

Yeardley's cropped gray hair was bristling. "I am in charge here, Lord Ratcliff, and I shall do the questioning." He looked at Mad Dog. "Now, sir, you have credentials to offer?"

Mad Dog flexed his fingers, feeling the tendons and muscles in his forearms tense and stretch. "I hold a bachelor of arts at Oxford and was a barrister at Lincoln's Inn." He paused, then said, "In addition, I served as a member of King's Counsel at the Star Chamber."

The sound of collective breaths sucked between teeth whistled through the hall. The Star Chamber of Westminster Palace was notorious as a secret court. It was not responsible to Common Law, dispensed with juries, could examine witnesses and proceed on mere rumor, and could inflict torture and any penalty short of death.

The startled look of recognition in Ratcliff's face was instantly replaced with a smug expression.

So Ratcliff remembered now, did he? Their last meeting, thirteen years before, had resulted in Mad Dog's ruin: with the annihilation of his emotions and the destruction of his mental faculties.

"Proceed then," Yeardley said.

With all eyes upon him, Mad Dog strode toward the female prisoner. Her eyes seemed abnormally large. He removed his straw hat and placed it gingerly upon her naked head, criss-crossed with minor cuts that doubtless had occurred while she resisted being shorn.

Her eyes glistened, then rapidly blinked back any suspicious moisture.

He faced the burgesses. He fell back on those years of studying law and finding ways of evading statutes as easily as if he had never fled the bar. "As Mistress Brown pointed out, no one has come down with the pox in the previous fortnight. Neither have the bachelors who gave over their possessions to Mistress Brown given up their ghosts."

His tone was casual, bantering, exactly right, he felt. "The primary charge against her, as I understand it, is of killing a cow by sucking it dry of its milk the night before the marriage ceremonies were conducted. I call Master James Harwell to testify."

The round little man with pipestem legs came forward, his flat cap in hand. He glanced nervously at his wife. The raw-boned woman gave a reassuring wink.

"Master Harwell," Mad Dog said, "what did Mistress Brown ask as a fee for her services for you?"

"A milk cow."

"Did you give her a milk cow?"

Harwell twisted his cap in his hands as if it were rosary beads. "Well . . . yes. And no."

"Prithee, would you explain your answer to the court."

"I gave her a cow that will produce milk."

"*Will* produce?"

"I gave her a heifer."

"Which means?"

"That the cow has not produced a calf yet."

"Which means, does it not, that until a cow produces a calf, the cow can produce no milk?"

"Aye."

Mad Dog turned back to the burgesses and the council members. "Which means, gentlemen, that a witch cannot suck a cow dry of its milk if it never had milk to begin with."

Murmuring erupted again. Yeardley pounded his mallet for order. "There still remains the charge that Mistress Brown killed the cow. That she has the Evil Eye. That with one eye green and the other brown, 'tis considered a sign of the Devil."

Mad Dog scanned the attentive faces. "Didst anyone witness Mistress Brown actually kill the cow?"

Not a single person stirred. Then Ratcliff rose from behind the table. The white ruff around his neck accentuated his falcon-red eyes. "I did."

"You assert that you were in the churchyard the night before the marriage ceremonies were conducted?"

An easy smile curled Ratcliff's mouth, a mouth as thin and lipless as an iron bear trap. "I do."

Mad Dog rubbed his jaw, wrinkled his forehead. "Now I am very confused, friend, because I have a witness who will testify otherwise. Wilt the Chesapeake maid Palantochas come before the bar?"

All heads turned toward the back of the room as the young Indian woman made her way to the front. Short of stature and slightly fat-padded, she was well known in the predominantly male community. Her deerhide moccasins made a soft thud against the floor's oak planks. Her limpid eyes flashed Mad Dog a searching glance.

"Palantochas," he said, "will you tell us what you were doing the night in question?" His words were distinct and deliberate.

She bit her lip, lowered her head, and her single black braid swung forward across her shoulder.

He nodded encouragement, hoping his backwoods diplomacy was paying off. He had learned ancient and modern languages, shone at math, read Francis Bacon and Christopher Marlowe, and studied under William Shakespeare at Blackfriars Theatre. Yet, here he was, defending an unscrupulous wench in a cow dung of a town.

In a tremulous voice, Palantochas said, "I spent the night . . . in the company . . . of him." Her finger pointed out Ratcliff.

Murmurs erupted. The room sounded like a beehive. Although many of the men had lain with the native women, few admitted it. To do so was as much as to declare oneself infected with the malady the Irish called the Country Duties.

"'Tis a damned lie!" Ratcliff said.

Mad Dog spread his hands. "Do any of the burgesses wish to question my witness?" He was counting on the members' reluctance to being possibly identified as one of the maiden's midnight customers.

"No one would believe the word of a misbegotten creature like this against mine!" Ratcliff snarled.

"I am finished with the prisoner's defense," Mad Dog said. "It hath been a pleasure to serve the Assembly."

Chapter Six

"Mad Dog Jones, doth thou take this maid to be your wife?"

"Aye, I do."

What a name! Mad Dog Jones! Modesty did not know whether to laugh or to cry.

While the minister read the sacred rites, she stood shorn of hair, barefoot, and dressed only in her smock—all because Mad Dog Jones was taking no chances. He was adhering to an old legality which Modesty knew dated back to medieval times that said a man was not liable for his wife's debts, provided he married her in nothing other than her smock. Even shoes and caps were prohibited.

"Modesty Brown, doth thou take this man to be your husband?"

How had she gotten herself into this mess?

One moment she was camouflaging a stolen snuffbox in London, and the next she was consigning herself to a living hell here in the New World.

The old minister cleared his throat. "Ummh . . . Mistress Brown . . . doth thou?"

Beneath raised brows, Mad Dog eyed her as curiously as she had the New World food called maize. She could guess what he was thinking—that she ought to be rejoicing that she wasn't going to be burning like an All Hallow's Eve bonfire.

As for herself, she was thinking hard. She was still required to fulfill her bridal contract with the Company or spend a year in the gaol. Having just spent a fortnight there, she doubted that a human could survive for a year. It was said even the freepersons who survived the year of seasoning were full of maggots and rotting above ground.

God rot the pious citizens of Jamestown!

There was also the bargain she had made with Mad Dog. She had the distinct feeling he wasn't the kind to give up easily what he felt was his. Nevertheless, he had another thought coming if he expected her to remain in this English colony long enough to rot.

"Mistress Brown? Did thou hearest me? Doth thou takest this man to be your husband?"

She sighed. "Aye, I suppose I do."

"I cannot take me commissions with me?" Gingerly, Modesty settled herself and her portmanteau of meager belongings in the prow of the birchbark canoe.

Mad Dog grunted. "They have been returned to their rightful owners."

"Yew had no right—"

"You truly art a scurvy wench."

"Yew are a lump of foul deformity."

"Thou art married to me now."

"A calamity it is!" She squinted suspiciously at him. "Wot be yewr real name?"

"You may call me master."

"I call no one me master."

"Egad. What happened to the willing hands and faithful heart you pledged unto me?"

"Yew got yewr fifty acres headright."

A wry smile curved his lips. "And I am out of pocket for your transportation costs. For which you shall serve me faithfully and willingly, I promise thee, wench."

"Me name's Modesty. How did yew know that Ratcliff had lain with Palantochas?"

"I didn't."

"But I heard her tell the burgesses—"

"How thy tongue doth wag."

She waved away a haze of gnats and said indifferently, "Yew are a unkempt churl."

"You were the one who bargained for marriage."

For the first time since they had set out in the canoe from Jamestown, he looked at her. Before, he had kept a hawklike gaze swinging in a steady arc from one side of the bank and its dark, impenetrable forest to the other. "Why me? Why didst thou bargain marriage with me, wench?"

"Modesty. Who else would be mad enough to marry me than a man called Mad Dog?"

Indeed, she thought ruefully, who would be mad enough to marry a woman accused of witchcraft, a fugitive felon? "Besides, Jack—yewr bondservant—told me how yewr fine words saved him from being broken on the wheel."

"You have heard of the saw 'jumping from the frying pan into the fire'?"

She figured she may have well done just that. The man's feral gaze seemed to pierce into the secret recesses of her mind. "For the cost of me transportation, yew could have almost bought a headright of fifty acres or bought an indentured servant—or yew could have taken yewrself a wife of yewr own choosing. Why me?"

"Do not flatter thyself." His searching glance swung to the somber glades of forest and back to settle on her. "In the bargain I sought satisfaction, small though it was, of an old score."

She was already humiliated, and his words wounded her. "Yew took me because no other woman would have yew. Look at yewrself."

The wintery gleam in his gray eyes halted any further words she had been about to utter. Still, with an inward shudder, she inventoried her new husband.

Like the Indians, he wore moccasins that

folded up below his knees. This time, however, deerhide trousers encased his thighs. The trouser leggings were tucked into the moccasins, and a leather jerkin was belted at the waist.

His thick dark brown hair, streaked by tropical sunlight and the seasoning of years, flowed like a lion's mane to fall heavy upon his shoulders. His skin was the color of burnt crumpets, his broad mouth as unpredictable as a river. At one moment she thought it scorned her, at another it took her by surprise with its deep, wry twist of a smile.

Indeed, there were many twists and unexpected bends to the man. Grudging admiration crept into her voice. "Yew played those web-toed burgesses like a fiddle. Plucking a string here and there, then yew leaned back, watching them."

His smile was just a quiver away from being a grimace. "Aye. I am a turkey buzzard. An avaricious creature, by my troth. I wait until a prey is helpless, then I strike. Dost not put thy trust in me. I use people, as thou dost, wench."

"Modesty." She should have been affronted by his poor opinion of her, but she was more intrigued by the incongruity of his character. A London barrister living like an animal at the edge of the world. A wild animal with the voice of a god.

He had a tall and powerful frame that held a leashed strength. His shoulders were strong and broad, and his arm muscles flexed from the unceasing thrust of paddle against water.

Her view, looking upriver from the canoe, was like gazing on an eternity of rushing water. The more she gazed, the more she realized the river's awful power.

In the New World, according to Mistress Pierce, other than a few Indian paths, the only roads were rivers, which, Modesty suspected, was why farms were granted in long strips along a river. Occasionally she sighted a farm amidst the trackless forest, but it had been several hours since she had last seen sign of human habitation.

At a place of vine-hung coolness, the wild man beached the canoe. She glanced at him inquiringly.

"We'll spend the night here. We got a late start, and Ant Hill is too far upstream to make in the time we have left."

Cautiously, she stepped from the wobbly canoe. She was sure there must be a trick to keeping the canoe upright in the water. She followed him ashore. "Ant Hill—yewr place?"

"Aye." In a clearing, he collected twigs and dead leaves for tinder, then opened his leather possibles bag.

"I hope the name isn't an apt description of yewr place." She slapped at a whining mosquito that had lit on her temple, where once rebellious curls had strayed from her cap. The shame of having her head shaved and then having to stand practically naked before the minister crackled like a flame inside her brain.

"Let's just say that Ant Hill is a far sight better than the Jamestown gaol." Hunkering down, he struck a glancing blow with the steel on the chunk of flint. At the glow of a spark, he began blowing, and nursed it into a small flame.

"Let's hope that yew aren't as barbaric as the good people of Jamestown."

From the canoe, he took out a fishnet of some sort of bark fiber and lines equipped with hooks that looked like fish bone. "I have the distinct notion that you have no idea of the concept of the word 'good.'"

She huddled before the fire, where the smoke warded off the pesky mosquitoes. "It has been me experience that goodness and virtue are seldom rewarded."

Her temporary husband sat on his haunches at the bank to spread his net in the shoal water. "Oh? What is?"

In the day's dying light, she watched an egret search the opposite shoreline for crayfish. "Quickness of wit for one thing. 'Tis far better to be wise than good, and better still to be shrewd."

He jerked in the net with its catch of fish. "Ahh," he said in a bitter tone, "'an excellent wife, who can find? For her worth is far above jewels.'"

"Proverbs." She rested her chin in her hand, grinned, and said, "'A joyful heart makes a cheerful face.'"

He looked askance at her. "So you can read."

He proceeded to clean, then plank the fish over the flame.

"Aye. Books *and* people. Now yew—well, yew're the kind of man who takes pleasure in the precise application of logic. No imagination to yewrself."

Over the fire's blazing streamers, he flashed her a disgruntled look. "And you think you are imaginative?"

"Aye." She shrugged. "'Tis like being a fairy. Yew can make anything happen."

"I trust you are not confused between a fairy and a fury. Or perhaps it is I who am confused. I would swear I have taken the latter for a wife."

She ignored him. "What kind of fish are yew cooking?"

"Shad. Do you ever stop talking?"

"Fairies are good talkers."

"If you've ever read Spenser's *The Faerie Queene*, then you know a lock put on the tongue is an excellent way to achieve silence."

"Never read anything but the Bible and a broadside about Jamestown." But his reference to silence made her realize that with nightfall the forest was alive with sounds of screeches, hoots, howls, and chatters. By now, a muggy fog shrouded the river.

Then she heard the trill of a clear liquid note, and the rough-hewn man across from her answered it with a warbled whistle.

She tensed. "What was that?"

He didn't reply but passed her a portion of the planked shad on a palmetto leaf. Behind her, the brush rustled. She whirled, almost dropping her food. A tall, dusky-skinned Indian stepped from the tangled copses. He carried a feather-tipped lance. His immobile face contained much dignity despite its smears of paint. One half of his head was shaven; a feather was tucked into the dark brown braid that fell from the other side.

Mad Dog said something in the Algonquin dialect. She picked up the word *pokatawer*, fire. Apparently he was inviting the Indian to join them, because he crossed the clearing to squat before the fire.

"Arahathee," Mad Dog patiently explained to her, "is the chief, the *werowance*, of the Monacans. The tribe lives above the falls at Rasauweak. The Monacans are actively hostile to the Powhattans and unfriendly to most English."

That was reassuring. *"Mawchick chammay,"* she said, using Palantochas's phrase for best of friends.

The Indian only nodded, but the condescension disappeared from his stony gaze.

Mad Dog darted an oblique glance at her before resuming conversation with the Indian.

While they talked, Modesty ate. The shad was surprisingly tasty. When it looked as if the two were going to talk through the night, she curled up beside the fire. She had not realized it, but her face and hands were sunburned during the river journey, so that she was chilled. Later she was partly roasted by the blaze and partly frozen, but too fatigued to move.

Sometime during the night she awoke. She thought she was alone, and terror rattled through her. Then she saw Mad Dog asleep on the fire's far side. The Indian was nowhere to be seen. Relieved, she went back to sleep, only to awake to find Mad Dog hunched down over her. She gasped. "What do yew want?"

His brows furrowed with disgust. "I believe I can control my raving desires for the while, mistress. 'Tis time to leave."

By the time they shoved off in the canoe, the morning fog had lifted. Later in the morning he pointed out a sleepy waterfront village. "Henrico."

Farther on, they passed a cluster of homes and a two-story waterwheel that he identified as Falling Brook.

"How much more traveling in this infernal country afore we reach yewr place? And where is yewr bondsman? Jack Holloway?"

"Earning his keep, as thou shall be anon."

"I am yewr wife, I remind yew. Not some indentured servant."

Amused contempt glittered in his eyes. "Aye, my wife for life, God help me."

"Oh, so yew believe in God, do yew now?"

The canoe had slid into a gentle current that momentarily carried it near the bank, and the dips of his paddles ceased. He rested, his arms braced against the paddles, though occasionally he pulled the boat along by hauling on cattails and overhanging oak branches, draped with moss. His hands were the most massive she had ever seen. "You do not?" he asked.

"I believe in meself. I believe a person gets wot she takes from life."

For a moment there was only the silence of the great forest. Then he said, "You get what you give." His eyes were empty. "And in the end, you give what you take."

He resumed paddling. His eyes had a faraway gaze. His manner was so remote that she decided silence was in her best interest, after all.

But not quite just yet. She felt that her suffering belonged to her alone, and she wasn't about to let a lawyer full of words get the last one. "Yew may have taken yewrself a wife, but it 'pears to me that I am the one doing all the giving. To have to work like an indentured servant the rest of me life in a rathole of a frontier settle—"

"—with willing hands and faithful heart," he reminded her with a black look that this time did silence her.

At length, when the western sun was balancing on the tips of spiraling pines and the parasol spread of ancient oaks, she sighted a long pier with a wharfhouse at its tip. A path of crushed oystershell led up through ragged grass to a clearing plowed with crops. On a hill were clustered several houses of various sizes.

Mad Dog banked the canoe and, collecting his flintlock, strode on up the path.

She grabbed her portmanteau and hurried to

catch up with him. So tall was he that the top of her coif came only to his chest. She had to double step in order to match his lengthy stride.

The main house was constructed of oak slabs chinked with mud and reinforced with moss and roofed with cypress shingles. She followed him inside.

The place had the clean smell of new wood. And it even a had a floor, a puncheon floor of split pine. By squinting, she could tell that the window frames were weather-tight. The room's furnishings were sparse—a ladder-back chair with rushing seat, a pine settle, and a short stool, not counting the long board table, of course.

The fireplace was of goodly size with an oven built into its wall. A lugpole with a variety of hooks, chains, and trammels hanging from it stretched across its mouth. A shovel, tongs, and a pair of bellows were piled at one edge of the stone hearth, and around its rim were heaps of cooking equipment: ladles, saucepans, skillets, pots, cauldrons, and the like.

She smiled. She hadn't done too badly for herself for the meanwhile, but she wondered how her other matchmaking attempts had fared.

"You can put your things in the bedroom." He nodded at another doorway that opened on what looked like a lean-to. "'Tis the original cabin I built of logs when first I came to the colony. There's a double chest—"

She supposed she should have expected

him to get around to this matter sooner or later. She set her portmanteau on the board table, put her hands on her hips, and nodded toward the bedroom. "Yew be wanting a wee one anon?"

His mouth quirked again, she wasn't certain whether with laughter or contempt. Or mayhaps both. He lounged against the entrance doorframe. Its tall lintel didn't even clear his head. "Well, now, you have agreed to be my wife, and I do not recall any stipulation such as the one you arranged for the Lady Clarissa and her husband, Reverend Dartmouth."

"How did yew find out about that?"

"Thorough investigation was part of my training in reading law."

She wondered how much else he knew about her. Had he learned about her nocturnal enterprise back in London? "I'd be pleased if yew'd tell me just wot me duties be."

"They're not that taxing. Be prepared for Juana to—"

"Juana? Another wife?"

At that, he grinned. "Hardly. Juana is as old as the bogs. A Spanish colonist who more than a decade ago was captured by the Arrohattoc. Even though she's free now, she prefers the forest creatures to society's creatures. When the whim takes her, she might drop in. To cook, clean, or just to sit in silence and dip snuff. So you will have occasional help during the day."

"And by night?"

He straightened, careful to duck his head, and crossed back to her. He stared down at her. "My God," he muttered, "we're both dreading this."

"Wot!" she screeched. "I got me pride. Yew think bedding with me is bothersome. How do yew think I feel about yew, a savage straight out of the forest?"

He frowned, tugged at his earlobe. "I think we had best get this over with now."

"Yew're mad!"

His eyes were slivers of silver. "Aye."

He scooped her up against him, and she knew her whole world had gone mad.

"'Tis broad daylight!" She protested as she stood beside the bedstead and glared at him. Her shaven head and bare feet disconcerted Mad Dog. Her feet were so small, with tiny toes. Without her hair, she was all ears and eyes. But those features appeared delicate. She seemed but a child. A small, defiant boy.

"'Tis no matter." He set about unlacing her bodice with the air of a man committed to work little relished. His high-top moccasins were already draped over her discarded peasant's pattens and buckled shoes on the bedroom hearth.

She sighed. "Here, let me." She slapped away his hands. "Yewr fingers are as thick as sausages." She turned her back to him and drew off her dress.

He began tugging his deerhide tunic over his head. She faced the other way. Late afternoon light spilled through the open window onto her thin shoulders. Her fingers fumbled with her new petticoat's points. "Do not tell me thou comes by thy name Modesty honestly."

"I swear yew bloody well come by yewrs honestly."

He reached around her and jerked on the ties. Her petticoat dropped to the floor. She stood clothed only in her plain smock. Visions flitted through his mind's-eye of ladies of the French court bedecked in all their enticing underclothes: the four-foot-wide farthingale that concealed the seductive curve of a hip, the corset that pushed up and thrust out the breasts, the multitude of lacy petticoats, the frilly smock, and lastly the fetching drawers, which English maidens, thank God, did not wear.

He took her by her shoulders and turned her to face him. "Thou art a virgin?"

"Find out."

Her wide, unappealing mouth was as rebellious and disapproving as a puritan's. But she sure as hell was no puritan. "I mean to."

Which wasn't true at all. He didn't have the slightest idea how to proceed with this recalcitrant woman. Any maiden he had taken to bed had been as impassioned as he. Here he was with his wife, God help him, and neither he nor she had the slightest inclination to fulfill their marital obligations.

He had really shot himself in the foot this time. For the opportunity of revenge, small though it was, and an additional fifty acres, he had taken on this misbegotten creature.

"Look, the longer we postpone this, the more difficult 'tis going to be," he said.

Those damnable eyes continued to glare at him.

He tried again. "Just what dost thou suggest I do? Take *two* wives? Take a mistress?"

"Give up sex."

Her frankness shocked him. "I'm not ready for that just yet."

"I didn't think so." She chewed on her bottom lip. "I suppose as long as we are married, we might as well make the best of it. I suggest"— she paused, and he would have sworn she blushed—"I suggest yew hold me hand first. Yew know, like yew see those gents doing with the ladies in the plays at the Globe."

"I truly am mad." But he bowed low. "Mad Dog Jones at thy service, my lady."

Her giggle startled him. He looked up to see a dimple at either side of her pale mouth. She dipped a deep curtsey, holding to one side the hem of her cambric smock. "Thou art more gallant than Galahad, sire."

"You are surprisingly good at mimicking."

She shrugged. "I cannot kiss yew if yew'll not bend down yewr head a bit."

"'Tis my pleasure to attend a maid whose beauty eclipses the sun." He had said the wrong thing, he realized instantly. Both of them knew she was no beauty. Never would be. In the silence that followed, he felt foolish.

She was studying him with earnest eyes. " 'Twon't work, will it? Me idea of pretending. Oh well, as yew said, let's get this business over with. We'll both feel easier for it."

She pulled back the covers and climbed onto the mattress, which he had stuffed with rags, cornhusks, and bits of wool. Watching her bottom wiggle beneath her thin cambric, he astonished himself by feeling a suddenly hot and elemental urgency.

Carefully, he unbuttoned the flap that covered his painfully sensitive erection and stepped out of his trousers. He slid beneath the covers to lie beside her. She lay on her back, her eyes squinched closed, her hands folded across her breasts. She looked like some sacrificial virgin. The image didn't befit what he knew about her, and was hardly encouraging.

His mind said to tell her to go to hell and then ride to Henrico's Bloody Bucket to down a tankard of ale. But his body clamored for a relief that it had gone without for over a year.

She opened one eye and peered at him. "If yew don't do something quick-like, I shall—"

"Will you shut up?" He pulled her against and half under him. There was no pretense on his part that he was engaged in lovemaking. As for her, she made no effort at pretending she was eager to please him. There was a certain dignity in her animosity.

Her hands clenched his shoulders as his knee spread her thighs. He entered her. There was no resistance of the maidenhead. He had expected none. Still, there was something curiously untutored about the way she moved beneath him. It was as if her body were trying to understand his.

His body responded, and he murmured inchoate phrases. Some grand, delicate balance was being created between him and her as they performed the assuagement of desire, the gesture of creation. He knew they were powerfully alive to each other, which was most strange.

And then he knew nothing in that brief moment of self-loss. Some moments afterward, he lay still upon her, trying to restore his breathing, to restore his sanity. His pleasure had been great, his relief extravagant. He dared to look at her. The way the sun shafted through the window . . . were her eyes glistening with tears?

His fingertips traced both sides of her jaw; then he tilted her head up and kissed her lightly. "'Twill be easier the next time." His words sounded awkward. Who would have ever guessed he had been the most gifted of speakers to come before the Star Chamber?

Wriggling from beneath him, she yanked the cover up over her meager breasts. "That will be a comfort."

Her truculent tone annoyed him. A tough little wench, she was. He rose.

As he tugged on his trousers, she asked, "Wot is yewr given name? 'Tis difficult to call yew Mad Dog in bed."

"You may call me by any name you desire. I only require that you come when *I* call *you*. Any other questions?"

"Aye. Where be me Jack?"

Chapter Seven

Rose laid her hand atop her stomach and felt the baby move. A little fist? Or a squirmy kick? Mentally she tallied the months left. Three, mayhaps four.

Fortunately, one of the two gowns provided by the Company had a high-waisted basque bodice, so she did not have to worry about letting out the seams of the brown moreen material. The poplin bertha concealed her breasts that seemed to grow fuller by the day.

A "peeping" sound brought her attention back to Bartholomew, wedged in the pew with his five-year-old brother between herself and Walter. The seven-year-old was tall for his age and had inherited his father's warm brown eyes.

Bart sat quietly, listening to Reverend Dartmouth read from the Common Book of Prayer, but she noted a mischievous gleam in the lad's eyes. Her own narrowed in inspection of her stepson, noted his knotted hand. With seemingly rapt face turned upward to the pulpit, she pried open the boy's hand to find a wooden bird whistle. She gave him a conspiratorial wink, which made him giggle. Nevertheless, she relieved him of his toy.

Three weeks earlier, she, her new husband, Bart, and Isaac had traveled to the fall line and the cabin of that wild man Mad Dog Jones to plead Modesty's case. How forbidding he was, listening to the message for help she had conveyed from Modesty. And its queer terms. All the while, he had said nothing. Only listened. And whittled.

When she had finished, Mad Dog had merely replied, "I'll think upon it," and handed fidgety Bart the bird whistle he had been carving.

That small kindness had touched her, as had the gallantry of the man's bondservant. Though he had been scything a field, he had paused to doff his straw hat as she passed by.

Rose, Walter, and the boys had been outside, preparing to climb aboard the lumbersome ox cart. The bondservant had knelt, offering her his knee as a step-up, and had said, "If Sir Walter Raleigh could do this for his queen, can I do less for a queenly mother?"

Imagine, her, Rose Crackston—no, Rose Bannock now—an ordinary country girl, being treated so chivalrously. She was quite certain that the bondservant, Jack Holloway, was a man of integrity, of noble heart, despite the stories circulating that he was a felon.

Services, held in the old Thomas Dale Church, were almost over, which today would be a relief. Not an eddy of air stirred in the hot, sticky, late August morning. Fortunately, the Lady Clarissa's husband, despite his normal reserve, was on Sundays a lively pastor who had a sense of drama.

Rose looked forward all week to these Sundays, when the men could socialize and conduct business, the women chat, and friends extend dinner invitations. Sunday attendance was mandatory in the colony unless no church was available, and then home readings from the Common Book of Prayer were expected.

Outside the church, the townspeople were already gathering: giving and receiving letters of business, reading advertisements, consulting about the price of tobacco and grain, and settling either the lineage, age, or qualities of favorite horses, for horse racing was an obsession with the colonists. Just as gambling was a ritual activity.

Isaac, no longer constrained by public censure, took off running, his arms spread wide, and then performed a cartwheel that landed him up against old Clem, the cowherder. "Whoa, lad," Clem said, picking up the boy and smacking the dirt from the seat of his knee breeches.

The old man's hooked nose almost touched his jutting chin. The children made fun of his contorted features, but children and adults alike delighted in listening to him play his German flute and in listening to his stories about the Pitch and Tar Swamp, where alligators devoured men alive and quicksand swallowed cows whole and mysterious lights guided lost souls out of molasses-like marshes.

The five-year-old cocked a crooked grin for old Clem and scampered away before Rose could bridle her stepson. "Isaac," she called, "don't go far."

Walter appeared unable to cope with the boys. She suspected he was still overwhelmed by the death of his wife two years before.

"Friend Bannock," John Rolfe called, crossing the churchyard to greet them.

It was at this same church that Rolfe's first wife, the Indian princess Pocahontas, was converted to Christianity and baptized. After her death in England, Rolfe had returned to Henrico and last year married Joane Perce, granddaughter of the Earl of Northumberland and daughter of Henrico's Lieutenant Percy.

Although Rolfe was only thirty-seven, his shoulders were bowed by rheumatism. A curious power gave grandeur to the nondescript man, so that he reminded Rose of a biblical patriarch.

Walter had told her that the local planter was well respected in the colony, and had succeeded in crossing purloined Spanish tobacco with the hardy native species.

Beneath her palm, Rose could feel her husband's arm tighten. Idle conversation was difficult for him. "Good morrow, Ma—Master Rolfe."

Joane, a frumpish little woman who contrasted with Rolfe's sticklike anatomy, said farewell to a friend and joined her husband. "Mistress Bannock, I've been intending to talk with you. Now that you have settled in at Falling Brook, the ladies in our quilting bee would have you join us."

Rose had been considered an outsider by the Henrico women, but now she knew that judgment had been passed on her and she had been found acceptable. "I thank thee, Mistress Rolfe. I liked Henrico and Falling Brook the moment I first saw them.

Falling Brook was little more than a cluster of ironworkers' huts on the outskirts of Henrico. She had learned from the settlers that the community had been named for the late Prince Henry. Sitting on a hill of a peninsula overlooking the James, Henrico had three streets of well-framed houses, a few storehouses, the church, and a tavern. The townspeople had already laid plans for a more stately church, a hospital to be called Mount May Lady, and even a university, by setting aside 10,000 acres.

Rose knew she could make a home for herself here. Here, she had a purpose. Walter and the boys needed her, as would her baby.

"I too have been awaiting the opportunity to talk with you about the House of Burgesses," Rolfe said to Walter.

Rose had heard that Rolfe had been elected last year to serve as Colonial Secretary for the General Assembly. "Henrico needs two burgesses to represent it this coming year at the General Assembly," Rolfe continued, "and I and Reverend Dartmouth, the incoming governor's new chaplain, would like to put up your name as one of them."

"Why—why me?"

Rose was as startled as her husband, but pleased that Rolfe would recognize in Walter a good man. She felt fortunate. Walter was truly considerate of her, helping her with those household chores she found difficult in her cumbersome condition.

"We are sorely lacking men of the gentry to represent us, men of your fine qualifications," Rolfe said. "A man who is both a businessman and a family man."

"Well, I don—don't know," Walter began. His bald pate began turning red.

"Mayhaps Master Bannock would like to think about it, John," Joane said kindly.

"Of course, of course." He clapped Walter on the shoulder. "Reverend Dartmouth will be coming by to see you, I am sure. If I can't persuade you, I am hoping he can."

Rose rounded up the boys, and they all started toward home, a cabin abandoned by one of the men who had been employed at the nearby iron works and furnace and who had decided to go back to England.

She waited until after the boys took off their

Sunday-meeting clothes, changed into yellow nankeen breeches and linen shirts, and ran outside to play before she broached the subject of which Rolfe had spoken earlier.

She was squatting before the fireplace to check on the samp porridge, cornmeal she had mixed with beef and various root vegetables. She had been cooking it slowly for three days, and knew it would be ready when she could lift it like a loaf of bread from the iron bake kettle. "I think ye would be a good burgess, Walter."

He put aside her garden hoe he was sharpening and crossed to her. "Here, let me help—help you." He took the heavy kettle by its handle and shifted it from the fire to the banked embers off to one side.

He was on eye level with her now. "I have heard ye talk about the need for a better road to connect the settlements," she said. "And a gristmill. And our own militia to replace the soldiers who come and go from England with no real care for our safety."

Was it the fire that flushed his cheeks? "Ye know—know I can't talk—talk as good as I sh—should."

"Ye do when it is something ye feel strongly about." She touched his wrist. "Like when ye talk me in bed at night . . . about your big plans for your sawmill, about your dreams for Bart and Isaac."

His fingers rubbed at his ragged mustache. "Me and the wife, that was the ti—time we liked to talk be—best." If his cheeks were flushed before, they could have caught fire now.

"Walter, ye have yet to kiss me," she said, feeling suddenly shy and quite the virginal maiden.

He rose quickly. "Best check the animals afore dark."

With wistful eyes, she watched him go. Did he still love his first wife?

Though not educated, Rose possessed a clarity of mind that came from one contented with a simple lot. But more and more, she was given to asking herself why, when all she wanted was to give a heart overflowing with love, she seemed to attract the very people who did not want to love?

Though it was midday, the cabin's thin horn-scraped windows offered scant light. Clarissa took the pick from the mantel and pulled out the betty lamp's wick to make the grease burn brighter. Accustomed to scented candles and glass windows, she found herself floundering in this backwoods hamlet.

Her father was a Dutch banker who had inherited an English title. Her mother had been a beauty who had seen to it that Clarissa was taught early to dance, sing, and play the clavichord like a professional. She knew that she would as soon commit suicide if she thought she had to live in this cultureless land of simpletons forever.

She thought of her silver, glassware, and books still unpacked in her trunk, a symbol of her determination to cling to hope. But as the weeks passed, she lost her confidence that she would ever see Nigel again. She saw that confidence as childish folly. Virginia was as big as a hundred Englands. It stretched far beyond the knowledge of man, white or Indian.

The rap at the door brought her back to reality. She lifted the door's latch to find Sally staring up at her with awe. The eight-year-old held a fire scoop. She grinned, showing a missing front tooth. "Ma sent me over to borrow a few hot coals."

"Come in." Clarissa stood aside and let the redheaded urchin enter. Taking the fire scoop from Sally, she crossed to the hearth.

"Ma forgot to bank the embers with ashes last night," Sally prattled, "and no amount of puffing and fanning is going to get any spark to blaze again."

Clarissa used the tongs to pluck a few hot coals from the fireplace and put them into the scoop.

"Pa would be in a real tizzy if he'd known Ma had gone and forgotten," Sally volunteered.

"Well, we cannot have that, can we?" Clarissa looked at the girl, really looked at her. She was dressed in a long muslin overblouse and a calico skirt and was barefoot.

Sally saw her looking and wiggled her dirty toes nervously.

Clarissa recalled how cheerless her own childhood had been. Great stress had been put upon an erect carriage, and she had been systematically tortured to achieve it. She had sat for a couple of hours every day strapped to boards to keep her from slumping. She had been forced to wear stays with needles built into them to prick her tired little waist when she relaxed for an instant. And she had been made to walk about balancing books on her head for poise. Even as a child, she had worn all of the panoply of her mother, including hoops, heels, and masks.

What would it be like to go barefoot?

After Sally scampered out, Clarissa headed for her retreat, a rustic bench of bent hickory saplings placed in the alcove of a grape arbor at the side of the cabin. As usual, the sweet smell of honeysuckle beckoned her beyond the arbor.

A few days after her arrival at Henrico, she had discovered the arbor, its rustic bench, and the honeysuckled arch which led to an almost hidden path through bramble and thickets down to a secluded section of the riverbank carpeted with budding raspberries.

Glancing around to make certain she wasn't observed, she sat down on the bench, removed her red-heeled shoes and, rolling down her garters, peeled off her fine stockings, edged with stiff lace. Like Sally, she wriggled her toes in the tufts of grass. "Mmmm."

Then, picking up her stocking-stuffed shoes, she plowed through the honeysuckle vines and gingerly picked her way through the thicket to the bottom of the hill. A small breeze ruffled the water. She stared across the broad river at the black wall of forest on the other bank. It was so silent out there.

How often over the past weeks she had stood there, hoping to espy an English ship sailing up the James with news. But she knew it would a full two years before Nigel could come for her.

At least she had known love. She had experienced his kisses, when both he and she were immersed in a wine-red rapture in which thought had no part.

He was thinking of her now. She knew it. She could imagine him in his cell. He knew she had fled to the Virginia colony. She had only to wait.

Chapter Eight

A covey of quail scattered into the underbrush at Modesty's noisy tread. She had never known such blasts of heat or such heavy rains that left only more steaming, hostile air. She sweated constantly except when the breeze blew faintly off the river in the mornings and evenings.

With a curse, she swatted at devilish mosquitoes that circled her, getting into her ears and nose. She shoved tangled vines and creepers from her path in her search for chestnuts. Since Mad Dog had brought her to his farm a fortnight before, she had developed a craving for the delicacy. Hot, steamed chestnuts and a tankard of Mad Dog's peach brandy before bed at night . . . aye, that was about as close to heaven as the likes of her would ever get.

Unless she counted Mad Dog's bed. And Mad

Dog's mouth. And Mad Dog's hands, stroking her breasts.

She could count on one hand the number of times in her two weeks as his wife that they had lain in lovemaking: one single time.

It was as if the day's intense sunlight exposed their aversion for one another. But under the cover of darkness, their tremendous awareness of each other made their sleep restless. Enclosed within the bed's mosquito netting, they would turn their backs on one another in an attempt to constrain that passion for lovemaking that had been demonstrated so tumultuously the day he had brought her to his cabin.

Mayhaps that was why Mad Dog brought out the gallon stoneware jug of peach brandy every evening to ease the tension that mounted each night before they went to bed.

Shifting her basket to one arm, she knelt amidst rank-smelling grass to pick some large trumpet-shaped violet flowers, when a voice commanded, "No!"

She whirled around. An old crone, as gnarly as a swamp cypress, pushed her way out of the bushes. She had straggly gray hair and a hide as tough and brown as pigskin. Over her calico skirt she wore a soiled, sleeveless tunic of tanned hide that fell halfway to her thighs. "Yew must be Juana," Modesty said.

"No!" she said again, pointing to the clump of tall, stalky flowers. "Jimsonweed."

Modesty lifted her shoulders to show her confusion. "Aye?"

"Jimsonweed. Jamestown."

Modesty understood—that the jimsonweed was a corruption of the name for the colonial capital. "Poisonous?" she asked, standing to face the witch of the woods.

"Drives *vacas* loco." The old woman made a corkscrew motion at her temple with an arthritic finger. "Turns *hombres* into fools who wallow in their own *caca*."

Modesty grinned. Between the old woman's English and Spanish and the hand gestures, she got the drift. "So does ale." She thought of the peach brandy.

Juana grinned, displaying tobacco-stained teeth. A wad of tobacco was tucked behind her bottom lip. "Ale is *bueno*."

Grateful for a visitor, even one with whom she couldn't communicate that well, Modesty said, "Come with me. We shall go to Mad Dog's cabin and drink." With her free hand, she made a motion of tipping a tankard to her mouth.

The crone nodded vigorously and fell into step beside her. "Mad Dog—you are his *mujer*?"

"His woman? His wife? Aye, he bought me." For now, she silently promised. What with the witchcraft trial, she might have to lie low for a while, but somehow, someway, she meant to find a way back to Jamestown and finagle passage back to England.

"Mad Dog bought me, *tambien*."

Modesty darted a startled look at the old woman. "He bought yew as well?"

"*Sí*. From the Arrohattoc. For many beads

and a bell." She slid Modesty a sly look. "You like to bed with Mad Dog?"

"What?"

"You like *che-ise?* All one with him? Under him?"

Modesty flushed. "About this much"—and she snapped her fingers to show how little she cared about bedding Mad Dog.

"*Sí.* Mad Dog big man." She spit a brown stream of tobacco juice. "Good in bed, I betcha."

Modesty refused to comment further on this delicate subject. By this time, they had reached the cabin. Modesty set her basket on the board table and dipped a gourdful of peach brandy from the crock into a leather noggin that she passed to Juana before pouring one for herself.

The old woman quaffed her own in one gulp, then gave a wide tobacco-stained grin and snapped her fingers. "This much." She snapped her fingers again and bobbed her head.

Modesty realized that Juana thought the gesture meant "a lot." She poured another nogginful for the old woman, who again tossed down its contents.

Then Juana padded over to Mad Dog's pipe box hanging on the wall. Used to hold and protect the long church warden pipes of breakable clay, the box had a bottom drawer for tobacco. The Spanish woman took a fresh plug of tobacco and dipped it behind her lip, then grabbed up the broom of hemlock twigs and began sweeping the dusty floor. "I work."

Modesty, who had done everything for herself, found this help to her liking. With that chore being attended to, she was free to prepare dinner, the light meal of the day—little cakes flavored with honey that she slid in the oven on a flat, wooden shovel. They were still warm from the oven when Mad Dog and Jack returned from work.

"*Hola*, Juana," Mad Dog said and strode over to the mantel to restore his fowling piece to its resting place. To Modesty, he said nothing. Neither of them spoke if they could avoid it. He crossed to the tin basin to wash his face and hands with the harsh lye soap.

Jack, his rough linen shirt filthy with grass stains, flashed Modesty a wink as he passed by. Gone was his scraggly beard. "Something smells good."

It certainly wasn't Juana. She gave off an offensive odor which reminded Modesty of rancid grease.

The hungry men ate quickly, as did Juana. Usually during the meals there was little exchange of conversation beyond the scope of the next day's work or an idle comment on the weather.

Jack shared the news that he had seen a family of intrepid raccoons feasting in the corn field. "I managed to frighten off the maize thieves," he said with his easy grin.

Modesty was learning that between the wolves, wildcats, and black bears, which Mad Dog said preyed upon the cattle, and the caterpillars that he described as rolling in like an invading army to devour the barley and wheat, farming in the colony was a precarious occupation.

While old Juana cleared away the trencher and spoons made of wood and horn, Modesty steamed the chestnuts she had collected. When she looked up, Juana was trotting out the cabin door without a backward glance.

Mad Dog was taking tobacco from the drawer at the bottom of the pipe box and appeared to think nothing of the old woman's silent exit.

Modesty placed an old shaving bowl filled with the chestnuts on the table and lit a bayberry candle against the encroaching darkness. Glad for the diversion of Jack's presence, she made the mistake of offering him a tankard of the potent home-brewed brandy.

He glanced questioningly at his master.

Mad Dog said nothing, only tapped the tobacco into the clay bowl of his church warden pipe.

Taking the man's silence as assent, Jack sauntered to the board table and hefted the jug of brandy to his mouth, then wiped it with the back of his dingy sleeve. His smile was whimsical, lovable, almost droll. "Like old times at Bridewell Docks, eh, Modesty?"

She nodded warily and darted a glance at Mad Dog. Calm as a lion at his waterhole, he sat on the stool and drank his brandy and smoked his pipe.

Jack swung a leg over the bench and sat opposite her at the table. Pouring himself a tankard of the brandy this time, he began to reminisce about the plague of 1605. Mad Dog set aside his pipe but continued to drink and listen.

"Aye, I remember that time well," Jack was saying as he stared dreamily over his tankard. "Each day was like a nightmare. I was a mere lad of thirteen at the time."

"Our house had a red cross painted on its door," Modesty said and took a fortifying swallow of the mind-numbing brandy. "And the words 'Lord have mercy upon us.' He didn't. Me brother took sick and died." The image of his bloated, black corpse was always with her.

Jack's blue eyes burned brighter than the candle. "My older brother got a job driving one of those dead carts." He took another deep draught of the brandy. "I would ride with him, calling out 'Bring out your dead.' The stench was ungodly."

Her attention was drawn to Mad Dog, who had put away his tankard and picked up a knife. She watched him begin to whittle new teeth for a wooden rake.

"You're handy with the knife," Jack observed. He was by now obviously quite in his cups or he would have remembered to address Mad Dog as Master.

Mad Dog glanced up from beneath the slash of his dark brows. "I perfected my technique while the Star Chamber was sitting."

"'Ow so?" Instantly, she regretted her question. His leering gaze told her that he, too, had drunk more than was his usual and that his tight rein of self-restraint was unleashed.

He continued to whittle. In the candlelight, the blade flashed with rapier swiftness. "As a barrister, I passed out sentences or let people go on the basis of favors, money, or property exchanged. I made no moral judgments. I based my actions on expediency despite the cruelty I deliberately incurred.

"Then, while the Star Chamber was sitting, I did something that I believed was in the king's best interest. Something quite horrible."

A look flickered across his face that Modesty couldn't identify. An awful look.

"I used every faculty and all my intellect to change its outcome. And it didn't work. I went insane. Bloody insane. I went running through the chambers off the Palace Yard, where the well-to-do prisoners from the court at Whitehall were temporarily kept. I killed all of them. Guilty or innocent. Male or female." He held up the blade and stared at it unseeingly. "I slit their throats."

In the silence of the room, Modesty's gasp was audible.

Jack shot unsteadily to his feet, tipping over the bench. His eyes roamed anywhere but at her or Mad Dog. "Time I was retiring."

Mad Dog pinned her with his steady gaze. "'Tis time we were retiring also."

If she had believed in a God, she would have dropped to her knees and blubbered a prayer right then and there. In lieu of that, she sprang up, accidentally knocking her empty tankard off the table. "I'm not," she declared. "I feel like dancing. All night." She held out her arms. "Jack, me darlin'?"

He swept her a gallant bow, then gave her a buffoonish grin. "I yield the floor to your husband, milady."

Her heart was pounding too loudly for her even to hear Jack take his leave. With terror, she watched Mad Dog advance, knife in hand, toward her. His slate-colored eyes were glazed from his hard drinking. Then, with movements too fast to follow, he sent the knife spinning haft over blade into the joust beam high above her head.

At the thud, her lungs noisily quaffed air like a thirsty horse at the trough. She looked above her, at the still quivering knife, and she quivered in response.

"Shall we retire?" he asked, this time with inordinate politeness.

She nodded.

He merely touched the back of her waist, guiding her toward the bedroom. If he became violent . . . she could only hope he was drunk enough that she could fight him off. She recalled a Jamestown wife at the church and her stories on how hard it was for wives living on isolated farms since there were no checks on a husband's physical abuse.

In the bedroom, the embers cast a wicked red light on Mad Dog's roughly hewn features. The enlarged pupils were twin fires. The slight curve of his mouth mocked both of them, their denial, their repressed passion.

Her chin trembling, she began to unlace her bodice.

"Your fingers fumble," he said in that low, richly modulated voice. His big hands moved hers aside and, with patience unusual in her experience with men, deftly stripped the laces from their eyelets so that her bodice fell away.

"'Tis that time for me monthlies."

"I know."

She could feel herself blushing, her cheeks surely as crimson as the glow of the banked coals. Of course, he would have espied her freshly washed rag strips draped across the elder bushes to dry.

With a whooshing sound, her overskirt fell about ankles. "And it matters not a whit to me, goodwife. 'Tis the blood of life. I have seen too much of death."

Only her linen smock guarded her nakedness—that and her coif. It covered her naked head. He reached to untie its strings, and she shrank away. "Please . . . yew know I feel shamed without me head covered." Stubby tufts of hair were growing back, as scratchy as the bristles she had scrapped from the hog that Mad Dog had slaughtered this morning.

"You don't have to feel shamed unless you choose to do so." Off came the coif. Then he did something strange: he aligned his hands at either side of her head and pressed. Gently pressed. "If I could but squeeze all the caprice and craftiness and carelessness from this fickle head of yours—"

"—yew would be bored," she said, surprising herself at her own audacity.

"I would have myself an obedient and trustworthy wife." He lowered his head and brushed her resistant lips with his. He paused.

In the silence, a log fell to pieces on the hearth.

He repeated his act. This time his mouth lingered on hers. His tongue separated her lips and stroked her tongue, as if daring her to respond.

She was inexperienced with this dallying. Sex was an act of urgency, to be rapidly engaged in and completed upon the spilling of the man's seed. Despite her mental resistance, she felt a glow of pleasure deep in her belly. Why not? she thought. Tomorrow, as intoxicated as they both were, neither of them would probably remember this.

Her tongue answered the challenge . . . dueled with his. Aroused, she grew bolder. Her tongue traced even the tops of his teeth, swept his mouth's hot, wet recesses. Their tongues entwined, withdrew, and engaged again. She reveled in the sweet taste of his mouth.

He made a sound in his throat that was like a muted roar.

At once, she ceased her seductive attempt at kissing. She tilted her head back to stare up into his hot, glittering gaze. Her mouth suddenly felt parched.

"Your training," he said quietly, "is more extensive than I at first perceived. A common wench with an uncommon passion. While you are not of the class of Lady Clarissa, still, how fortunate I am to find a woman who can match my own passion, after all."

His words seared her soul like a hot iron. Her damp lashes blinked back a betrayal of weakness and let a slow, contemptuous smile curl her lips. "Passion? So far, yew have behaved like a randy goat."

Like flint struck by steel, his gray eyes gave off sparks. His voice, however, resonated with languid curiosity. "Do I now?" He drew her smock down over her shoulders. His callused hands caressed her flesh as they moved the linen down the length of her arms.

"Aye, yew do." Her breasts were bared. Her nipples, burned under his gaze, grew hard. She wanted to cover her breasts, but her arms wouldn't move. His touch had a lethargic affect on her.

"Amends are in order then." He drew the shift on down past her hips and let it slide to the floor. "You have to understand that at an early age I discovered sexual pleasure," he said casually, "and I continue to rediscover it endlessly." His hands were on her hips and then easily sprang loose the knotted drawstring that secured the damp rag strip between her legs. It, too, slithered to the floor.

With a gasp, she covered her eyes with her hands.

126

"There is no need for embarrassment," he continued casually as he shrugged out of his leather jerkin.

She peered between her fingers. His bare chest gleamed in the firelight.

"I find the feminine body, including all its attendant functions, most exciting." He unbuttoned the flap of his trousers and his thick cylinder of flesh sprang free. "You see, I was the Prince of Revels at Middle Temple and sometimes my appetite for passion still manages to rear its lusty head."

As she closed her eyes again, she wished she could close her ears as easily.

"Exploring the pleasures of a woman gives me insatiable pleasure." She heard the soft thud of what she guessed were his moccasins. "I suppose hedonism is for me second nature." Tenderly, he kissed the hollow of her neck where it sloped into her collarbone.

The muscles low in her groin tightened spasmodically. Her head lolled to the other side, giving him full access to her shoulder. She could feel his erection pressing into her belly.

"For instance, merely your musty scent awakens in me a fierce desire for you."

He brushed a kiss on the rise of her breast and at the same time grasped her upper arms, moving her slowly backward until her calves met the bedstead. Her eyes closed, she was disoriented. It seemed the mattress rose up to enfold her. When she felt his mouth shrouding her navel, and his tongue plunging into its well, her lids snapped open. The ceiling's smoke-blackened beams loomed above her. "Please . . ."

"I delayed in revealing the scope of my sensual nature," he said, "until I judged you ready to participate."

With an indrawn breath, she clasped his head, tunneling her fingers through his long hair, digging into his scalp.

His lips traveled the path between her ribs up through the shallow valley created by her breasts. One hand cupped her breast and his fingers tweaked its turgid nipple. She gasped at the sharp pleasure the action caused.

"I see now I have underestimated your ability." Braced on his elbows, he moved further up over her. Softly, he kissed each of her lids. With concentrated tenderness, his forefinger traced each of her aureoles. "Your skin, where it is untouched by the sun, is smooth beneath my fingers and quite lovely.

She was beguiled by this gentleness, until he suddenly mounted her. She cried out, arched toward him, only to feel him drive deep inside her.

Then he dipped his head, his wild mane sweeping her face, and lathed her nipples with light, passionate kisses. This alternation of sensitivity and fierceness was only the beginning of the exquisite passion to which he subjected her, mind and body alike.

Toward dawn, she stirred within his arms. Both their bodies were misted with perspiration. She stretched languorously, feeling drained yet, paradoxically, replete. With a contented little sigh, she tentatively explored the tender spots of her damp inner thighs.

"Modesty?"

"Mmmm?"

"Don't mistake unbridled carnal devotion for affection."

Chapter Nine

Goodwife Dartmouth. How strange the name sounded to her ears. No longer was she the Lady Clarissa Lockridge. She was the wife of the Right Reverend Patrick Dartmouth, who never suffered an impious thought.

She, who had been accustomed to carriages, was riding pillion on a nag that managed to find every pothole in the well-traveled trail. Her arms tightened almost imperceptibly around Patrick's middle.

She could only be relieved that he could know naught of the impious thoughts that bestirred her own middle. Or of Nigel's more than chaste kisses when last they parted. She had bribed the guard to let her and the satirical poet see each other, if only for a few minutes. Within days of those too few rapturous moments, she had been banished to the country home in Kensington in preparation for a hastily arranged marriage to the Duke of Clarence.

Compared to Nigel, Patrick was so deadly dull.

Compared to London, Jamestown was deadly dull.

The bleak little hamlet of Henrico could not even be called alive. Patrick had related the history of the place, which originally had fifteen lots of one acre each. The town had developed because tobacco planters north of Jamestown wanted a convenient tobacco inspection site.

Henrico's palisaded fort was a company compound that included a longhouse, a log church, and a store. Outside the compound, separated by a muddy pasture, was the company barn, a tavern that was little more than a privy, and a cluster of crude cottages, one of which she and Patrick shared.

Well, shared was not entirely accurate, she thought with a relieved sigh. At night she took the bedroom, he the loft.

"Thou art tired, Mistress Dartmouth?" her husband asked, mistaking her sigh.

"Aye. How much farther to the Jones farm?"

"Not much farther. Mayhaps another half hour."

The trail wound beneath gnarled mulberry trees, feathery green acacias, and magnolia bushes. They spread a cooling canopy against a steamy summer sun that made her green riding jacket, finished with hand ruffs, uncomfortably

132

warm. In the branches, magpies and wrens warbled notes that contributed to a stirring symphony of mating calls.

Just beyond the wall of trees flowed the James. The trail followed it all the way through the valley to Jamestown. The river was all ears and a great gossiper. For scores of miles westward, word had gone through the upper reaches of its valley that brides had been coming to Jamestown and that bachelors on the scene would have prime choice.

The bachelor Patrick Dartmouth had been on the scene, but Clarissa suspected he had not planned on fetching back a bride.

Now, the man was hoping that the great gossiper would likewise spread the word of the Christian god to the Chickahominies, Mattaponi, Pamunkey, and Powhattans, all members of the powerful Algonquin Confederation. Patrick had told her that this network numbered some 200 villages.

His fervent devotion to this religious cause aroused within Clarissa both admiration and a certain jealousy. Was she of so little beauty that he noticed her not?

As for him . . . well, if his features didn't look as if they had been chiseled by an amateur sculptor, he might be considered of passable appeal. His thickly lashed hazel eyes could be passionately warm when he spoke of his hopes of converting his Indians.

At last, the Jones farm came into view. She would be glad to see Modesty. The nimble-witted woman was a diversion, despite the accusations that she was guilty of all sorts of chicanery. Only six women lived at Henrico, and they were old beyond their years, worn out by the land and lost hopes.

Clarissa fought back a shudder. In a few years, she would be like those women. She had to be careful. She couldn't let down her standards in the midst of people either hopeless or indifferent to their situations. She thought of the girl Sally. What chance did she have?

Patrick trotted the mare past a snake-fenced pasture where eight or ten head of cattle grazed, then past fields of oats; flax for linen; tall, tasseled Indian cornstalks; but not the ubiquitous, noxious tobacco plant. Closer in, just beyond a peach orchard, were a swine pen, a tanning shed, and a large barn and corral.

Near a large, sturdily built cabin, Modesty was working the kitchen garden. She squatted between rows of bushes bearing a yellow crookneck vegetable called squash, or *Askutasquash*, the Indian term. The foods of the New World were strange and unsavory to Clarissa's taste.

Sighting them, Modesty rose, arched her back, rubbing the small of it, then started toward her visitors. Her strangely colored eyes were alight with amusement. "By me troth, Clarissa," she said, wiping her grimy hands on her apron, "I never thought I would see yew astride a horse. Good morrow, Reverend Dartmouth."

"Greetings, Mistress Jones." Patrick dismounted and held up his hands to help Clarissa down. Those long, slender hands easily closed around her corseted waist. He lowered her to the ground so that she stood toe to toe with him.

She peeked up at him from beneath the narrow brim of her fashionable black riding hat with its bows and ostrich feathers. Her nearness seemed to have no affect on him.

"Thy hat isn't tilted enough," he said. He adjusted its brim slightly forward, then turned back to Modesty. "Thy husband, is he within calling distance?"

Modesty's mouth curled in a big smile. "Yew can be certain that me husband, wherever he be on the farm, already knows of yewr arrival."

Clarissa felt a great pity for the woman, married to such a beast of the wilds as Mad Dog Jones.

Patrick had a higher opinion of him than she did. "The man has a peculiar sense of honor. I mean he believes more in what a person is than what they say. He's a man who does things by instinct rather than by decision," he had told her.

Apparently Mad Dog Jones's present preference for solitude had deteriorated him into something only a little more civilized than the New World wildlife.

Reluctantly, Clarissa admitted to herself that she was most fortunate. Of the Jamestown bachelors, she had selected the most refined, a mild-tempered husband she could control through pretty manners and a reproving gaze when needed.

Or rather, Modesty had selected Patrick for her. For this, Clarissa turned to give the waiting woman a most grateful hug. She avoided staring at her white coif, where tendrils should have been visible beneath its plain, banded edge. Modesty's overskirt was gathered up, peasant style, around her waist. Her coarse stockings were dirty, and she wore pattens over her shoes.

Unconsciously, Clarissa's hand went to her lace steinkirk, held in place by an heirloom ruby brooch. Patrick's income, while not large, was at least guaranteed by the Company, so that she did not have to work the fields. His tutoring fees and whatever gratuities his parishioners could afford in the way of a chicken or a bushel of corn were extra blessings.

Blessings? Egad, now she was sounding like her Bible-spouting husband.

"Come on inside out of the heat," Modesty was saying. "A tumbler of spring water should cool yewr calluses."

Clarissa had to smile. She picked up her long, full, trained skirt and followed her inside. "My backside *is* getting callu—" She broke off when she realized Patrick was regarding her with intent interest. His full lips, which should have belonged to a hedonist, twitched.

Fortunately, at that moment Modesty's husband entered the cabin, his musket in hand. Perspiration sheened his sun-baked face and dampened his shirt. His glowering scan took them in.

Clarissa had to fight back a shiver. To extract herself from his view, she swiftly seated herself in a ladder-back chair in the corner and became inordinately occupied with stripping off her gloves.

The cleanly kept room, bright with mid-morning sunlight streaming through the open shutters, was as scarce in furnishings as her own. Wildflowers, whose names she wasn't familiar with, sat in a gray crock painted with some sort of whimsical creatures.

Mad Dog tossed his straw hat on a peg and wiped his forearm across his sweaty forehead. "Well met, Reverend Dartmouth."

"Since we art neighbors," Patrick said easily, removing his felt sugarloaf hat, "we have come to call."

Modesty's husband propped his musket against the fireplace and took a clay pipe from the pipe box. Lighting the pipe, he said, "I would hardly call eight miles a neighborly distance."

Undaunted, Patrick took a seat at one end of the settle and draped his arm across its back. "Aye, that is true. I've come with special purpose."

Modesty poured water from a pitcher banded with blue figures. Sweat stains formed half moons beneath her underarms. "A preacher with a purpose." She brought tumblers of water for Clarissa and Patrick and passed a third to her husband. "I should have known."

He accepted the tumbler, and a brief look passed between the husband and wife that Clarissa couldn't read.

Then he said, "Modesty tends to hold the Church in contempt. You know, that little misunderstanding about witchcraft." He swigged down the water, and Clarissa watched with fascination as a stray droplet trickled down his thickly muscled neck. He set the tumbler on the mantel.

"I was not in favor of that unfortunate piece of business," Patrick said.

"None of the contract brides believed it of you, Modesty," Clarissa said and really meant it. The woman might be devilish, delightfully so in fact, but she certainly was not the Devil incarnate.

Modesty sat on the stool and clasped her earth-smudged hands around her knees. Her eyes narrowed, and Clarissa knew it wasn't from her usual squint when straining to make out something. Rancor glittered there. "No, but enough people were willing to believe I was a witch that Ratcliff almost got by with burning me at the stake."

"He's still setting fire to the faggots of innocent victims." Mad Dog drew on the pipe's long stem, then added, "At least his allies are."

Modesty looked at her husband sharply. "Wot do yew mean?"

Mad Dog exhaled a wreath of smoke that was lost in the dusty sunlight. "Word among the Po-

tomacs is that Ratcliff is intriguing with the Powhattan tribes. Stirring up trouble against the
settlers on the colony's frontier. The chief of the
Monacans warns there may be an attack at the
fall of the leaf—in autumn."

Real fear tightened the muscles at the back of
Clarissa's neck. "Why would he do such a
thing?"

Mad Dog shrugged shoulders that she
couldn't help but notice were almost as wide as
an ell's bolt. "If the Indians cause enough trouble with the settlers, Yeardley could find himself replaced. Ratcliff is next in line. He wants
the governorship."

Modesty frowned. "Why? The scoundrel is
making a fortune in flesh trading."

"A governorship is worth several fortunes.
The colony is the rendezvous of a fortunate
white few who grow rich through their privileged position."

He sent Clarissa a reflective glance, then said,
"These are not your English gentry but bour-
geois plutocrats who work for their own special
interests. Ratcliff could even be knighted, as
Yeardley was last year. All Ratcliff must do is
demonstrate that he is able to control the Indians and the governorship is his."

Listening to him talk, Clarissa was struck by
the extraordinary texture of the man's voice, a
softly modulated baritone. Black velvet came to
mind. She had expected—well, less cultivation.

"That is one of the reasons I came to see thee,"
Patrick said. "About the Indians. Word has it

that thou hath been here since the year after the first colonists arrived, since 1608. And that thou walks freely among the Indians. That they trust thee."

Mad Dog said nothing. Just waited, one massive hand cradling the bowl of his pipe.

" 'Tis my concern for the Indians that led my ministry here. I desire to teach them civility and to educate them that they might understand about God and learn the Gospel story. My hope, ultimately, is to build an Indian school at Henrico."

Mad Dog tapped his pipe bowl against the hearthstone. "You will have to kill their leader first. Itopatin, their *werowance*, is a puppet. His younger brother Opechancanough pulls the strings. Opechancanough hates the Christians."

Patrick's sandy brows furrowed. "Why is that?"

"When a child, he was taken by the Spanish to Spain, Mexico, and Santo Domingo. In those eight years he was indoctrinated by both the Jesuits and the Dominicans. Gradually, he came to see only hypocrisy. While in Havana, he escaped and made it back here to his homeland. He fiercely resists the introduction of English faith, language, or manners among his people."

"But how can we be held accountable for what the Spanish did?" Clarissa interjected. "Their Catholic—"

"I make no moral judgments, Goodwife Dartmouth. What is, is."

"Do you have no values, no—"

Modesty interrupted her with a hollow laugh. "Me good husband values expediency. That be his God."

"I see." Looking at nothing in particular, Patrick nodded, as if coming to a conclusion, then slapped his hands on his thighs. "Well, then, I suppose that brings me to the second reason for my visit. I take it thou hath a particular end in mind regarding thine affairs. Dost thou think this expediency that thou, uh, value might dovetail with serving as one of the two burgesses from our borough?"

Mad Dog braced his forearms on his widespread knees. "I also value my solitude."

Clarissa leaned forward, addressing Modesty. "Master Bannock, Rose's husband, has agreed to be our other burgess."

"Rose lives in Henrico?"

"Nearby, at Falling Brook. Master Bannock has constructed his sawmill close to the new ironworks."

Modesty raised winged brows. "Bannock's—uh—eloquence is rather limited, is it not?"

"True, the man stutters," Patrick answered, "but he is sincere and conscientious. With thy training and eloquence, thou would make an excellent representative for us," he said, directing his words to Modesty's husband. He rose and picked up his hat. "I would like to take back thy acceptance to Henrico with me."

Clarissa stood and walked to the door. For some reason she couldn't fathom, she felt com-

pelled to back Patrick in his bid for Mad Dog as
a Henrico burgess. Then, too, she truly enjoyed
Modesty's company. "We could visit with Polly
and Annie and the others in Jamestown during
Assembly time, Modesty."

Modesty rose from the stool. "Jamestown
could go up in its own smoke for all I—" That
big smile of hers appeared suddenly, and she
accepted with a surprising alacrity. "Well, of
course, I wouldn't mind seeing Polly and Annie
again."

"What dost thou sayeth, Master Jones?" Patrick smiled, and Clarissa thought that mayhaps
her husband was not so dour after all. "As a burgess, thou could pursue thy own matters of expediency."

Mad Dog stood. "I'll think upon—"

The door swung open, and a man of medium
height entered. Dressed in the thigh-length tunic and knee breeches of a field hand, he had
curling wheat-blond locks that fell about his
ears and vivid blue eyes. They quickly assessed
Clarissa, then his mouth curled in an almost
comical smile. "Milady." He doffed his flat cap.
When he straightened, his eyes were openly
daring.

Clarissa nodded, feeling herself blush. So this
was Mad Dog Jones's new bondservant.

"Holloway?" Mad Dog asked, his harsh gaze
leveled on his bondservant.

The man called Holloway relinquished his vi-
sual hold of Clarissa and turned to his master.
"I came in search of bandaging." He held out

his left palm. The fingers were sliced across the middle joints and bleeding. " 'Twould seem that I am none too proficient with the scythe yet."

"I'll take care of it," Modesty said, coming forward.

He started toward Modesty but brushed too close to Clarissa, causing her to drop her gloves. "Here, let me," she said, thinking of his injured hand, and stooped to collect her gloves at the same time as he did. They bumped again, each laughing.

It was the first time she could remember laughing in months, maybe years. Behind that peasant facade she wanted to believe there existed something fine, noble, and dignified.

Having finished the midday meal, Jack took part of his hour's respite on his bed of hay in the barn's loft and admired the ruby brooch he had pilfered. His dexterity, he reflected with wry amusement, might be said to be inborn. His mother had been a prostitute who had taught him to rob guests with whom she had just lain.

He had tried to give up thieving. Run off to sea, he had. But even as a deckhand, he tended to fancy valuables other than his own. A delight in the captain's gold sword hilt inlaid with rubies had resulted in a forced flight through the back streets of Santo Domingo.

"Jack Holloway!"

He looked over at the ladder just in time to see Modesty emerge from the loft's trapdoor and charge toward him. "Scurvy thief! Unscrupulous scoundrel! Shifty cur! I could wrap a horseshoe around yewr neck!"

He got up his arms just in time to ward off a blow from her fist. "Whoa there! Modesty. My love. Wait. Give me a ch—"

A left punch walloped his cheekbone, and his head snapped to one side. "I saw yew cop the brooch."

"My hand, you're hurting—"

"Afore I'm finished with yew," she panted, "that hand is going to be the only thing that feels good on yewr miserable body, Jack Holloway."

Blindly, he grabbed at her flailing fists. He latched onto one and jerked her down beside him. Her knee shot up, and he dodged so that it just barely missed its target. It took several seconds of tussling before he could pin her beneath him. "Since when did you qualify for sainthood?"

Those marvelously mismatched eyes glared up at him. He could almost hear her teeth grinding. "Is yewr noggin filled with pea soup? Wot do yew think will happen when Clarissa finds her brooch is missing? A hue and cry will be sent up—and, wot with the felony charge, I'll be the likely suspect!"

"Now, now, Modesty." He flashed her one of his appealing smiles. "For all Clarissa will know, the brooch could have fallen off during the trip here or back."

"Lady Clarissa to yew." Her eyes narrowed. "Or have yew already copped a familiar feel from her?"

"She's too hoity-toity to bugger, for my taste."

"Jack Holloway, yewr taste in women is most catholic. Any of them and all of them."

He had to chuckle. "That is one of the things I find fascinating about you. You are not only clever, but not likely to be shocked even by the most outrageous sallies."

He was slightly surprised to realize that he really meant what he was saying. Modesty was not a regular beauty, not even really pretty. Her looks caught a man off guard because they depended on wit and expression rather than on bone structure. A painter could never truly capture her sparkle and vitality that came from her confidence and determination.

With a celerity of movement, she rolled from beneath him and sat up. "Yew be a bloody fool." She began plucking bits of straw from her calico gown. "Yew laugh when others fret. Yew remain at ease when most men shout out their rage. Yew'll swing from the gallows sure as a leper has lesions."

"I intend to sell my life dearly."

"Count yewrself lucky Mad Dog bought your indenture papers. Most planters want to get all the work they can from their bondservants, since they can keep them but a few years."

"Lucky? With luck I can put away enough booty, such as this brooch here, to get me passage to Hispaniola and rig up my own brig and buccaneers."

"So the sea calls yew back once more. Yew'll never settle down, will yew, Jack?"

"Never. And neither will you." With his poor bandaged hand, he took her hand and held it against his heart.

Her mouth crimped. "Cut the drama, Jack. But 'tis true, I have no plans to settle down, either. Not here, at least. Not alone with a man so skilled with the knife as Mad Dog."

He abandoned his effort. "Freebooting, Modesty, living off only your next heartbeat and a song in your soul, that is what gives a dull life flavor."

"An interesting philosophy," drawled a male voice.

Both he and Modesty jumped. At the sight of Mad Dog, his crossed arms propped atop the ladder's top rung, Modesty jerked her hand from Jack's grasp. "I—I came up to—to rebandage Jack's hand." She drew a roll of linen strips from her skirt's placket hole.

How much had Mad Dog overheard? Jack wondered.

Modesty dipped her homemade brush into the tin cup of turpentine, then dabbed the bristles into the dollop of blue-green paint on the rotten piece of hickory plank. She had to make short, rapid strokes just below the crock's stoneware rim, because her self-made paint tended to dry too quickly.

Then, too, her strokes were hurried because there was yet the lard to be rendered and soap to be made from it. Fortunately, old Juana had appeared yesterday like some leprechaun to shuck the corn, and just as mysteriously vanished. Like the river, she carried gossip gleaned from her roamings up and down the valley.

This was the best time of day for Modesty to desert drudgery and escape into enchantment for an hour. Mad Dog and Jack had eaten their midday meal after Clarissa and her husband had departed, so she did not have to worry about the two men returning until late from the fields they were clearing of stumps.

If Jack returned at all. Her vivid imagination could just envision his handsome body, now tanned by the hot summer sun and muscle-honed by the strenuous labor, hewn into quarters by Mad Dog's axe. After finding her today with Jack in the barn loft, Mad Dog could have easily gone on another killing spree. However, he had merely informed Jack that work was waiting.

But that fulminating glance . . . She could well imagine what fate awaited her when Mad Dog returned this evening.

No, she didn't want to. She knew all too well that her husband hadn't come by his name because his mother had experienced a flight of fancy at his birth.

She attributed her bizarre fascination with him to his rich, melodious voice. At night, it made it all too easy for her to forget the wild man she lay with. It caressed her, beguiled her, excited her. And then his body took over, and she was lost. At least, her body was. Her mind— well, she was still in possession of it.

147

And it was busy formulating plans for leaving this pisshole of a country come General Assembly time next July. Reverend Dartmouth's suggestion had provided the means for her to get to Jamestown. Now, she just had to find a way to buy passage back to England.

By the time she set foot on English soil, more than a year would have passed. If she were careful, used an alias, she could avoid apprehension. Alas, her circumstances would not be as lucrative as when Jack had been her employer. Still, with her skill with the brush and pen, she could find a way to make ends meet.

She brushed another stroke onto the butter churn. A shadow fell across her improvised pallet. Her scalp prickled. Indians occasionally appeared without warning, padding across the open field like gray wolves in single file. Sometimes they even strolled into the cabin, uninvited. They would dip a finger into Mad Dog's inkwell, give the grinding mill an experimental turn, or peer into the wavy looking glass.

Once, Arahathee had entered the cabin without warning. Like today, she had been furtively painting and had jumped more from guilt than surprise. She knew Mad Dog considered the Monacans valuable allies. As a peace offering, she had quickly sketched a rough character of the half-naked top-knotted warrior. He had seemed genuinely pleased.

As she glanced over her shoulder now, she almost wished that this latest visitor were an Indian. Musket in hand, Mad Dog had entered the room as silently as the deer from whose skin his moccasins were made. His eyes were as chilly and gray as the Thames in winter.

He stood so close, she could smell his woodsy scent. He reached toward her, and she shrank from his powerful hand, but he merely plucked a piece of straw stuck in her coif.

She stared at the straw, then up at his unyielding expression. " 'Twas not wot yew think."

"How do you know what I think?"

She swallowed. "Jack and me, we go back a long time."

"Partners in crime?" He crossed to the hearth to take up the scourer for cleaning his musket barrel and screwed it into its ramrod. "As long as both of you understand your prior partnership is not to continue. In any form. Have I made myself clear?"

The way he rammed the rod in and out of his musket barrel made her nervous. He never took his eyes off her. How could anyone withstand that unwavering glare? It snared people.

One time when she had been picking huckleberries, she had espied him through the trees. He was standing still as a rock. Curious, she had crept closer through the underbrush. Motionless, he had let squirrels mistake him for a stump and play about his feet. Ten or fifteen minutes later, he had snared one of them for dinner that evening. He was a man of frighteningly infinite patience.

"Aye," she said at last, grudgingly. "Yew have made yewrself clear."

He settled a heavily muscled thigh on the board table's edge and laid his musket and ramrod on the bench. He tapped a knuckle against the empty crock, making a hollow thudding sound. "You were preparing to make butter?"

"Yew're bearbaiting me." She jammed her brush into the mug she used to hold her other brushes and palette knife. "Go ahead. Strap me to the dunking stool for neglecting me duties. Or better, mayhaps, slit me throat."

He picked up one of her brushes and ran a testing finger through its bristly tip. "You made these?"

"Aye. From bristles from our hogs."

He put the brush down. "And the paint?"

"I crushed the green clay along the riverbank and mixed it with the oil from our ground flax seeds."

"Innovative, are you not?" He picked up the butter crock to examine her work. "You have a steady hand. But what in God's name is this design?"

"A fairy ring." She compressed her lips, awaiting the next sharp sting of his words.

Instead, his voice seemed filled with sincere interest. "Tell me about it."

She eyed him warily. Surely he was baiting her again. "About wot?"

He looked as if he had lost his patience. "About the fairy ring. Why the faces, wench?"

"Modesty." This time, she was the one without patience. "A fairy ring is a circle found in fields where fairies have been dancing. I happen

150

to like to paint their faces into the ring." Elves, gnomes, brownies, pixies, nymphs, leprechauns and banshees, trolls, even Beelzebub himself. Hadn't she married him incarnate?

"I believe I am well acquainted with the legend," he said drily, "that fairies sometimes become visible to a person who has stepped inside the ring. I suppose you have stepped inside one?"

She placed one foot on her bench in a truly brazen manner, braced her elbow on her knee with her chin propped on her fist, and smiled broadly. "Nay. I am a fairy meself."

"Oh, are you now? I suppose you are Titania?"

"Titania?"

"The fairy queen. More lovely, more innocent than any other. She almost lost all, but for the protection of the gentle and powerful strength of the fairies who saved her by their love."

There he went again, needling her about her innocence and her past. But with that transfixing voice, as smooth as fresh cream and as potent as Trinidad rum, one was almost willing to disregard any insults.

"In faith, master, I am but one of yewr ordinary fairies—angels forced to leave heaven because of a wrongdoing."

"A former angel?" One black brow climbed. "Now, somehow I find that difficult to—"

"Aye, I am. But a human being came to fairyland and married me, he did. Then brought me to his home. Yew do know 'ow the fairy tale goes, don't yew now?"

He put her churn down, planted a forearm on his thigh, and leaned toward her with a positively wicked smile. "No. Do tell me."

"Why," she said quite earnestly, "the human being must follow strict rules in order to remain married to a fairy. For example, a human husband must never scold or strike his fairy wife or refer to her being a fairy. If he does, the fairy immediately returns to fairyland."

"I should be so lucky." He collected his musket and rose to leave but at the door paused and looked over his shoulder. "Do not get any ideas in that scheming head of yours about going with me to Jamestown for General Assembly. I have no desire to have my good wife arrested for further nefarious deeds. You have already cost me dear enough."

She was gripped by a terrifying sensation that he understood her better than she understood herself, and that it was the unsympathetic understanding of an antagonist.

Chapter Ten

Modesty pulled on Betsy's warm teats, one after the other, with rhythmic movements. Often, the milking could be tedious and monotonous, but sometimes pleasantly soothing. A rhythm of life, it was. The steam rising off the milk in the crisp, early morning frost. The rooster tiptoeing along the fence. The husky rustling of the corn tassels.

The pumpkins yet to be harvested lolled lazily in the garden, as large and orange as last night's full moon. A hunter's moon, Mad Dog had called it.

The picture seemed idyllic, until her thoughts stopped drifting and she remembered that she was married to a man who was likely to cut her throat with his whittling knife if the whim took him. Didn't he brand his cattle by a personalized notching of their ears?

Next thing she might know, he would be notching hers. She had indeed jumped from the frying pan into the fire. She could choose between the risk of roasting in Jamestown or having her throat split at Ant Hill. London, with its hazard of Fleet Prison leering at her, seemed infinitely preferable.

On the surface, she and Mad Dog had taken on a rhythm of life in their relationship. Rising early by candlelight, they ate a silent breakfast, then off to their own chores. At midday she would carry lunch to him and Jack if their work took them far afield.

Lately, though, both men had been working furiously in the tannery. The salted meats and tallow that Mad Dog exported went neglected. At sunset the men were back for dinner and after the meal would return once more to the tannery for a few hours more of concentrated work.

In spare words, Mad Dog had told her that it took a full year to turn a new hide into good leather: removing the hair, scraping the inside, soaking and turning the hides in vats of tannic acid and the bark of sumac and chestnut. Lastly, there was the currying of the hide to smoothness and softness. It was a smelly process. Only Juana smelled worse.

Some evenings, she would show up in her usual will-o'-the-wisp way and teach Modesty how to spin the flax tow she had combed into yarn, or help dip candles in the candle wheel.

Once, the spry old Spanish woman even climbed on the cabin roof to drop a live chicken down the chimney—her method of cleaning a chimney that wasn't likely to put chimney sweeps out of work.

But after the candles were snuffed and Modesty and Mad Dog were at last alone, the nights were something else. No rhythm to them at all. She never knew if Mad Dog's passion would be wild and tempestuous, like the storm-tossed *God Sent*, or gentle and sweet, like a lamb nibbling carrot tops from her palm.

"Had I udders as large as yewrs, Betsy, then yewr owner would sit up and take notice, verily." She chuckled at the image.

It was almost as if she were indeed an invisible fairy, so little note did he take of her. Discounting the nights, naturally.

Compared to someone of Lady Clarissa's station, she was lacking in appeal. Not that his opinion mattered a whit to her, except for his permitting her to accompany him to Jamestown.

She had to find another way to get there—safely. The colony's capital was little more than a living cemetery, but at least she would have the opportunity to buy passage for England before the good citizens decided to serve her up as skewered chicken.

At the sound of a clanking bell, she ceased her milking. Through the haze of the Indian summer morning, she sighted the square sails of a sloop. Betsy turned those round, long-lashed eyes on her as if to inquire what the holdup was. "Not now, Betsy. We've visitors!"

She pushed back the stool and collected her half-filled pail. Sloshing the milk, she set off in a quick pace for the cabin. Why would a merchant ship be upriver this late in the year? Mad Dog had made it clear that by this time, before the arrival of the gale season, most of the trading vessels had already set sail for their respective countries.

She left the pail on the table, smoothed her skirts, and tucked into her coif the errant wisps of her newly grown hair. Duck curls she derisively called them. She hurried back outside. The sloop was already putting in at Mad Dog's long pier. Juana came trotting out of the woods to investigate also.

Ant Hill had not had visitors from the outside world since Clarissa and her husband had called to visit almost three months before. Anticipation of having contact with other people, and finding out the latest news, filled Modesty with excitement. Her feet fairly flew down the oystershell path, while the reclusive Juana hung back.

Modesty's life on the Thames, England's major trade route, had taught her much about ships. This one was an old, rotting three-masted merchant caravel, barely serviceable. But to Modesty the *Roter Löwe*, bronze cannons and all, was a beautiful sight floating upon the James. By the time she reached the dock, the East Indiaman's gangplank had been lowered.

The Savage

A blubberous, red-cheeked man who could have easily been rolled down the gangplank was followed by a lanky, hard-eyed man in a sailor's Monmouth cap. Aboard deck, a score or more hands scurried to secure the ship's rigging.

The fashionably dressed man in the forefront doffed his Copotain hat with its high conical crown to reveal short, sparse flaxen hair. "Captain De Ruyter, madam." The middle-aged man bestowed a half bow and a full grin. His lips were as naturally red as his cheeks. He wore a wide-sleeved, short cloak with a falling collar and wide breeches gathered at the knees. "You are—?"

"Master Jones's wife."

A flicker of surprise passed over his apple-dumpling face. "My first mate, Schouten," he said, indicating the taciturn man behind him. She had seen plenty like him and the *Roter Löwe*'s crew on the Thames waterfront. They had prowled the ports of the world and would as soon rob you of your life as your purse.

"Is the master at home?" De Ruyter's English had a distinctly Flemish accent which she could identify from her working for a flemish calligrapher, and his gestures were distinctly effeminate.

"Aye. He should be here shortly." Of that, she had no doubt. "Won't yew come on inside and—"

The captain had transferred his gaze beyond her, and she turned to see Mad Dog, his musket cradled in his arm, striding toward them. "Ho, Mad Dog!"

"Henrick. I had begun to doubt you made the trip this year."

"And miss out on your quality hides? Not on your life."

"My bondservant is in the tanning shed now, finishing with their bundling."

De Ruyter winked. "I'll furnish a detail of my hands to load the hides, if you will furnish us a glass or two of your brandy."

Mad Dog raised a brow. "Brandy this early in the morning tells me your constitution is made of iron."

De Ruyter grimaced. "I drink it to wash down the foul taste of your English duties."

"Then brandy it is. And bread and cheese to ease its passage."

"I see you have taken yourself a—wife."

Mad Dog wrapped an affectionate arm around Modesty's waist. His smile was more cynical than fond. "Ahh, yes, my charming help-meet."

"Me beloved husband." Modesty ground her heel into his soft moccasin and was pleased to see him wince.

Once inside, she found Juana already preparing a repast of cornbread and hard cheese. Putting her alehouse experience to use, Modesty poured drinks for the three men who straddled the board table's benches and discussed Bristol, which was the destination of Mad Dog's hides, and the price they were expected to bring.

"The price my employers receive does not make it worth my while," De Ruyter complained. "Not when I have to forfeit your colony's custom duties out of my own return from the Dutch East India Company."

Mad Dog's hands gripped his tumbler. "So you fattened Yeardley's purse again, eh?"

Juana, her leathery face set in disapproving lines, supplied the men with a wooden trencher of cheese and day-old cornbread. Schouten snapped up a hunk of both.

De Ruyter wiped the ale from his upper lip. "Let the other foreign vessels put in at the port of customs and pay the duties. Not this Dutchman. Tell them, Schouten."

"Ya, this is our last time to put into the English colony." He popped the cheese in his mouth, revealing yellowed, crooked teeth.

De Ruyter leaned forward. "You see, I plan to buy guns and ammunition manufactured in Liége, Belgium, take the cargo to Africa's Niger delta, and barter with an African king there for his captives. Then I will take the captives and sell them into slavery at the Santo Domingo sugar fields for five times the cost of the gun cargo."

The year before, a Dutch ship had brought twenty-odd Negro slaves, the first in the colony. Mad Dog had said that Yeardley and Ratcliff had bought most of them.

"After that," De Ruyter continued, "I load the *Roter Löwe* with sugar and return to Liége to buy more guns. And Santo Domingo," he finished slyly, "does not charge such high custom duties."

"What will your employers say about this?" Mad Dog asked.

"The Dutch East India Company be damned." De Ruyter swallowed the last of his brandy, then said with a conspiratorial smile, "They can count the *Roter Löwe* lost at sea."

Modesty set a basket of dried oysters before the men with a thud. They were busy talking and did not take note of her sour expression. While she openly acknowledged herself as mildly unscrupulous, hoodwinking from the well-to-do, men like De Ruyter and Ratcliff who had no qualms about trading in human flesh disgusted her.

Nevertheless, her mind was racing. How to get De Ruyter to drop her off at Jamestown?

Granted, she had nothing to barter for passage, not even her body. Not when flesh came so cheaply for men in the captain's business. Unless. . . . Why hadn't she thought of it before!

She smiled and poured the men another round of brandy—and yet another.

Through narrowed eyes, Mad Dog watched his wife liberally fill the guests' tankards. That big smile of hers—she was up to something.

But then so was he. Apparently their plans shared the same modus operandi.

He drank little after that first tankard but encouraged the two men to drink heartily. He hefted his tankard more than once in a toast.

160

"To sugar, slaves, and Santo Domingo."

And again. "To the success of your new trade."

"Here, here," Schouten said. His sullen expression had been replaced by a sloshy grin.

When Modesty disappeared out the door, Mad Dog generously poured the contents of his tankard into De Ruyter's and excused himself.

"Whither goest thou?" the befuddled captain asked.

Mad Dog stood at the doorway and watched Modesty. "To check on the loading."

She did not head down the path to the dock but set off in the direction of the outbuildings. He doubted that she was seeking the privy.

With a cordial expression, he turned back to his guests. "Raise another bumper. I shall return shortly."

He caught Juana's attention and in Spanish told her to summon Arahathee at once. The old woman nodded stolidly, spit into the fireplace, and trotted past him out the door.

Next he found Holloway in the tanning shed, beyond the paddle vat where a few pallets of hides still awaited loading aboard the ship. Modesty was not with the bondservant.

Curious, the relief he felt. He doubted the woman's fidelity. She made it quite clear how barbaric she considered him. He had never thought about taking a wife again, and certainly not one as coarse as Modesty.

Yet she was his wife now. And he could not deny that sometimes he hungered for the warm touch of another. After all, he was human, although his wife expressed considerable doubt about that.

At first, after the killings, he had wanted only to retreat from life, retreat from his conscience. Then he realized there was nowhere to hide. He had thought that if he could stay alive in the charnel house that was the Virginia Colony, he could put an ocean's distance between himself and civilized society's heavy hand of authority.

But colonial life had little to offer him. And the pleasures and comforts of normal human relationships, the things that gold could not buy, were not to be had at all, doomed by his guilt. Still, like a fool, he yearned.

Holloway left off securing a pallet with rope and straightened. Despite the mild weather, sweat beaded his suntanned face. "Aye, master?"

"I want to stage a party."

The bondservant's fair brows met over the bridge of his nose. "You what?"

"Take all the remaining kegs of peach brandy in the springhouse and give them to the seamen. I want them to drink heartily. Do you understand?"

With a grin, Holloway wiped the sweat from his brow with his arm. "I do not understand your reasoning for all of this, but I think it a most splendid idea. I shall set myself about this delightful task."

"Something else. I desire you to remain sober. Quite sober."

The man looked crestfallen.

"Stay with them. Entertain them." In truth, the bondsman had the makings of an actor. Shakespeare would have appreciated his talent. "I will explain later."

There was still his wife to deal with. Pride prevented him from asking his bondservant if he had seen the wench. She could not have gotten far.

He bypassed the privy and entered the barn. At his footsteps, a piglet ran squealing. In the far stall, the bay mare welcomed him with a whinny and a steaming stream of piss. Betsy placidly ignored him. In one corner, the hiding place of harvested pumpkins was exposed by the dusty sunlight filtering through the door. He stopped, listened, and thought he heard movement in the loft.

Moldy hay cushioned his footsteps as he crossed to the ladder. Scaling its wooden rungs, he cautiously stuck his head through the loft's trapdoor. He should have known.

Her back three-quarters to him, Modesty was plowing through Holloway's trunk. She tossed a woolen cap over her shoulder. Next a pair of knitted stockings went flying. Then an "Aha!" issued from beneath her breath. He watched her hold up something to the slivers of sunlight between the clapboards.

"I do not think you could wear Lady Clarissa's brooch with quite the same aplomb."

She twisted around, losing her balance on her knees. One arm flung out to brace herself, and she ended up in an awkward half-reclining position. "Yew are becoming clever at spying!"

"A spy and a thief. We make a pair, do we not?"

"I did not steal the brooch!"

He climbed into the loft and, ducking his head under the low beams, crossed the straw-strewn floor to hunker down before her. He held out his palm. "Give it to me."

She made a fist. "I was going to see that it was returned to Clarissa."

He pried loose her fingers. They were nimble, her nails short and ragged, her hand hard. "By way of Captain De Ruyter?"

Her mouth made a petulant moue. "All right. All right. I was going to buy me passage back to England. Look, yew don't want me any more than I want yew. I burn the bread, I spoil the butter, I knot the yarn. Juana can do the chores much better."

He studied the brooch, so brilliant in the loft's dim light, then studied his wife. So tarnished. "But I don't fancy Juana in bed with me," he said quietly, calmly.

Her face crimsoned. In another woman he might have called it a virginal blush. Or was she merely warm because of the stuffy, hot barn? "How many men have you known?"

"Thousands."

So she wished to play with him. He drew his thumb across the heel of her hand. She swallowed. His thumb continued on across the pad of her hand and then dipped into the center of her palm. He felt the tremor ripple down through her arm and into her hand. "To whom did you first give yourself?"

"A—a baron."

He lowered his head and kissed her palm. He heard her telltale rasp. It amused him. "Was it everything you expected?"

"And more." Her voice had a hard edge to it.

His head dipped, and with his tongue he licked the spot where his thumb had been. Her breathing sounded like the far-off rasping of a sash saw. The sound told him he was succeeding with his own game.

He raised his head. Her lips were parted, her breathing shallow, her pupils dilated. "And what did he pay you for your maidenhead?"

If those pupils had been torches, he would be in flames. "The gent paid me with his garberdine."

"His overcloak?"

"It was the blizzard of '07." Her eyes stared back in time. "I was twelve and homeless and freezing."

This was followed by a careless shrug, but he knew enough about reading people to believe her. He felt somehow less for having begun this game.

Admittedly, the woman intrigued him. One never guessed where her words would land. She was as haughty as a marquise with the ingenuousness of a child and the cunning of a Medici. "A maidenhead for warmth," he muttered, staring down at her roughened hand. "The equity of the exchange is somewhat unbal—"

"Me maidenhead for me life."

He looked up. Her jaw was set in stony lines. Everything about her was hard. "I'll see to it that the brooch is returned to Lady Clarissa."

"I am sure yew will." She yanked away her hand.

His shoulders shook in silent mirth. He stood up. "Our visitors will be drinking heavily. The rest of the day, stay here in the loft, out of their way. And out of mine."

She peered up at him with calculated innocence. "Does that go for tonight, too?"

He felt a profound sadness for her destroyed innocence, then the feeling vanished with lightning speed. "If you are not in my bed when I am ready for you, I shall come and get you. Wherever you are. I will never again lose what is mine."

"Yew are the Devil's dung!" she screeched as he descended the ladder.

He knew that already. That was something he had to live with the rest of his mortal life.

He left the barn, noting that Holloway was following his orders and rolling a heavy oaken keg down the oystershell path toward the dock, where several slovenly seamen were already prying off the lids of two other kegs. The Jamestown cooper had charged Mad Dog enough shillings to make those kegs with their pliable willow-branch hoops.

At the cabin, De Ruyter and Schouten were feeling no pain. They were singing, in fact.

Their forearms braced on the board table, they leaned toward each other, grinning, their voices lifted in off-key lewdness.

> "In the spring of the year,
> when the gism is too thick,
> there is nothing so dear,
> as the sassafras stick."

Juana would not return with Arahathee and his braves for several hours, enough time for Mad Dog to fashion the shape his vengeance was to take. It was no wonder he appreciated nothing in life. Because until he took his revenge, he would be consumed with a tormenting, bottled rage. The sight of Ratcliff, still alive, had uncorked it. Vengeance, blind and sterile and contemptible.

"Mad Dog!" De Ruyter called. "You are neglecting your company. Come join us."

Mad Dog filled their noggins to the brim, drew a small measure for himself, and settled down next to Schouten. The first mate's lids were at half mast. "Your wife? Where ish she?"

He sipped the potent brew. "In the privy. With the runs." That should blot the man's lust.

Schouten's lids dropped, and he nodded. "It hashppens."

"Hickory dickory dock," the jolly captain launched into another ditty. "His mouth slid up my cock." He tittered and laid a stubby finger across his lips. "Sssh. The mistress mustn't overhear."

Mad Dog settled in to watch them and wait. As a young man, he had been left an enormous fortune of 120,000 livres a year by his maternal uncle. A wastrel those early years, he had drunk with the best but kept his head, more of an onlooker than a participant as life leaked away and night after night repeated itself.

His disgust gave way to a calm thoughtfulness. What he had in mind bordered on sheer stupidity. Yet with perfect timing and a little luck it was just possible. . . .

The afternoon's late shadows subsided across the puncheon floor. Merrymaking could be heard coming from the ship. De Ruyter had passed out, his head lolling in the split brandy. Schouten was staring witlessly at nothing, when Arahathee appeared in the doorway. Schouten eyed the Indian dubiously, shook his head as if to clear it, and resumed drinking.

Arahathee, dressed in buckskin breechcloth and tunic, cradled a new musket in his arms. The hilt of a knife protruded from the high top of one moccasin. He stood tall, bronzed and majestic, as befitting a *werowance*.

"*Wingapoh*," Mad Dog said, calling him by the Algonquin term for good friend. He rose and indicated to Arahathee to follow him outside. The braves, numbering fifteen, fell back for their leader and Mad Dog.

On the landing below, the sailors appeared not to have taken notice of the visitors. The seamen were staging their own party, laughing, singing, shouting. Two were so drunk they were dancing like a couple and toppled from the old sea-bucket's deck into the river.

Mad Dog led Arahathee and his warriors around to the back of the cabin and squatted beneath one of the peach trees. Its leaves had changed to a dull yellow, others littered the ground. Arahathee dropped down opposite him. His thin lips quirked and he nodded toward the ship. "Plenty of firewater."

Mad Dog grinned. "The musket you carry. Where did it come from?"

"A dozing Powhattan."

"That is not good news, my friend." The day the *Sparrow* had put in at Jamestown, Mad Dog had staggered down its gangplank and set out walking with his knapsack along the James, vowing to continue on until he had outdistanced the sound and smell and sight of a sickened society and himself.

Arahathee, at that time yet to be a chief, had found Mad Dog nearly six weeks later. Wading through a swamp and wandering in a daze, he had been eaten up by mosquitoes and had a rash that oozed and itched miserably. His features had been hardly recognizable. He had learned that the red rash came from the oil of a poisonous ivy, unknown in England.

The Indian's amusement had infuriated him. Perhaps his weakened attempts at driving a punch to Arahathee's midsection had aroused the man's admiration; certainly not his pity, for the Monacans, all the Indians, were incapable of that feeling. Pity could destroy a soul.

Arahathee had taken him back to the Mona-can village and instructed a wife to coat Mad Dog's rash-blemished body with a paste. In time, he healed and was permitted to come and go among the Monacans, from whom he learned their methods of planting, the faces of the moon, and many other particulars that enabled him to survive in the wilderness.

In turn, he had taught Arahathee how to read a compass, a device the chief still considered magic, and shown him the workings of a lock and key. The latter had absolutely delighted Arahathee.

Mad Dog had learned that the Indians were not simple-minded but quick of apprehension, subtle in their dealings, exquisite in their inventions, and industrious in their labor. Far more than he could say for his countrymen at James-town.

Now he shared his plans with Arahathee in the Algonquin tongue. "I am taking over the ship in the river."

Arahathee inclined his head and said nothing.

"The ship's chief and his subchief buy and sell people as slaves. I am giving to you the chief and his subchief to sell or keep captive, as you wish."

Humor at the irony of the situation glinted in Arahathee's jet black eyes.

"Those of the men aboard ship who wish to remain in my service, may. I wish the others to be escorted ashore—safely—by your warriors and set free at the mouth of the river." With over a hundred miles of formidable forest and river between Ant Hill and the cape, he doubted that the men would have any desire to return.

"The ship?"

"The ship is to be used to destroy my enemy, Ratcliff, and his estates."

Arahathee nodded. Ratcliff's alliance with the Powhattans, the Monacans' enemies, had not found favor with Arahathee. He frowned. "Why not kill the man, burn his crops?"

"That is not my way." No, he didn't go for the jugular. He planned to peck the man apart. A field here, a shipment of tobacco there. A piece of flesh here, an eye there.

And he knew just the man to be the instrument of his torture. The perfect pirate. Since his own wife desired the man, the sooner he implemented his plan, the better.

Chapter Eleven

"You want me to wot?"

"Paint over the name of the merchant caravel." In the fire-lit bedroom, Mad Dog traced the bow of Modesty's lip with a callused fingertip. "With your artist's eye, you could do that quite splendidly."

The amber glow highlighted his cheekbones so that they looked like pottery shards. His irises were like the silver glass beads the Indians coveted. And his kisses were as heady as the colonial brandy in which she had seen the Indians in Jamestown too liberally indulge. His woodsy smell in itself was highly arousing.

She knew he toyed with her, that he amused himself by awakening her grudging desire to an unsustainable passion that left her weak with the ache of wanting. Then he would chuckle with amusement when she was reduced to asking him to take her.

"Change the *Roter Löwe*'s name? To wot?" His plan to ruin Ratcliff was becoming more devious by the day. Mad Dog had the knack for taking small openings and changing them into big opportunities.

"Oh, use your imagination." His fingertip mapped her chin, moved down her neck, and rested in the hollow of her throat. "You are so good at doing that."

Heat flooded her cheeks at his veiled meaning. Exploring his wondrously built body was a never-ending pleasure for her. Mayhaps because her sight was so poor she used her hands and fingers, her lips and tongue, so skillfully.

"'Tis a marvelous gift you have," he had once told her in a voice suspended somewhere between exquisite agony and tortured ecstasy. That time had been mid-morning. He had returned with a turkey he had shot and wanted her to dress and boil it—and had stayed to dally away the morning.

Strange, to be so intimate with someone and yet not address them either by name or an endearment. His name did not fit in the environs of the bedroom, and he had taunted her that her given name did not befit the less than virtuous woman he had taken for a wife. Of course, neither of them had an endearing feeling for the other.

A smile curved her lips. "*Roter Löwe* uses ten spaces. So does the name I have in mind."

Thrill to the most sensual, adventure-filled Historical Romances on the market today...

FROM LEISURE BOOKS

As a home subscriber to Leisure Romance Book Club, you'll enjoy the best in today's BRAND-NEW Historical Romance fiction. For over twenty-five years, Leisure Books has brought you the award-winning, high quality authors you know and love to read. Each Leisure Historical Romance will sweep you away to a world of high adventure...and intimate romance. Discover for yourself all the passion and excitement millions of readers thrill to each and every month.

Save $5.⁰⁰ Each Time You Buy!

Each month, the Leisure Romance Book Club brings you four brand-new titles from Leisure Books, America's foremost publisher of Historical Romances. EACH PACKAGE WILL SAVE YOU $5.00 FROM THE BOOKSTORE PRICE! And you'll never miss a new title with our convenient home delivery service.

Here's how we do it. Each package will carry a FREE 10-DAY EXAMINATION privilege. At the end of that time, if you decide to keep your books, simply pay the low invoice price of $16.96, no shipping or handling charges added. HOME DELIVERY IS ALWAYS FREE. With today's top Historical Romance novels selling for $5.99 and higher, our price SAVES YOU $5.00 with each shipment.

AND YOUR FIRST FOUR-BOOK SHIPMENT IS TOTALLY FREE

IT'S A BARGAIN YOU CAN'T BEAT! A Super $21.96 Value!

LEISURE BOOKS   A Division of Dorchester Publishing Co., Inc.

GET YOUR 4 FREE BOOKS NOW — A $21.96 Value!

*Mail the Free Book
Certificate
Today!*

Get Four Books Totally FREE — A $21.96 Value!

▼ Tear Here and Mail Your FREE Book Card Today! ▼

PLEASE RUSH
MY FOUR FREE
BOOKS TO ME
RIGHT AWAY!

Leisure Romance Book Club
65 Commerce Road
Stamford CT 06902-4563

AFFIX
STAMP
HERE

His hand glided over her hip and down the length of her thigh. "And what is that?"

The lightness of his touch evoked just the opposite desire in her. She wanted to be taken in maddening, demanding lust instead of this drawn-out love play that strung her nerve endings so taut she quivered. Her breath caught, her lids fluttered, in anticipation of the moment that his hand would move inside her thighs. "Yew shall see."

He cupped her shoulders and gently pressed her onto her back and lowered his head over hers. His long hair formed a dark canopy for their faces. Where her fingers deftly wielded a paintbrush, his lips deftly feather-brushed her own. "I *would* see. All of you."

The kiss she expected, hungered for, was not forthcoming. Instead, to her astonishment, he shifted his massive weight. Braced on his forearms, he slid lower over her.

She felt his beard-shadowed jaw abrade her chest. His hair, tickling her skin, followed in the wake of his tongue-tipped kisses. Kisses that moved even lower.

She tried to focus her thoughts elsewhere, to retain at least the freedom of her mind. She visualized the task he had set her. "The figurehead would have to be recarved, also," she murmured. "To match the ship's new name."

"I'm good with a knife," he said, his words smothered between her breasts.

Envisioning his aptitude with the knife at

splitting throats, she felt the hair at her nape stand on end.

"But I am also good at other things," he continued, as did his adroit kisses.

Her nipples hurt, they were so hard with her pent-up need. She wished he would kiss them or tweak them as he sometimes did until she groaned and shuddered in quick release.

She had a notion that she surprised not only herself but him as well at how quickly her body responded to him, over and over again. However, he neglected her pouting nipples. Keen disappointment and frustration were undoing her effort at maintaining her detachment.

When his lips reached her belly, she thought he would kiss her navel, as he had done once before. She trembled with delicious excitement. Her hands covered each of her breasts, her fingers finding her nipples. She sighed.

"It is this I wish to see," he muttered thickly and parted her thighs before she realized what he was about.

With bewilderment and embarrassment, she tried to squeeze her legs together.

Easily, he kept them spread and lowered his head to view her most intimate parts by the revealing light of the flickering coals. "Ahh, you are like a rose." She could feel his warm, ragged breath, his fingertip lightly tracing the intricate folds of her skin, separating each one. "Your pink petals unfurling one after the other . . . to reveal that inner bud . . . glistening with creamy dew."

Her fingernails dug into his forearms, hoping to stop him, but his tongue found the engorged bud and began stroking it.

She squirmed, wiggled her hips, anchored by his large hands. Inconsistent with her hips, her hands grasped his head and held him. Her fingers raked through his lion's mane as she felt the ecstasy of release flow through her.

Later, with their backs turned to one another, she whispered, "I know now why they call you Mad Dog."

He said nothing, but she could tell he was listening.

"Backward, it spells God damn."

His low laugh was almost savage.

It was she who was damned. She had to find a way to leave.

His arms folded across his chest, Jack stood just inside the wharfhouse, sheltered from the wind, and watched as Modesty carefully lowered herself from the ship's fo'c'sle to the scaffolding that dangled against the vessel's swelling side.

The fifteen remaining members of the *Roter Löew*'s crew went about rerigging the less than seaworthy vessel, but more than one sailor cast a peek at Modesty's trim ankles encased in white woolen stockings.

Squatting men were busy with needle and cord, sewing and lacing the great pieces of canvas into more serviceable sails.

A strong northern wind buffeted the scaffolding. Modesty gripped the scaffolding rope with a white-knuckled hand, while the other began painting the name of the caravel's new home port in cobalt blue.

Jack heard footsteps on the pier's wooden planks and turned to see Mad Dog. The wind billowed his employer's black cloak and long hair, making him look like some fiend swooping down upon him. Jack waited until Mad Dog entered the wharfhouse and was within earshot, then said, "She's extraordinary."

Mad Dog arched a devilish brow. "The ship or the girl?"

He grinned. "I'm damned either way I answer that."

"You are damned if you fail to serve me precisely as I have instructed. You understand me, I trust?"

"All too well."

Jack was ostensibly to serve as an intermediary agent for the planters: With their power of attorney, he was to take orders from the colonial planters for goods required from London—farm implements, horses, weapons, clothes. The task should take no more than four or five months.

In exchange, he would carry their cash crops—tobacco, flax, corn—to England, where he would trade them to the representatives of London's merchants, the factors, in exchange for the ordered goods. Of course, no cash was to change hands other than the commission Jack took.

From among the planters whose business he was to solicit, he was to gain Ratcliff's trust. In representing him, Jack would gradually build Ratcliff's debt to the various London merchants until that debt destroyed Ratcliff's estate. A demonic plan which its deviser calculated should take no more than three or four years.

At the end of that time, Mad Dog had promised Jack that the vessel would be his to sail the high seas, and that his indenture papers would be given back to him.

Jack eyed Mad Dog warily now. "You are taking a risk in trusting me, a notorious felon. What's to prevent me from making off with the ship as soon as I set sail from here?"

That slow smile sent shivers rippling down the muscles at either side of his spine. "I share this with you that you may be enlightened. I am the fourth Baron De Villiers through my mother, and my father is the Lord High Admiral of the British Navy. Should I request it, he will most devotedly hunt you across the seven seas. He will explore every cove and inlet of every island until he finds you. Rest assured of that. If you cooperate, I am sure it can be arranged for you to receive the highly prized privateer papers which would permit you to legally ply your nefarious trade."

Jack was awed by the man's lineage, but he managed to respond with merely a shrug. "Doubtlessly your father is a figure who wields much power. So why not let him destroy Ratcliff? 'Tis obvious he could do so as easily as he could squash a cockroach."

Again that unnerving smile. "I reserve for myself the right to that great pleasure."

The practice of decorating a ship's bow with allegorical sculptures symbolizing the ship's name had seemed ludicrous to Mad Dog's father, whose wife was a scion of an ancient Norman family. "'Tis the foppish French who are responsible for such an asinine thing. Humph, decorating a ship. By God, next the French Navy will be decorating their seamen's cocks!" his father had fumed.

Mad Dog had been a mere fourteen at the time. He made a quip that played on the word *seamen*, bringing a stern glance of disapproval from his father, a member of an old, close-knit Essex family of minor gentry.

Now Mad Dog felt rather asinine, perched on a scaffold like some damned pigeon while trying to re-carve the figurehead. Ironic, he thought, that the warrior Ajax had been a madman. And here he was converting the madman into a water sprite—under the direction of the wench he called his wife. She had yet to paint the ship's name.

November's chilly wind buffeted the platform against the ship's planking, and his knife slipped. A crimson slash bisected his thumb pad. "Damn!"

Modesty cried out from the ship's bow directly above him. "Are you all right?" Her face was as white as her coif. Tendrils of hair coiled from beneath its edge and draped over her neck. Her rapidly growing hair had a lustrous health and soft curl that her former locks had lacked.

Mad Dog wiped his hand on his buckskin breeches. "Aye."

He waited until the gust of wind abated, then went back to carving. The foremastmen were taking in the top sails, a swabber washed the deck, and the boatswain was coiling the tackling and arranging the marlin spikes. The fifteen sailors who had elected to remain and serve under Jack Holloway appeared steadfast enough.

"Can yew make her a little more—er, feminine?" Modesty asked.

With a grunt, he picked up his chisel. "I never claimed to be a sculptor."

"Well, she looks more like a seahorse than a sprite."

He flung her a scornful glare. "Don't you have duties that call?"

"'Tis exactly that about which I wish to speak."

His mouth pressed flat. The wench was exasperating and would test the patience of a monk. "Why is it that I have a foreboding?"

"You recall you asked me to paint the ship's name?"

"Aye? And what is it to be?"

She hesitated, as if she were about to request some rare boon, then blurted, "The *Maidenhead*."

His hand halted its work on the figurehead.

He glanced up at her. Her expression was at once both guarded and waggish, like a feminine Falstaff. In spite of his consternation with her, he had to chuckle. "So you have regained that prize possession. Symbolically speaking, of course."

Her big smile transformed her pinched face into a portrait of dazzling features. Bemused, he stared up at her.

"Yew might say that. But 'tis not about the name I wish to speak," she said, her words a little rushed, a warning to him that something was afoot. Of course, that was to be expected whenever the wench was around. "Have you given thought to the papers Jack will need? The credentials he must have if he is to convince the planters that he would represent them most honestly?"

"Is this something we have to discuss now?" Cannily, she had picked a time when he was at a disadvantage—dangling from ropes and she placed in a position of superiority above him.

"And there are the ship's papers, also." She lowered her voice, even though they were alone at that part of the vessel. "And if you expect to falsify Ratcliff's bills of lading and—"

Granted, she was right about the need for official documents. He hadn't thought that far ahead. He was only just formulating the strategy for forcing Ratcliff into financial failure. "Cease priming me and get on with it. What is it you have in mind, wench?"

"Modesty." She looked quite pleased with

herself. "Why, only that I am a master forger."

He could feel his eyebrows climbing the rungs of his forehead. "You, naturally, have—er, your own credentials?"

"Well, I have none of me work with me, but I can testify that I trained under the best."

"But of course," he said dryly.

She looked affronted. "Well, I did! I worked under Joos de Hondt himself no less!"

Mad Dog was impressed. The Flemish calligrapher was also a scientist and cartographer who had migrated to London just before the turn of the century. He later had become famous for the first wall map of Europe. "That was during one of your more reputable periods of activity, I take it?"

"No." She wrinkled her nose in disgust. "It was during one of Joos's disreputable periods of activity."

Laughter burst from him. "I should have known."

She ignored his remark and leaned further over the figurehead. Her voice lowered even more. "Mad Dog, why wait years for yewr revenge? I can furnish yew with what yew need! Now! Have Jack bring me back Ratcliff's signature, and I can falsify a mortgage of the estates. All Jack would have to do would be to file it in London with the Company and bring back the lien on Ratcliff's property. Ratcliff Manor and every single candlestick in it would be yewrs within the year!"

He picked up on her drift. He could buy up

Ratcliff's paper debts at a fraction of their face value and have them reimbursed in full for himself. "And in return?"

"And in return, yew let me go." She hurried on. "When Jack comes back from soliciting the planters, we can sail with him when yew go to Jamestown for the General Assembly. While we are at Jamestown, yew and I can arrange to be divorced. Just in time for me to take passage back to England with Jack. It all works out quite nicely, doesn't it?"

She looked so hopeful. He hadn't realized how miserable she was at Ant Hill. All at once, he recognized the trail of signs she had been leaving, which he had been too obtuse to read. "The water sprite." He gestured at the figurehead. "And the nymphs and leprechauns and fairies you paint. All this preoccupation with these fantasy beings—they're your way of coping with the unbearable, are they not?"

Her bewitching, mismatched eyes held a nostalgic expression. "The people of the nether world are like wise children who never grow up. They are never malicious as adult humans can be, only mischievous sometimes. And the human world can't hurt them."

He couldn't stand what he saw in her eyes and fixed his gaze instead on the coarsely carved water sprite emerging from the warrior. "I am not one for grand gestures," he said gruffly, "but if your work proves worthy, then divorce you I will."

* * *

A freshly gilded water sprite graced the ship's bow. Within less than a fortnight the caravel was ready to sail under her new guise, the *Maidenhead*. So, too, was Jack Holloway.

He was in possession of a letter of introduction from Thomas West, twelfth Baron De La Warr and grandson of a first cousin of Queen Elizabeth—courtesy of the magnificently mendacious Modesty.

For his role, Jack was bedecked in the garb of a gentleman. A fashionable narrow swordbelt that followed the shape of his waistline was buckled at his side; a plumed hat was rakishly tilted over one eye; his high, standing collar had been stiffened with buckram; his blue velvet doublet with points of red ribbon and slashes in the sleeves revealed the red silk lining; and lastly, high bucket boots were ornamented with ribbon knots and spurs.

A tuck here, a feather there, a bit of ribbon, and Modesty had redesigned the apparel of the vanished Captain De Ruyter.

Jack wriggled his scrunched toes. The boots were a wee bit small, and De Ruyter's hose were somewhat baggy in the seat. The doublet was too short-waisted, so that the peasecod, the pad in the center front of the doublet, barely covered his cod.

He knew he could convince the average colonist of his genuineness, but a greater test lay just downriver, at Henrico. So it was for that village he first sailed.

The miserable wretches who had agreed to

stay on obeyed his orders readily enough. After all, his command could be no more brutal than that of De Ruyter, and at least the sailors were assured of continued employment. A dependable first mate would be helpful, but Jack had to count himself lucky just to have his own ship.

He blew a gallant kiss to Modesty, who waved good-bye from the wharf. His lot could be worse. He could still be confined, as she was, under the hawk-eyed watch of Mad Dog.

Mad Dog had estimated that there were thousands of miles of navigable waterways in the colony and well over a hundred plantations to visit between now and General Assembly time. They were widely scattered along the banks of the James and Chickahominy Rivers, Chesapeake Bay, the Pamunkey and Rappahannock Rivers to the north, and even a few as far north as the Potomac and the Susquehanna.

Jack bypassed the profitable Varinas tobacco plantation and Falling Brook to put in at Henrico, a little less than an hour's journey for the *Maidenhead*. The town's inhabitants, delighted by a ship's arrival, turned out at the wharf.

And he was delighted to learn that the good Reverend Dartmouth was away at the ironworks on Falling Brook. The rector's house was in little better condition than the others, whose timbers were rotted by the damp. Clarissa greeted him at the door. A white coif covered her golden hair. But not even the somber gray of her dress could detract from her pure beauty.

The Savage

There was the instinct for the dramatic about her.

Was she making an effort to fit in with these backwoods people?

His eyes roamed her wonderful oval face, remarkable for its classical lines, aquiline nose, violet-colored eyes veiled by long dark brown lashes, and clear-cut mouth. "You haven't changed since last we met, nigh five months ago."

Her eyes scanned his attire. "You have."

She had unwittingly followed his lead. Good. "May I enter, mistress?"

Her gaze darted beyond him, to Clem, the old cowherder, leading the hamlet's cows across the muddy green, then to a plump woman pinning a wet apron on a hemp line strung between two hickory trees. The chill wind whipped at her scarlet tippet and batted the white apron back and forth.

At last, Clarissa's gaze came back to him. Her hands twisted an embroidered, lace-edged handkerchief of lawn. "People will—"

"Leave the door open. The afternoon is not so chilly that a few moments of fresh air wouldn't revive you."

Without waiting for her reply, he removed his hat and stepped past her. He glanced around. The main room, while as sparse in furnishings as that of Ant Hill, was made more personal with small family portraits that adorned the plastered walls. "Nobility evidently runs in your family."

Parris Afton Bonds

"I suspect the same of yours." Her eyes searched his face, as if seeking confirmation.

He quashed an impulse to laugh. "But not wealth. My forebears have a tendency to squander their inheritance. By the time I came of age, my inheritance had been wasted by relatives, and I found myself in debtors' prison."

"I suspected that. Somehow I just knew that life had treated you unfairly."

She was close to the mark, and it made him nervous, made him feel vulnerable. That need to feel important reared its deceiving head. He decided to put his guise to the test. He unrolled the document tucked beneath one arm and passed it to her.

Rapidly, she scanned the forged letter of introduction from Thomas West.

"The baron always had faith in my mercantile abilities and arranged to buy my papers from Mad Dog Jones," he explained with a smoothness that surprised even himself. "He put up the major portion of the capital for this venture."

Her hands, no longer magnolia-white, rerolled the document. "Thomas was a friend of my father's."

He could feel the sweat break out on his palms. "What a small world." He mentally cursed Modesty for her selection of patrons.

"Indeed." She passed the document back to him. "You know Thomas died en route to Virginia last year?"

He swallowed hard and studied her face for

a sign that she was on to him. Her gaze was guileless.

"Aye. It was a big setback. Cost me six months of servitude before West's last instructions caught up with me."

Timing had always been a factor in his luck. Now was the time! He fished in his string-drawn purse of suede and held out in his palm the object his irate employer had given him with the warning to restore it to its rightful owner. "Your brooch. I found it outside Mad Dog's cabin. I've been wanting to return it to you at the earliest moment possible."

She clapped her hands. "Oh, this was my mother's! I was heartsick when I lost it!" She threw her arms around him. "Thank you, thank you, Jack!"

He clapped his arms around her slender waist. His nostrils quivered at the fragrant scent of her hair. He closed his eyes to savor the sweet moment. Aye, timing was with him again!

"Uhmmm."

He spun around. Patrick Dartmouth stood in the doorway.

What perfect timing, Clarissa thought.

"Patrick, dear," she said easily, and picking up her voluminous skirts, circumvented Jack and went to her husband's side. "Look what our dear friend has returned to me. My brooch! Remember, I lost it. On our trip to Ant Hill."

Patrick removed his black cloak and buckled hat and hung them on wall pegs before he even bothered to glance at the piece of jewelry in her hand. "It pleases me to see you smiling once more."

Her husband's indifference exasperated her. He was never stirred to anger, not even jealousy. He would bore her if she didn't find his attitudes so quaint. At least he and Nigel could stage a lively debate on the meaning of life.

What did it take to arouse deep feeling in her husband? Oh, not the passionate conviction of his faith, but the unbridled emotions of the heart. Lust, rage, envy, greed, love?

Not that she truly wanted love from him. It was the tedium of the hamlet that drove her to do perverse things like toy with her husband's psyche. She spent her days in toil. Hands that had been meant to play the dulcimer and harpsichord had lost their loveliness from washing, rubbing, and scrubbing. Her scented gloves now bedecked a scarecrow in her herb garden.

Smiling, she whirled back to Jack. His handsome features wore a wariness that amused her. He was such a trusting soul. He really believed that her kiss of gratitude had been spontaneous. Fortunately for her, she had seen past him to Patrick approaching. "Won't you stay for dinner? I would adore hearing more about your venture. And about Thomas. He was a most dear man."

By now she knew Patrick was aware of her lie about not being able to cook. Luckily for him, she had an affinity for cuisine, for all too often a distressed parishioner would appear at their doorway for spiritual counseling and stay for supper.

Jack accepted her invitation, and the boiled mutton, hasty pudding, stewed tomatoes, and prunes with cinnamon and ginger tempted the man's palate, while he related more to her and Patrick about his enterprise. "You see, by taking orders from all the planters, I can buy in quantity and thus obtain a better price for the planter."

"Perhaps thee might wish something for the house," Patrick suggested to her. He took a swallow of the mulled apple cider. "A loom? A washtub?"

"La! You are always so practical." She pushed away her plate and leaned forward. "I would desire a harpsichord." She did not glance at her husband to see his expression. "Of course, such an expensive item is out of the question. In its place I would have a looking glass."

"A looking glass could never do full justice to your beauty, milady," Jack said.

At that moment, the ship's bell rang the hour, and he excused himself from the table, saying, "We sail with the tide on the morrow."

After Jack was gone, Clarissa began removing the tinware and the salt cellar from the table. "Isn't Master Holloway charming?" She had forgotten how exciting dinners were at her parents' table, where notables, literati, and intellectuals had assembled.

Patrick's narrow face was set in noncommittal lines. He turned to the mantel for his pipe.

"A bit of the gasconade for my taste."

She set the tin-glazed plates in the bucket of water she had drawn earlier from the new well. She glanced at her wash-reddened hands and silently despaired. Enough! The dishes could soak. A whimsical notion diverted her attention elsewhere for the moment.

Removing her taffeta apron, she picked up her embroidery and seated herself on the bannister-back chair. Patrick sat only an arm's length away, facing the hearth's dancing flames. "You do not like Jack Holloway?"

Smoke puffed from his pipe as if it were a chimney. "In faith, I do. How could anyone not like the man? Droll, personable, entertaining. Yet, I doubt the man's honest intentions."

Her needle plied rapidly in and out. "How can you say such a thing? 'Twas he who returned my brooch."

"There is something about him that—"

"Aye, there is." She devoted inordinate attention to her cross stitchery. "He is truly a virile man."

The puffing ceased. After a moment of silence, Patrick asked, "Does thee think so?"

She had to refrain from gritting her teeth. "Aye." She could think of nothing to add, though.

"Because of the way he looks at thee?"

She glanced up, careful to keep her features expressionless. "Looks at me? How is that?"

He shifted his gaze to the fire. "As though he would like to touch thee."

She let a small frown of puzzlement knit her brows. "In what way, husband?"

"Like . . . like. . . . "

"Aye?" she asked in an innocent tone. She leaned slightly forward, her lips parted.

There was only the sound of the fire crackling. Patrick's voice cracked with it as he answered, "Touch thy hair."

Her hand drifted up to her coif. "But 'tis hidden."

He, too, leaned forward, loosed the strings tied beneath her chin in a bow, and tugged the coif from her head. Her hair tumbled loose over her left shoulder. She heard his breath suck in. His hazel eyes darkened even further.

Her throat tightened. Her stitchery lay forgotten. "Do you think he desires only to see my hair?"

"Nay." He swallowed. "I think he yearns to run his fingers through thy locks."

"Show me how," she whispered. Her breathing came shallowly and rapidly.

He stretched out a trembling hand. Slowly, his long, slender fingers combed through her tresses, beginning at her temple and stroking downward to where they curled over her left breast—and lingered there. "Like frothy butter," he muttered.

Her breasts rose and fell with her labored breathing. It was as though his fingertips scorched her swollen nipple through the material. Her eyes locked with his. "Where else would he touch?"

He shot to his feet. "Nowhere, because thee is mine."

She closed her eyes. She had not realized how starved she was for a man's touch. Her face upturned, she waited.

His footsteps moved past her.

Scarcely believing he could have rejected her, she opened her eyes. The cabin door was open, revealing the night's frigid darkness.

And her coif lay abandoned at her feet.

Chapter Twelve

From their card house of a cabin, Rose watched in the early dawn's light as her husband in name only trudged in the snow's drizzle toward his sawmill. Looking like a long-legged heron, Walter picked his way along the cattail-lined shore. His steps left quickly vanishing footprints in the thinly layered snow. She thought it a symbol of how unsubstantial his relationship with her was. Tenuous. Gossamer. Trifling even.

Three other men, shouldering iron axes and ripsaws, waved at her as they strode off in the opposite direction toward the white-shrouded forest. She worried about them. Winter's high winds made tree-felling hazardous.

Construction was almost finished on the sawmill, but as a consequence the improvements on their wattle-and-daub house had been postponed. In inclement weather the roof was a sieve, and the wind whistled through chinks in the walls and the single window's poorly set shutters.

Rose hugged her shawl more tightly about her bloated body and turned back to the fireplace. Water dripping from the mortar-gaping bricks hissed in the flames. She walked to the trundle bed where Isaac was curled into a ball beneath the woolen blanket. Bart was built like his father, and his feet, long for a seven-year-old, dangled over the rope bed.

She tousled Isaac's rumpled straw-colored hair. "Gruel's ready to eat."

"Sleep," he muttered into the crook of his arm.

"No, not sleep. Study. And you too, Bart."

Bart burrowed deeper.

She crossed in ungainly steps to the small green-and-white dome-topped chest which held a few worthless heirlooms, a boxwood comb, and a hornbook she used to teach the boys reading and ciphering.

She wished she knew more, but alas, the boys knew almost as much as she. "'Urry up, get dressed, you two lazy dunces! Mid-morning draws nigh."

One of Bart's bare feet sought shelter beneath the blanket. She grinned and tugged it off both boys, who wore only flannel nightshirts, disdaining the nightcaps she had made them.

"Ohhh!" Isaac groaned and blindly groped for the blanket.

"Fire's burning low. I'll get another log. I want you two up and dressed by the time I return."

The cold air nipped her cheeks and hands. Feeling as though she waddled like a duck, she started across the yard toward the woodshed. Her labored breathing frosted the air.

She would be glad when her time was upon her. By her calculations, she was a week past due. At this dawdling pace, her baby would be born on Christmas Day. What with the chicken nesting in the willow cradle Walter had fashioned, their cabin could almost pass for a stable with a manger.

Tiny icicles fringed the woodshed's flat roof. The door's wooden hinges had swollen, and drifted snow sealed the door around its bottom. She had to jerk with both hands to open it.

She didn't like going inside because of the myriad vermin that crawled everywhere. The English countryside had not been like this. With nostalgia, she recalled mellow sunlight and soft mist and gently rolling hills.

She left the shed door open for the weak wintery light. Her gaze searched the musty-smelling premises carefully for lurking bugs. Satisfied, she stooped, collected two split logs, and with a low grunt of effort rose to go.

Sounds other than her own halted her. She turned and peered out the doorway. Two Indian savages were running across the yard toward the cabin. Tomahawks in hand, they kept their bodies lowered in a half-bent posture and moved stealthily.

There was really no time to think. Rose only knew that she had to draw their attention away from the boys, to do something without bringing the boys to the cabin door. She threw the logs down, and their thudding noise spun the savages in her direction.

The Indians sprinted toward her with their tomahawks raised for the kill.

She froze, as stiff as the icicles overhead. Then, frantic with fright, she got out the word, "Friends!" She thought she shouted, but her words came out no louder than a chick's peep.

At least the two Indians did not bury their tomahawks in her skull. After an argumentative exchange of words she could not understand, the shorter of the two grabbed her upper arm and shoved her forward, ahead of him.

She stumbled, caught her balance against the trunk of a denuded oak. Her arms encircled it, as if it were the leg of some giant from whom she was pleading protection.

The other warrior, who wore a wreath of weasel skins on his naked pate, gestured toward her swollen middle.

She did not mistake his gesture, that of gutting with the knife. "No!" she gasped.

The first Indian shook his head and moved his hand up and down, as if signaling patience.

Once again, she was pushed forward. The two were herding her away from the cabin, across the stubble of winter cornfields and toward the forest. Briers caught at her apron and tore at her skirts. She was shivering, both from fright and from the cold. Her captors were draped in layers of animal skins and seemed not to notice the cold.

On through the forest they traveled. The Indians laughed when she could not keep up with them and prodded her with the hafts of their weapons. Once, when she fell, the weasel-crowned Indian made as if to lay open her stomach then and there.

Crying, she scrambled away and pulled herself upright with the help of a densely vine-clad sycamore. She was panting heavily. The Indians watched her, as if gauging her endurance.

Time. That was what she needed. If she could stay alive until the boys missed her and went for their father, she might be rescued. Might be. She banished the last thought from her mind and with a resolute nod indicated that she was capable of moving on.

The journey resumed. She had the sense they were moving parallel to the river, though she could neither see nor hear it. If that were so, then they were moving into Powhattan territory.

The tribes of the Powhattan confederacy were known to be friendlier to the colonists since Master Rolfe had taken the *werowance*'s daughter for his wife several years earlier. Rose's hope grew.

Occasionally a gloomy sun peeked between the sky's gray layers of clouds. Its paltry light was filtered even more by the dense lattice of branches.

Toward midday, when she thought she could not take another step, her two captors halted. From leather pouches they produced jerky and berries that looked to her like English capers and squatted to partake of the meager fare.

Nothing was offered to her. She took the opportunity to sit. She explained away the pains that were shooting up her stomach as stitches in her side that came from unaccustomed physical exertion. She concentrated, instead, on how to stay alive.

What fate awaited her once the savages reached their destination? Should she try to escape before that? Only if an excellent opportunity offered, she decided. Time was still her best ally.

Too soon the repast was finished, and her captors were prodding her forward again. She was being swallowed up by the wilderness. Brambles scratched her face. On her cheeks, tears of frustration and fear froze in their tracks. Paradoxically, her flesh was feverish. Her eyes felt as if they were burning.

Just when she was ready to whirl and yell at her captors to go ahead and kill her, they emerged into a clearing that fronted the sluggish James. Eerie vapor rose from the water.

At the shoreline, the short Indian delved into the brush and tugged forth a canoe. He nudged her into it. The two pushed it through the shallow water until they were knee-deep themselves. Then, with Rose ensconced in the middle, they climbed in and began paddling through the cold mist. Snowflakes melted upon hitting the water but clung momentarily to her lashes.

Her captors were making for the opposite shore. Spiraling tree tops began to take shape. When the water became choppy, she realized the canoe had entered the confluence with another lesser river; most likely, she judged, the Appomatucks.

The longer they traveled, the more distance they covered, and the more frightened she became. No one would ever find her. Worse, the pains in her abdomen were coming more frequently. There was no denying the fact: She was about to have her child . . . if she was not killed first.

There was also the possibility that she and her baby might be kept as slaves. She had heard too many descriptions of the hideous atrocities inflicted on slaves.

With that thought in mind, she was prepared to leap from the canoe. She could not swim, but a swift death by drowning was better than prolonged torture.

At that moment of decision, a monster of the deep rose from its sleep to thrust its head through the mist and block the canoe's way.

"Ahee!" cried out the weasel-skin-clad Indian. So startled were the canoe's occupants that their abrupt movements toppled it, and they were flung into the freezing water.

Rose floundered, sank, and struggled to the surface again. Her clothing weighted her. Her body, tortured by the cramps of childbirth, rendered her helpless. She cried out once, then felt the river sucking her downward to its burial bed.

The woman had to weigh twenty stone if not more. Her flailing arms threatened to beat Jack senseless. But then he had to have been already senseless to dive into the frigid water. The fleeting sight of the white woman wedged between the two Indians had shocked him, so that when the canoe capsized he had dived from his ship into the water without thinking.

The thrashing woman put his own life at peril. Scenarios played out before his eyes in quick succession: the *Maidenhead* sailing the high seas, he on the quarterdeck directing his crew of buccaneers; the glittering towns of the West Indies prostrate before his privateering warfare. Glory, gold, and gentlewomen awaited him.

The aristocratic face of the Lady Clarissa flashed in the back of his mind, but what he actually saw was a panic-stricken face, scratched and reddened and with hair straggling like seaweed across it.

Her cries of "'Elp! 'Elp!" told him this was no aristocrat but a coarse commoner.

"Stop struggling!" he shouted.

He was wasting his breath. Alternately she battered him with her open hands and clung to him as if she were determined to drag him under the surface with her.

The two braves were already swimming off in steady strokes and soon disappeared in the frosty mist. Good sense told Jack he should swim off, too. He was tiring quickly.

Foolishly, he grappled with the woman instead. She lashed out at him, striking him against his temple with the heel of her hand.

He had no choice. His fist clipped her jaw with enough impact to knock her unconscious.

His arm locked beneath her chin, he swam toward the canoe. It had righted itself and bobbed on the water between him and the shoreline. The water was numbing cold. He wasn't sure if he had the strength to reach the canoe, much less cling to it in hopes of keeping the two of them afloat.

Let her go! Let her go!

Like a dunce, he ignored the inner warning, that instinct for survival that so many times had saved his hide. His lungs felt as if they were caving in, collapsing on him like a pair of bellows. His ears rang with his pounding pulse.

Somewhere out of the mist, he heard his crew's searching shouts of "'Ello? 'Ello?"

Timing was his once again! An eddy swirled the canoe's bow out toward him. He lunged, grabbed hold, and held on for dear life. It seemed forever . . . and finally he felt his boots drag bottom. He staggered onto the tree-lined shore and dropped his burden. He fell face forward. The sand grated against his cheekbone.

At first, all he could hear was his breath rasping in and out of his throat and lungs in great gasps of indrawn and expelled air.

Then he heard the woman. She was groaning and throwing up water.

He rolled to his side and looked back over his shoulder. "For the love of God, woman, will you shut the bloody—"

His words choked in his throat. The woman lay on the sand behind him like a great beached white whale. He crawled toward her. "What the—" Again, his words were robbed by what he saw. The way her wet dress clung to her distended stomach. She was with child!

With a tortured moan, the woman gripped her belly and rolled into a fetal position.

"My God, if you're aren't having a baby!"

"'Elp me." Her words were like the rusk of a boat being dragged upon sand.

He recognized her now from her and her husband's visit to Ant Hill when she had delivered Modesty's marriage proposal. Apparently she didn't recognize him. Time and Modesty's alterations had changed his looks more than he had realized. "What—I don't know what to do."

Her blanched lips formed a gargoyle's grimacing grin. "Neither do I."

He broke out in a sweat. He scanned the water for his ship, but fog enshrouded everything. No help there. How far back upstream was Bermuda's Hundred? He had spent a couple of days with the various planters there, introducing himself and taking orders for English goods after leaving Henrico.

The young woman's teeth were chattering. He removed his doublet, wrung it out, and laid it over her. It wasn't much help, but it was better than nothing.

She stretched out her arm. "Please, 'old me 'and."

Her hand was small, like a trusting child's. "What be your name?" He knew he was prattling like an old spinster who lives out her lonely days spinning yarn before a fire and suddenly has a visitor. But he was at a loss as to how to help her.

"Rose. And 'oors?"

"Jack. Jack Morley, the Earl of Monteagle." The lie came easily, as lies always did whenever he felt inadequate, unsure, worthless. What the bloody hell, even if he and this young woman survived, he would never see her again.

"An earl," she said with wonder and awe.

"I was on my brig, the *Maidenhead*, when I spotted you in the river."

"The *Maidenhead*." Her little gasping laugh sounded forlorn in his ears. "The man I thought I loved . . . not me husband . . . he wanted me maidenhead." She paused and drew a fortifying breath. "But not me."

"The cad," he mumbled, knowing he might as well be castigating himself. It was likely that somewhere there existed one or more women he had bedded and abandoned with child.

Her fingernails dug into his palm.

He waited until the spasm passed, then, to keep her talking, asked, "Where do you live?"

"Falling Brook, just beyond Henrico. 'Oor ship put in there, did it not?"

"Aye," he said cautiously, wondering how much she might have heard about his enterprise.

She screamed out her anguish. Her body writhed with another thunderbolt of pain. She released his hand and rolled from side to side, her arms wrapped around her stomach once more.

The sight of blood staining the white sand galvanized him into instinctive action. "Sshh," he said, stroking away the wet strands of her hair clinging to her cheek and forehead. "'Tis going to be all right."

He went about trying to make her comfortable, removing her buckled shoes, stripping off her wet woolen hose. Her feet were no bigger than his palms and blue with cold. He chafed first one foot, then the other, with his hands.

"Thank . . . thank 'oo." Tears trickled from the corners of her eyes. "'Oo are a 'ero. A knight worthy of the Round Table."

Something that might have been integrity cringed inside him. "You are delirious."

He began stripping away her bloodied underskirts and pushed her overskirt above the dome of her stomach. "I recall something about clean linens and hot water," he said, talking to keep her mind off her pain. And off his ignorance in such matters. "We come up lacking with clean linen, but your wee one could not have picked a prettier spot to be born. Lots of water."

Her answering laugh was more a groan.

He felt for his dirk, tucked into his belt scabbard. He could only hope her outcries did not attract any more savages.

Her hand latched onto his arm. He bent over her again. "Isn't there something about pushing? Are you trying?"

A tight laugh issued from the slit of her mouth. "Do 'oo want to try?"

He winced at her coarse accent. He had not rescued an aristocratic mermaid but a Billingsgate sturgeon. Life was like that for him. Always the leftovers. "Where do you hail from in England?"

"Middlesex."

"A country girl are you now?" His mother had been a country girl, from Hertfordshire. He tried to imagine her as this one was. Young, naive, giving birth to him, a child she didn't want.

"The Indians in the canoe?"

"Kidnapped me, they did."

"Well, we'll return you. When the mist lifts, the *Maidenhead* will be prowling the waters, looking for me." He hoped.

"Ohhh!" she gasped and shut her eyes against the pain. Her mouth was a gash.

His teeth worried his lower lip. "Try pushing again. Maybe that will get this over with more quickly."

"I don't 'ave to try." She was panting. "The babe is shoving 'is way through."

"Oh. So 'tis a boy you've decided it's to be?" Her hair was drying, and it spread across the sand like spilt ink. Beneath her pallor, a natural pink color could be detected on her cheeks. "Rose," he murmured, thinking how perfectly her name fit her complexion.

"Aye."

Before he could reply, she screamed out. Quickly he clamped his palm over her mouth. "I think 'tis best you hurry the wee one."

Her back arched. Her heels dug into the sand. Her teeth sank into his palm. God, he felt so helpless.

Then he saw it. A small portion of the baby's head. "Looks like your babe is tired of waiting!"

As he watched the wee one enter the world, exultation overcame him. This was rapidly replaced by a feeling he had never experienced, reverence. The only time he had been near a church was when he had robbed the lottery shack on St. Paul's cathedral steps. He had felt no reverence then.

This was something more even. The great mystery of life was unfolding before him. A supreme secret, if he could but grasp it before it disappeared.

He heard a sputtering little cry, like a kitten's mew, and put out his hands to receive the baby. "'Tis a boy," he whispered. "Just as you predicted."

"Another boy!" she sighed.

"Another boy?" He used her petticoat to enfold the reddened, wizened, bawling gift. Black downy hair matted the small head. With wonder, he touched one tiny ear, shaped like a cockleshell. The flailing fists were no larger than a musket ball.

"Aye," she said, smiling softly and looking for all the world like a lovely Madonna. "I 'ave meself two other sons. Stepsons, really, but I love them as if they were me own. Me 'usband will welcome another 'and at the sawmill. Let me see me babe."

Relieved to be rid of the squalling infant, he laid it in the crook of her arm. And with the act, the great mystery evaporated from his mind.

Chapter Thirteen

With Jack no longer there to help, turning up the land for the spring crop was taking longer than Mad Dog had anticipated. Would he ever see the cagey chap again?

He wiped the dribble of light rain from his brow with the back of his hand before picking up the mattock. He needed a plow, but such an implement was so heavy that four horses or a span of oxen would be required to pull it.

Raising the flat-bladed pickaxe above his head, he swung downward in a mighty arc. The mattock broke up the soil and cut roots of bramble and nettle that were impertinent enough to grow on land he had declared his.

Thinking of the impertinent woman who had turned his sanctuary into a Bedlam, his tempo increased.

The hoyden didn't know the meaning of logic or reason.

With the strike of the mattock, the loosened earth exploded.

She was harder to read than a Pamunkey war trail. He never knew what to expect from her next.

He swung again, his muscles straining his deerhide tunic. Clods of damp dirt showered the ground around his high-top moccasins.

A fortnight ago, he had picked up his pipe, only to find minuscule trolls painted in cobalt blue dancing in a ring around its clay bowl.

Again the mattock smashed into the earth.

For all he knew, at that very moment she was forging indenture papers to sell him off as a bondservant. A clever wench, his wife was.

He could feel agitation churning in his loins. He dropped the mattock and turned his face up to the March drizzle. Any colder and it would be snow. He swallowed the rain water and sputtered and laughed at the thought he entertained.

By God, he must be mad after all, but he would do it.

Maybe this was his opportunity to make things right. His chance to turn around the horrible consequences of his rapacious act thirteen years ago.

He did something that was in complete contradiction with his meticulous nature. He left the mattock where it lay, in the rain, and strode off toward his cabin.

He passed Juana on her way to the spring-house. Her sharp old eyes scrutinized him. He realized she was wondering what he was doing, returning from the fields so early in the day. Then her tobacco-toothed grin revealed itself. She knew.

He strode on.

He found Modesty at the board table. Across it were scattered fresh vellum, unsharpened quills, a perforated wooden sander, and a wax wafer to seal missives. She kept a candle burning for sealing with wax.

Ever since undertaking her enterprise, she had been working industriously. Her craftsmanship was astonishingly good, and could pass even his discerning eye.

Her tongue tipping her teeth, she was penning her cursive words. Over her shoulder, he read, "This bill of sale made the twelfth day of February in the year of our Lord one thousand six hundred and twenty-one between Lord Richard Ratcliff and. . . ." Her head was bent low over the parchment, the better to see her handiwork. Her brown hair, highlighted with blistering red, curled a good two inches below the plain edge of her coif.

"So this is how my shillings are being put to use."

She didn't even look up as she picked up the penknife to sharpen her quill. "I am turning shillings into pounds for yewr foe's undoing."

He was glad her gaze was trained on the

quill's end or else she would note how undone he was.

"Juana says that Henrico hosts a fair come Mayday," she continued, dipping her pen into the brown ink that she made by mixing vinegar and ox gall. "I want to—"

He fought to bring himself under control, his features impassive, his voice callously indifferent. "I want you." What had happened to his usual eloquence? At that moment he was barely articulate. He fingered a flaming lock at her nape. "Now."

The penknife halted.

He placed his hands on both her shoulders. His voice was low, as rough as her poorly hackled spinning thread. "In my bed or here at the table. I care not a whit where."

Slowly she looked up over her shoulder. Her mouth was set in a hard line, but deep in her eyes smoldered that astounding passion of hers. "I am yewr wife, not yewr whore."

He tugged just enough on her hair to tilt her head further back, exposing the long, smooth column of her throat. "Wife, whore, it makes no difference to me."

She shook off his hand. "Yew stink of manure." She returned to sharpening the quill.

Her nonchalance infuriated him. She must have seen from the corner of her eye as he drew back his arm. She ducked, but his aim was not for her but the accoutrements littering the board table. With one backhanded swipe, he sent them falling, fluttering, rolling.

She gasped. Dropping her quill, she shrank as far away as the end of the bench allowed. She held the penknife pointed at his midsection. "I choose me lovers."

He advanced on her. Would she stab him? Did she hate him that much? "Aye, you did. You married me." He leaned over, took the penknife from her, and sent it thudding into the wall.

"When a man has the key to a room," she said stonily, "the woman inside can hardly be said to be doing her own choosing."

Wrapping one arm around her waist, he slid the other beneath her legs to lift her as easily as he would a bale of hay, and spread-eagled her upon the table.

She broke his hold. Spitting and spewing, she aimed a well-placed kick at his crotch. He dodged at the last second. She lashed out blindly with pummeling legs. Her shift and skirt were riding up beneath her buttocks, exposing hose-encased calves, bare thighs, and a glimpse of a triangular patch of short, wiry hair.

His eyes must have betrayed the excitement the erotic sight instantly aroused in him, because suddenly her legs stopped their thrashing.

Her expression changed from one of impotent fury to blatant sensuality, as if she knew she held the winning hand. Braced on her elbows, her thighs tantalizingly parted for his intimate view, she asked in a husky voice, "Where is Juana?"

He unbuttoned his breeches. "She won't return for a while. She's wise in the ways of a man and a woman." To his ears, his voice sounded strangled. "As I think you are." He lowered himself over her. "Mayhaps you are a witch. Mayhaps you have bewitched me."

She opened her arms and thighs to enfold him against her and take him in. "Oh, no. I told yew," she whispered against his ear, "I am yewr ordinary fairy."

Slowly, rhythmically, he began pumping into her. "Ordinary you will never be."

Her soft white thighs closed around him. Her lids drifted closed. Her lips parted. She sighed. "Neither are yew, Mad—" Her eyes opened. "What is yewr real name?"

A humorous bent seized him. "Just call me your coxswain."

Her response of low laughter was delightful. Gradually her hips began responding in tempo to his. Then they were pounding hard, meeting each of his thrusts. She was engulfing him.

"Oh, God," he groaned.

He felt it coming, that indescribable feeling he always experienced when making love with her. Colors would explode on the back of his lids. He would lose himself, if only for an instant, but in that time he would be given that elusive taste of eternal ecstasy.

When clarity was restored, he lay flaccid between her damp thighs, his head on her clothed bosom. He realized that she was tenderly stroking his tumbled hair.

"Yew were most fortunate yew did not strike me just then," she murmured idly. "Or else I should have returned at once to me fairyland."

He mentally counted on his fingers. This was March. No, she wouldn't be returning to fairyland. At least not before the year was out.

" 'Then said Boaz unto his servant that was set over the reapers, Whose damsel is this? And the servant that was set over the reapers answered and said, It is the Moabitess damsel that came back with Naomi. Then said Boaz unto Ruth, Go not to glean in another field but abide here fast by my handmaidens.' "

Patrick paused. Every one of the thirty-six upturned faces in the little church was enrapt with his reading of the biblical story. His gaze fell on her, and Clarissa shivered. He spoke with extraordinary power, with a charisma that during biblical times was said to have come from the Holy Spirit.

Her husband returned his gaze to the printed page. " 'And Boaz said unto the elders, and unto all the people, Ruth the Moabitess, have I purchased to be my wife. So Boaz took Ruth, and she was his wife and he went in to her. And she gave birth to a son.' "

Clarissa flushed and pricked her finger on the wild rose she held. Patrick's blunt prose made

her uncomfortable. Nigel's flowery verse had
never filled her with so much . . . unrest.

That was it. Unrest. And spring fever.

Spring! The year had gone so quickly!

"So on this auspicious day," her husband was
saying, "we gather to rejoice in the birth of a
son four months ago to Master Bannock and his
wife."

Clarissa stared at the spot of blood on her fingertip. The rose had been Patrick's idea. On
their way to church that morning, he had seen
it and picked it. He had an affinity for plants
and animals. All living things, in fact.

Was life like the rose? One couldn't have the
pleasure of its beauty without suffering the pain
of its thorns? What would Nigel have to say
about that? In less than a year, he would be free.
And then what?

"If the parents will bring the infant forward
now for the christening."

In the pew to Clarissa's left, the parents
moved to stand in front of Patrick. In Clarissa's mind, Rose Bannock was like her name-
sake, a wild rose thriving amidst the squalor
of a barbarous land. Now that she was no
longer round with child, she was almost waif-
like. By her side, Walter stood inordinately
tall and very proud of the sleeping infant in
his wife's arms.

Patrick glanced at her, and Clarissa remembered the cue. With the wild rose in hand, she
went to stand beside the couple as godmother.
Her fingers touched Patrick's as she passed the

rose to him. At the tingly sensation, her breath fluttered in her throat.

She peeked at him, but he seemed not to have been affected, as she had been. He was in such mastery of himself. And here she had always thought she had been the one in control of her emotions.

Holding the rose by its stem, her husband dipped the bud in the small brass bowl of water, then lightly touched the baby's downy head. "I christen thee Jack."

"Get your starboard tacks aboard and haul taut off your lee sheets," Jack ordered a bandy-legged sailor.

Jack turned his face to the stiff breeze sweeping in off the ship's stern. Five months and both foul and fair weather had taken him places along the Virginia shoreline that not even the colony's intrepid adventurer, Captain Smith, had mapped. Colonists still talked about the captain wherever Jack had stopped, although he now spent most of his time in England when not exploring faraway places.

A couple of days was the usual amount of time Jack spent visiting each community. Sometimes he partook in their games of nine-pins, billiards with the common farmer, or gambled either at horse racing or piquet with the more well-to-do planters. Often he was reduced to watching a demonstration of the community militia, as if he were some visiting dignitary.

Some communities had names evocative of England, like Charles Cittie, Surrey, Warwick, Isle of Wight, Elizabeth Cittie. Others, plantations, were evocative of grandeur, such as Martin's Hundred and Mount Ratcliff, his last port-o'-call before returning to Ant Hill and then sailing for England. With the stack of orders from other planters whose trust he had gained, he was well positioned to dupe Ratcliff.

As the ship approached Mount Ratcliff, Jack stood at the railing, impressed by the brick manor house which loomed ahead. Like a monarch on the throne, it sat on an emerald knoll with its horseshoe-shaped staircase serving as a footstool. Not shutters but glazed windows overlooked the lazy-flowing Chickahominy. Like loyal subjects, smaller, timbered outbuildings clustered in the background.

Jack had learned as much as he could about Ratcliff and the manor from the settlers without arousing suspicion, and they had told him that the bricks for the manor had been imported from England at the expense of the Virginia Company, and the stone for the staircase had been quarried in Ireland. Bricklayers and masons, initially hired to work on Jamestown's municipal buildings, had been commandeered by Ratcliff for his own private use, as had fifteen of the bondservants with whom Jack had been transported.

Leaning on a stout cane and identifying himself as Ratcliff's overseer, a man of short stature greeted him at the landing. Believing Jack to be of the gentry, the little man appeared anxious to please. "Oliver Munger." He bobbed his head and doffed his felt hat.

At that, Jack saw the man's ferret eyes and knew he would have to tread carefully. Men like Ratcliff's minion were sly and, like bloodhounds, scented immediately activities of an illicit nature.

Munger conducted him from the dock, up the grand staircase, into the manor and then to the library where Ratcliff awaited him. With a thinly veiled air of condescension and a contemptuous curl of his lips, Ratcliff extended a beringed hand, indicating an upholstered X chair. "I have heard word of your enterprise. You represent—"

"Myself. John Holloway, Esquire." Jack removed his plumed hat, gave a half bow, then sprawled in the chair with the insouciance of an aristocrat. "And I represent interested planters."

Below the white crest of hair, unblinking bloodshot eyes inspected him. "By taking large orders for items, you can purchase them more cheaply—is that it?"

He waved a languid hand. "And thereby add pounds to your coffers."

Now the eyes flickered with interest. "Perhaps you would like a glass of Alicante while we discuss business."

"'Tis a fine Spanish wine," Jack said. "But I prefer the Portuguese Madeira or Fayal."

The lashless lids slid half-closed, as if to conceal the thoughts behind the reddened eyes, but Jack knew his offhanded remark had not gone unnoticed. His unpleasant stint with a Spanish galley had served him in good stead.

After that, Ratcliff was most cordial, even to the extent of showing him around the estate. The clever man had a purpose in mind. That, Jack did not doubt.

His practiced eye took in the storehouses filled with hogsheads of tobacco, as good as ready cash. He noted the elegant furnishings, and was reminded of comfort long denied. He observed the numerous indentured servants and five black slaves, all guarded by equally starved English mastiffs.

"A ship that will deal in slaves can bring untold profits to its master," Ratcliff told him.

Jack calculated that the estate represented wealth beyond what his trade would ever bring him.

Wealth. The word enticed him. As he knew Ratcliff was doing. The word "wealth" warred with that other word, freedom. Freedom that went with the danger of the high seas. Go over to Ratcliff's side, and wealth could be his for life.

He was almost tempted to divulge Mad Dog's plan. It was a heady feeling to know that it was in his power to play off the two sides against each other. Modesty's role in it however made him waver, as well as the fact that Ratcliff had almost succeeded in having her burnt as a witch.

The Savage

Having finished the tour of the estate, Jack and Ratcliff were beginning to climb the horseshoe staircase when a man in tattered clothing came running around the corner of the building. He had been badly beaten. Something, a whip most likely, had laid open one gaunt cheek and his left forearm.

Panting, he addressed Jack. "Please, m'lord. I ask for your protection!"

Obviously, the man, pitifully thin, did not recognize him. With horror, Jack realized that this indentured servant was one of the men with whom he had been transported the year before. Elias Johnson. Then Elias had been a strapping man.

Ratcliff glowered down at the servant. "You forget your place."

At that moment, Munger showed up with his cane. "There you be. You'll pay mightily for this." He tugged at his hat brim. "Me apologies for the disturbance, your worship."

Without thinking, Jack asked, "What has the fellow done?"

"A laggard servant, he is!" Munger replied. "And disobedient, as well. He deserves more than a beating with the whip."

"Sire," Elias implored. "My master is inhumanly cruel. As God is my witness!"

Elias, Jack knew, was not one to whine. The fellow had won his spurs in 1603 battling the Turks in Hungary and certainly knew about hardship.

"Another servant," Elias hurried on breathlessly, "Alice Abbot, died two months ago from beatings. By my troth, I counted five hundred lashes inflicted on her at one time! Her body was full of sores and holes—that were rankled and putrefied."

At that moment, Jack knew with which side he would align himself. "The fellow has arms that look like he once rowed in a galley. Fatten him up, and I could use him aboard my ship."

Ratcliff's mouth curled in anticipation. "'Twill cost you. The bondservant is a hard worker."

"Not according to Munger here," Jack commented dryly. "A laggard, did he not term the bondservant?"

He was thinking quickly. In the past five months, he had learned about the widespread practice of gambling among the Virginians. All ranks seemed to be desperately given to it, even to the point of putting up their servants as stakes.

Gambling, whether over cards or horses or humans, brought together in a single focused act the planters' competitiveness, independence, and materialism. All based on the element of chance.

Wagering represented a social agreement in which each individual was free to determine how he would play, and the gentleman who accepted a challenge risked losing his material possessions as well as his personal honor.

Not that either he or Ratcliff had personal honor.

Five months and a thousand miles had devoured all the pounds and notes Mad Dog had advanced him. Unless. . . .

"Still and all, I shall wager with you at a game of whilst for the old chap."

"Your stakes?"

"This." Jack drew from his embroidered waistcoat the black silk hatband with its gold buckle, of which five months earlier he had relieved the right Reverend Patrick Dartmouth.

"More than once, you know, it has crossed my mind to wager with you at a game of cards."

Modesty grinned. "Yew're only saying that because yew're losing." She discarded the queen of spades and drew from the stock the five of diamonds.

"Or to sell you off to Arahathee," Mad Dog mumbled and played the jack of spades and took a card from the pile.

Outside, rain fell steadily. To Modesty, it seemed that enough had fallen during April to float Noah's ark. With both her and Mad Dog confined to the cabin, boredom had driven her to suggest a game of piquet with an old deck that had been found aboard the *Roter Löwe*.

She played her king of hearts and, spreading her remaining cards face up on the board table with a flourish, announced, "Carte blanche!"

He scanned the cards, then narrowed his eyes on her. "You cheated."

She mustered an indignant look. "I did not! 'Tis a curmudgeon yew are. Now hand over another tanner."

In the last three days, she had amassed enough sixpences to replenish her pens and brushes when she got back to London. She would set up a stall and charge the pudding-heads for letter writing and document deciphering. She might end up as poor as a churchmouse, but she wasn't about to play blind man's bluff with bailiffs ever again.

"Yes, you did cheat," Mad Dog said, each word distinct. He folded his arms and fixed her with his flint-eyed gaze. "Now you can either show me how you rooked me or you can clean the privy."

Just the thought brought a sour fluid to her mouth, but she managed an indifferent air. "So, build another privy."

He lifted a brow, and she knew he wasn't about to buy her bluff, that at the first sign of the rain letting up, he'd send her to the outhouse with a scrub brush and a bucketful of lime.

She sighed. "All right." Never one to surrender without trying to strike a bargain, she added, "But in exchange, yew got to take me to the fair at Henrico come May Day."

"So done."

"Watch." She shuffled the cards. "Cut them."

Eyeing her suspiciously, he did so.

"I'll tell yew now that cutting a deck has naught to do with preventing yewrself from being swindled. 'Tis just a formality the card swindler allows yew. To distract yew."

With a flourish, she ribbon-spread the cards, face down, fan-wise across the table. "Now this one"—she tapped the card with her finger—"is the high card, the king of spades."

She flipped it over, and his brows yanked up at the sight of the king of spades.

It took her the better part of an hour to show him how to watch for the designated high card while shuffling, and to drag his left thumb across it to palm it in the left hand, and then bring it back to the bottom of the deck. "See, yewr left hand crimps the card so that it lies bowed when all the other cards are flat."

She indicated the concave card. "When yew perfect yewr rhythm, the other players will be watching the eye-catching way yew brandish the cards and will not look for the little things."

She glanced at Mad Dog and could tell she had once again managed to impress him with her peculiar skills. "So what do yew think about advancing me passage fare back to England?"

He rose from the table and stared at her as if she were one of those colonial insects never seen before. "I think you would swindle your own mother, wench."

"Modesty. And remember. Yew promised to take me to May Day at Henrico."

"I'd like to take back that promise and the one I gave when I pledged to take you for my wife."

She watched him stride from the room. She sighed. Well, she had failed to get the passage fare from him.

Now what?

Chapter Fourteen

During her brief residency at Jamestown, Modesty had learned that cargo ships sank, tobacco prices fell without warning, bondservants suddenly sickened and died, and storms and droughts ruined crops. Nothing could be counted on—except change. Modesty knew that Mad Dog relied on the remoteness of Ant Hill to prevent it. And yet here he was, committed to leave his sanctuary all because of her caprice, the wench he had taken for a wife.

On this first day of May she rode pillion behind him. His bay mare trotted along the river road, bordered with jack-in-the-pulpits, anemones, dogwood, and violets. "Rose must have her baby by now. I wonder whether 'tis a boy or a girl. By me faith, 'tis even possible Clarissa is in the family way. I bargained with the good reverend for celibacy in his marriage to her, but me doubts that the two have kept the pledge."

"Egad, wench, you chatter like a magpie."

She latched onto a handful of his hair and tugged sharply. "And yew, me lordly lion, art a dullard. 'Tis May Day, a time for fun and frolic." She firmly believed that his problem was that he didn't know how to unbend.

From the sounds of revelry drifting down-river, Modesty knew that the inhabitants of Henrico had started early with bending the elbow to raise a bumper of ale. Now at midday, they should be well in their cups.

The top of a towering eighty-foot maypole, bedecked with hawthorn blossoms and streamers of colored ribbons, came into view before the river road opened onto the village green. It had been transformed into a maze of stalls, stages, and game areas. Settlers from outlying areas swelled the population that had turned out for the holiday.

Youths wrestled, a man who looked like an old satyr played a German flute, a plump young woman displayed her handicrafts of quilts and rugs, and merchants hawked their wares. A steady stream of carousers poured in and out of the chicken coop known as the Bloody Bucket, where spirits like ale, beer, and wine lightened their own.

Next to the tavern was a stable, its floor strewn with fresh straw for the holiday. With a less than optimistic expression, Mad Dog dismounted and held up his big hands to assist her down.

She braced her hands on his shoulders. Her smile teasing, she said, "Careful, yew might betray yewr fear."

He glanced sharply at her. "What are you talking about?"

She took her hands from his shoulders. "Yew're afraid yew might have a good time with other people. Then yew would need them, wouldn't yew?"

"Ply your tawdry art trade, wench," he growled, "and leave thinking to the intellectuals."

His words cut deep. She whirled from him and stalked from the stable into the sunlight and the mass of people.

Her name was called out, but not by Mad Dog. It was Rose who hailed her. The swarthy young woman cradled a baby in her arms. "Modesty! I 'ave missed 'oo so!"

"Oh, let me see yewr baby, Rose. A boy or a girl? When did yew have—"

"Before Christmas." With a mother's pride, she passed the baby to her. "Jack be 'is name."

Modesty gazed down at the cherubic face with unblinking eyes as large as Spanish doubloons. "Why, he's a splendid lad." She peered at Rose. "Yewr marriage—'tis a good one?"

"'Oo did well when 'oo bargained with Walter for me."

Modesty noted that Rose had not exactly answered her question.

"The boys?" She glanced around, searching for Mad Dog rather than the Bannock boys. Where had he gone?

"They be with Walter, watching a juggler."

She passed the baby back to Rose. "And Clarissa and her husband?"

Rose pointed to the church. "Decorating it with flowers. Come on along. The Lady Clarissa will be filled with joy to see 'oo."

Accompanying Rose, she drifted toward the church with reluctant footsteps. The desire to see Clarissa warred with her distaste for religion.

Inside, it took a moment for her eyes to adjust after the bright sunlight. Then she saw Clarissa. The aristocratic woman stood beneath a box-like pulpit set high on a pedestal and reached by a small flight of steps. She held an armful of spring flowers that she passed, one by one, to her husband.

It took a moment for Modesty to realize what he was doing—braiding the flowers around the stair banisters. "A mite pagan, isn't it, Reverend Dartmouth?"

His gaze searched the back of the room. "Good morrow, Mistress Bannock." Then surprise came to his face. "Mistress Jones? How farest thou?"

"Modesty!" Clarissa deserted the pulpit and headed down the aisle toward her. Her husband followed in the wake of flower petals shaken from their stems.

Modesty kissed her cheek. "Yewr beauty puts

the flowers to shame, Clarissa." She nodded at the yellow violet the minister still held and asked him, "Yew're not afraid the villagers will burn yew for such sacrilege?"

His smile was gentle. "Does not the Bible say that as a flower of the field, so a man flourishes?"

"Does God say anything about a woman flourishing?"

Rose rolled her eyes. "Modesty, 'oo 'ave not changed a whit."

The minister held out the violet to her. "For you. Like the wildflower, you have flourished here in this garden wilderness. Or don't you see it yet?"

With suspicion she eyed the flower, then him.

Clarissa smiled. "Give up, Modesty. A man of God is impossible to argue with."

Memories of harsh lessons taught by her Bible-quoting stepfather set her mouth in a grim line. "Aye, I know." However, she took the violet and tucked the stem underneath her cap, so that the yellow blossom peeked out just above her cheekbone. With three pairs of eyes upon her, she felt self-conscious. "Well, me husband has wandered away. I shall see yew all anon."

With Mad Dog, she never knew what to expect. If he were like any of the other menfolk that day, he could be drinking, gambling, or wenching. But he wasn't like any man she knew.

She refused to go in search of him like a scold. Instead, she would make the most of enjoying the celebration. She mingled with the people, taking in everything. The smell of wild goose turning on a roasting spit. An unpenned dog in heat. Boys pitching horseshoes or participating in foot races; girls playing tag; old men playing ninepins, young men staging bouts with cudgels.

Watching grown men foolishly compete to catch a greased pig brought laughter to her lips—which was her undoing.

A pug-nosed man in a flat cap, obviously inebriated, grabbed her hand. "Here she is! Our comely queen for May Day!"

She tried to tug away, but he held fast. He was adamant about proclaiming her the May Day Queen in an even louder voice. "May Day Queen! May Day Queen."

Others took up his refrain. She found herself being led by a procession of revelers toward the May Day pole, standing in a field of strawberries. Their gaiety was contagious. Off came her coif, down came her hair. Laughing, she let one country maid crown her with a wreath of flowers.

Then, holding one of the ribbons streaming from the pole's top, she joined with a dozen other merrymakers dancing and frolicking around the Maypole until it was covered in bright ribbons.

Gasping with laughter, she collapsed on her back in the strawberry-scented field alongside a reveler, the very man who had proclaimed her queen.

The mirth bubbling on her lips died away as she stared up into Mad Dog's glowering eyes.

"Are you finished cavorting?"

He always had to go and ruin everything. She sprang to a sitting position and tugged her skirts down over her stockinged calves. "Aye!" Anger boiled up inside her and scalded her tongue. "I am finished with yew!"

Thoughts of a prurient nature occupied Mad Dog's mind. Persistent visions of Modesty's lithe, nubile body had been there for a month now, since May Day.

He had spent that May Day in conversation with John Rolfe, discussing important matters. After a year under Yeardley's relaxed rule, the colony was being given a new governor, Francis Wyatt. What the planters were most afraid of was the restoration of the arbitrary government that had existed before the General Assembly of 1619, when the king could do what he liked.

Mad Dog realized that, like the planters, the outside world could and would intrude upon his self-imposed isolation and would affect his life. He realized that he could no longer remain apart from humanity.

He also realized that he found his wife highly desirable, since that May Day when he had watched her abandoned dancing. She was no longer the spitting cat with claws unsheathed in protection. She purred, she stretched languorously, her tiny tongue licked her lips as if in replete satisfaction. What had happened to her anger?

He could not take his eyes off her, and he knew she knew it.

Instead of moon watching, he watched her.

Watched her budlike breasts. Were they fuller these days?

Watched her taut stomach. Was there a slight curve to it?

As if his thoughts summoned her, he spotted her moving down the grass-worn path toward the springhouse. He remained sitting, his back against its stone wall. He had chosen the spot because it was the coolest, with the water running through shallow troughs dug into the springhouse's dirt floor. The "brummph" coming from inside told him that a bullfrog had found a home for the warm June evening.

"Wot are yew doing?" she asked. He couldn't tell if she was surprised or not by his presence. In her arms she toted a crock of butter.

He removed the long pipestem from between his lips. "Moon watching."

"Wot?" Real curiosity underlay her question. She drew nearer, only an arm-span away. Her stocking-clad ankles could be seen from beneath the hem of her underskirts. He raised his gaze to her face. Did her cheeks seem to have a soft glow? Were her eyes more radiant? Or was it his anxious imagination?

"Moon watching. I would think that surely fairies, even ordinary ones like yourself, would be thoughtful moon watchers."

She hesitated, then lowered the crock and dropped down beside him. Her blue serge skirts clouded around her. "Remember, 'tis not wise to mention the fact I am a fairy, or I shall disappear."

Was she teasing or had she gone as mad as he and truly fancied herself a fairy? He could never quite tell about her. She could be a damnable irritation.

"So what is this business about moon watching?" She drew her legs up against her and folded her arms around her knees.

"'Tis serious business here in the colony," he said with a straight face. He, too, could indulge in the fancy of the backwoods people. "For instance, the best time to cut brush is in the months of June through August, when the old moon that day is in the sign of the heart."

She nodded, as if prompting him to continue.

"Well, pole beans should be planted when the horns of the moon are up, to encourage them to climb, but a building must not be roofed then, for the shingles will warp upward."

He glanced at her to see how much of what he was saying she fully believed. Her face was turned partially away, her gaze raised to the moon. Her hair was gathered beneath her coif, and her neck was bare to his avid eyes.

He cleared his throat and went on. "During a full moon a slaughtered cow will give juicy meat, and during a waning moon a slaughtered pig will produce only dry meat. Under a new moon a man should hay his meadows, but not—"

"What about during the dark of the moon?" She shifted her gaze to him. "What should a man do then?" Waiting for him to speak again, her eyes lingered on his mouth.

His voice sounded to him like the bullfrog's just inside the springhouse. "A man should plant his root crop."

"And have yew done that?"

"Aye." He met her gaze and held it. "More than two months before, when I took you on the board table."

The moon's muted light could not conceal her heated blush. Swiftly she lowered her chin to her knees. "Wot if the . . . seeding . . . did not take?"

He took her chin between his thumb and forefinger, forcing her gaze to meet his. It seemed as though not a breath of a breeze stirred the sultry evening air. "I would plant again. And again."

She stared back at him. "Wot if I tell yew me body has already accepted yewr seed? Then would yew leave off planting?" Once more, her voice was inflected with curiosity.

"I know your body very well. Better than you." He searched her face and regrettably found his answer. He released her chin and touched her bottom lip with his forefinger. "You are still ripe for planting."

Her wide triumphant grin revealed bright teeth. "But 'tis not the dark of the moon."

He ran his thumb over her bottom teeth, so charmingly uneven, as was her breathing. "Mayhaps not, but by the days I have reckoned, 'tis nonetheless your fertile time."

Her eyes grew wide.

He grazed his lips against hers and whispered in a voice that was husky with urgent desire, "I had thought to come to you later tonight, in our bed, but here is just as well, where the soil is fecund and the moon can watch."

Her eyes were smoky with the same desire that possessed him and which he knew he had awakened within her. "I think I would not conceive if I truly found your touch distasteful."

"Can you deny that 'tis good, this passion that links us?"

"'Tis unnatural," she whispered.

"'Tis as if we are obsessed." There was no other way to explain such an unlikely coupling as his with this low-born woman. He didn't give her a chance to speak but cupped her small face in his hands and buried his tongue between her lips.

She made a soft noise that seemed to him to be half sigh, half whimper.

He tore off her coif and pushed his fingers through her soft curls. By now he was past all restraint. He caught her shoulders and pressed her sideways until she lay beneath him. The scent of fresh, damp soil filled his nostrils. And her scent. Sweet, light.

Her arms slipped up around his shoulders. She broke loose from his rapacious kiss. Her breathing was raspy. "Can you deny that yew love me?"

He raised his head. "Love you?"

Her mouth twisted. Her eyes were bleak. "I can see that the thought has never crossed yewr mind."

"No," he said bluntly.

Her body squirmed beneath his. "Let me up."

"No. Wait." He anchored her wrists against the earth. "You're not given to foolish sentiment, are you?" He heard the doubt that had crept into his own voice. "Surely you are not in—"

"Nothing has changed, has it?" she said in a tone as harsh as lye. "So, am I still allowed to leave when we get to Jamestown?"

She deserved honesty. "Things have changed. I want a son from you."

Her breath hissed. "Wot?"

He rolled off her and onto his back. He flung a forearm across his forehead, stared sightlessly up at the mocking moon. "'Tis my second chance at righting a grievous wrong. I will not let this opportunity slip through my fingers."

She tried to push herself upright, but his right leg still pinned her to the ground. She half twisted toward him. Those oddly colored eyes blazed. "Yew would breed me as yew would yewr—yewr heifer?"

He moved away to sit up, his legs spread and his arms braced on his knees. He massaged the bridge of his nose, letting his fingers follow the flare of his brows to knead his throbbing temples. "I want another son."

"No wonder they call yew Mad Do—another? Another son?"

"Aye." He buried his face in his palms. His ragged voice was muffled. "My son would have been nineteen this year. The same age I was when he was born."

"He died in the birthing?"

"No." He raised his head. His hands knotted together, he stared like a blind man into the nightmare of the past. "Christopher was six years old when he died."

"I am sorry," she said softly. "It seems so unfair when wee ones die, before they even have a chance to live."

He went on, knowing that he must talk. After thirteen years, he had to uncage his monster. "I was the youngest ever to be appointed to the Star Chamber. It consisted of men from the King's Council, a group of royal advisers. I was arrogant with my privilege and my power. Careless of the feelings of others, including my wife and Christopher. I had no time for them. I was busy consolidating my influence at the Court of King James, as was my rival, Richard Ratcliff."

Her skirts rustled as she drew near him on her knees. "So that is where yew know the man."

He glanced down at her piquant face. "What do you know of the Star Chamber?"

She visibly shuddered. "It passes judgment without trial by jury. It uses torture to obtain confessions."

241

"Aye. The court is so named because it holds unregulated, secret meetings in the Star Chamber of Westminster Palace to try persons too powerful to be brought before the ordinary, common-law courts. James used the Star Chamber to crush opposition to his policies.

"It came about that William Lilburn, a barrister at Lincoln's Inn, was a devout puritan and wrote a seditious article attacking stage plays and actors in general. At the time, the queen was taking part in a rehearsal for a ballet, so an attack upon the Crown was implied. Everyone involved was arrested, from Lilburn himself to the paper's publisher to the people involved in distributing the article.

"It so happened that the Star Chamber was sitting during this incident. Ratcliff offered up a perfunctory plea in behalf of the charged. I was surprised he accepted the thankless task, because it certainly wasn't one that would gain him additional favor with James.

"I saw the opening and immediately took up the opposition, determined to demonstrate my eloquence, my skill, my unswerving loyalty to the Crown. I demanded that everyone involved in the matter be executed that very day. 'Everyone?' Ratcliff inquired."

He stopped. The image of Ratcliff's guileless half smile would haunt him all of his life. Now the smile personified had intruded into his colonial sanctuary.

"I should have sensed that something was amiss," he continued at last. "Ratcliff acceded too easily to me. But my mania for power overrode my intuition. 'Everyone,' I replied. And in so doing I ordered my own son's death."

He heard her quick inhalation.

"You see, I had taken Christopher and his nursemaid with me to Westminster Palace that day." He paused, then forced himself to dredge up every ugly detail. "My wife and I had argued earlier that morning about the lack of attention I gave our son and her. Her carping annoyed me, and I refused to take her with me but brought him along. When I was summoned to the Star Chamber, I left him and the nursemaid in the Strangers' Gallery to witness another debate."

He paused, then said in a quiet voice, his words spaced by pain, "Somehow my son gained possession of one of the pamphlets. A palace guard caught him with it and arrested him."

"But he was just a child!" she protested.

He shrugged. His shoulders felt so heavy. "Children have their ears shorn off or their nostrils slit for stealing something as petty as a potato."

"I know," she said bitterly.

"When I returned to the Strangers' Gallery for Christopher, the hysterical nursemaid told me what had happened. I went at once to find my son, but he had already been taken to the Palace Yard and hanged."

"And that is when yew went mad," she murmured.

"Aye."

"Do you think that Ratcliff was responsible for yewr son possessing the pamphlet?"

"I never had the time to find out. I had to flee England." He grunted. "Regardless, I was the one who ordered my son's death, not Ratcliff."

"But yew didn't knowingly do it!"

"Does age or relationship make a difference? With careless cruelty, I condemned the guilty and the innocent. My son happened to be among the latter. Afterwards, I truly didn't care any more one way or the other about blame or responsibility or honor or power. I simply didn't care about anything."

Or at least he had thought so . . . until he had seen Ratcliff again at Jamestown.

In the silence came the soft murmuring of water running through the springhouse troughs. After a moment, Modesty said, "Then—if yew are already married—we can't be."

He heard the hope in her voice and took perverse delight in dashing it. "We can still enjoy the great comfort we derive from being married to each other," he said, his tone heavy with sarcasm. "My wife committed suicide that same day upon learning of Christopher's death. She drank poisoned wine."

He was irritated with himself that he had suffered a momentary weakness and revealed his soul's torment to this wench he had taken for a wife. He came to his feet and stared down at her coldly. "Now you know. So give me a son and I'll give you a divorce."

She sprang up, her hands clenched at her sides. Her eyes glittered with scorn. "No wonder yewr wife preferred suicide. But if I thought we had to stay married, I'd put poison in *yewr* wine!"

"If I thought we had to stay married, I would drink it."

Chapter Fifteen

Beneath the noonday sun, the curling hair on Mad Dog's bare chest was damp with sweat. He was cutting thatch for roofing and then binding the bundles with hemp cord. His well-honed body moved with a modicum of effort.

Modesty closed her eyes and shook her head to clear it of his tantalizing image. She wanted to hate him for using her, for teaching her the addictive pleasures of his lovemaking. She grumbled at her lot, but she had to admit he gave her care, safety, fairness, and bravery.

And she had to admit that the love consuming her with such an intensity was an agony. No, worse. It was a happiness that mocked her with its elusive fulfillment. If only she could make her mind a blank, her body rigid and unyielding whenever he came to take her unto him.

Since last night, when he revealed his appalling past to her, he had not approached her, had not even come to bed. She knew he was still wrestling with the demons of his memory.

Just as she knew he would nevertheless come to her before the week was out . . . and before her fertile period was over.

With a forlorn sigh, she opened her eyes and espied through the river birches a ship gliding into view. She had learned from Mad Dog that great fleets of tobacco ships sailed each year down through the rivers and creeks of Virginia to the mouth of Chesapeake Bay to head out through the capes for England, returning a few months later with all kinds of manufactured goods—the latest books, gowns, silver bowls, stockings, carpenter's tools, and farm implements.

But this ship was familiar. It was the *Maidenhead*. Mad Dog was already striding down the hill to the pier. He passed through the wharfhouse to wait at the end of the dock for the long-awaited vessel to put in.

Wiping her paint-wet fingers on her apron, Modesty started down the oystershell path and emerged from the cool shade of the wharfhouse to join Mad Dog on the dock as he watched, his hands planted low on his hips. Aboard deck, sailors were scurrying to shouted commands to lower sails and anchor.

Within minutes, Jack was striding down the gangplank. For just a moment, she had the keen sense of being back in London at the alehouse and Jack swaggering in, bedecked in fine clothes, his feathered hat tucked under one arm. His starched ruff was dazzling white against his suntanned face, his curling locks unevenly streaked with varying shades of gold by the relentless sun.

Over a year had passed since his capture at the Bridewell Dock Grog Shop, and her infatuation for Jack had been replaced by a consuming love for Mad Dog that was like a strange and sublime fire.

By the time she reached the caravel, the two men were deep in conversation. A third man had joined them. He was slender, and a scattering of freckles adorned what would have been a pleasant face were it not for a welted scar rippling across the right cheekbone. He wore canvas trousers and a sleeveless leather jerkin.

Jack broke off and swept her up in his arms, oblivious to Mad Dog's presence. "Modesty," he rejoiced, "I thought of you a hundred times!"

Uncomfortable under Mad Dog's speculative gaze, she wriggled free. "Once for each time yew lifted a purse?"

His expression one of affronted innocence, he held up his palms. "Not once, by my troth. For the first time, I have been selling myself, my word, my integrity."

She almost laughed, but she could see he was quite serious.

"'Tis true," the scarred man put in. "Jack here saved me arse even."

"My first mate," Jack said, introducing the

man. "Elias Johnson. And what he isn't telling you is that I won him off Ratcliff in a game of cards."

"Yew cheated," she asserted.

"I told you, I'm a changed man. I found out that I could not give up the role as planter representative, though verily I wanted to bolt several times. But there was a yoke of responsibility that attached itself to me like a tick each time a planter entrusted me with his crops."

"I am glad you did not bolt," Mad Dog said drily, "or else I would have had to take time off from planting to hunt you down. And hunt you down I would."

"On my honor, I behaved." He paused, then flashed her that roguish grin that Modesty knew had captured many a female heart. "Well, that's not entirely true. I did feel compelled to relieve a certain gentleman of his gold-buckled hat band."

This time she did laugh. "I am comforted. I would have been sorely distressed to think a sense of decency corrupted yewr great gift."

"As I would yours," Mad Dog told her. He draped a possessive arm across her shoulders. "Shall we show our planters' representative samples of your great gift?"

She sobered. "If me forgeries don't pass muster in England, 'tis *yewr* head, Jack."

He rubbed the back of his neck and said in a bantering voice, "I'm mighty attached to it."

Laughing, almost as if in camaraderie, the

four strolled along the wharf and back up the shell path toward the cabin. Even stolid-looking Juana displayed her stained-toothed grin for Jack and trotted out a keg of the potent peach brandy.

Mad Dog tugged on a full-bodied shirt with sleeves gathered at the wrists. Then he settled onto the low stool and lit his pipe. The wreath of smoke concealed the expression in his winter-gray eyes, but she knew he was watching her and Jack. Speculating about the depth of their relationship, was he now?

Pleasure that she could make Mad Dog jealous exhilarated her. She laughed more, talked more, and mildly flirted with her old friend as well as his first mate. After a while, she flung her quiet husband a measuring glance.

He looked unimpressed.

A frisson of fear traveled down her spine. She had always felt somewhat smug about her skill at distracting a dupe. Beautiful she might not be, but boring she never would be. Or so she had thought.

Had she overestimated her asset? If it wasn't jealousy that had flickered in Mad Dog's eyes, what was it? She reviewed the conversation of the night before, and with a sickening feeling realized that it wasn't love but merely proprietary interest that he had professed.

"Well, Modesty," Jack was saying, "are you going to show me your handicrafts?"

Setting aside her noggin of brandy, she drew the rolled sheaths of parchment from the double chest and unfurled them on the board table. "What do yew think, Jack? Yew are the master of make believe. Will they do?"

He quaffed the last of his brandy before putting down his own noggin to better view her work. With narrowed eyes, he scanned the documents, then said, "If you can duplicate Ratcliff's signature onto these, then, aye. We should be able to bring down the mighty man. At the most, I'd say nine months."

"Nine months," Mad Dog whispered with arrogant male assurance. His breath tickled her ear and made her tingle all over. His hands held her wrist against the wharfhouse plank walls. "Nine months from tonight and you bear my child."

She felt as if her heart were galloping. Her senses were extraordinarily acute: the wall's rough cedar planking abrading the back of her hands, the moldy scent of green dampness, the slap of the water against the pilings, the dance of rain pelting the cypress shingles. And now the taste of his mouth, his tongue leisurely exploring her lips, her teeth.

She pushed away. "Yew are so sure?" she rasped, her voice all but drowned out by a clap of summer thunder.

They had walked Jack and Elias back to the caravel after dinner, bidding the two men good night when the rain had started. As they turned to leave, her hurried steps had thudded against the wharf boarding. Mad Dog's command to

"Wait" had stopped her heart as well as her steps.

He aligned his hands on either side of her face. His eyes were silver stars against the dense darkness of the wharfhouse. "Aye, I am sure. As I've never been before. Can you not feel the white-hot heat between us? Our passion is as fierce as the summer electrical storm. Tonight you will conceive my son."

She wanted to feel his mouth possessing hers again in a kiss that dominated all her thoughts and feelings, so that she would not remember that this was not love, only lust.

But instead he tore off her coif and buried his face in the soft cloud of new hair that drifted loose about her face. At the same time, he grasped her skirts and pushed them up around her hips.

Her hands, released from their human manacles, fumbled feverishly at his breeches' buttons. Hot and hard, his erection pressed against her belly. Her hands cupped his massive organ, and she went on her knees. She had never experienced this urgency, this need of him before. Mayhaps he was right. Tonight was meant for his filling her with his seed.

"No," he said hoarsely as her mouth explored his length. He pressed her on down onto a bed of coiling hemp and began kissing her everywhere. He seemed out of control. Her neck, her cheek, the rising mound of one breast—they all felt the heat of his torrid kisses.

Yet it was with gradual love play that he

sheathed himself inside her folds of wet, soft velvet.

She groaned with pleasure, and he clapped a hand over her mouth. She had forgotten the nightwatch aboard the *Maidenhead*, anchored only yards away.

Then his taking of her, so fierce, so furious, altered its tempo. This was unexpected, uncharacteristic of their volcanic passion. His lips returned to lavish silken kisses over her cheeks, her temples, her chin. He stroked her damp hair back from her face. "Ssh, slowly, my accomplished adventuress."

"Why? Why this . . . this tenderness?"

His dropped a kiss on the tip of her nose. "Why, simply because I want my son conceived in tenderness."

With that, he began a concentrated control of his movements in and out of her. She could feel his total focus on her body. The result was an ever-expanding awareness of the two of them moving in a cooperative unison that brought a much more explosive ecstasy.

The prolonged pleasure was unsustainable. Her hands curled, her legs stiffened, she arched into him. His mouth absorbed her outcry. Afterwards, she could not look at him but kept her eyes closed.

He kissed away the inexplicable tears that seeped from beneath her closed lids. "'Tis all right," he said, holding her against his length and stroking her reassuringly, as a man would a wild mare he is trying to induce into captivity.

It was more than all right. It was like dying and going to heaven. But she wasn't going to tell him that if he didn't know. Instead she said, "If I am indeed carrying yewr child now, then I have a right to know yewr real name."

He grunted, tried to move away, but she held fast to him. "A son shouldn't have a father named Mad Dog," she said, running her fingers over his beard-stubbled jaw.

"Inigo."

"Wot?"

"You heard me," he growled. "Inigo. Inigo Jones."

Her peel of full-throated laughter was irrepressible.

Chapter Sixteen

Before proceeding to London, the *Maidenhead* put in at Jamestown. Disembarking for the Publick Times were the burgesses and their families from upriver Henrico, as well as the governor's new chaplain and his wife. Watching them leave the ship, Jack felt the knots ease from his shoulders. His masquerade had not been detected. He wondered how well he would fare as he mingled with the crowds.

Jack knew from his business encounters with the colonists that every July Jamestown's population of three hundred doubled almost overnight for the convening of the General Assembly and the courts, as well as for the Publick Times.

Since it was the social, cultural, and political center of the Virginia Colony, all sorts of people descended on the capital to seek pleasure as well as to settle their legal concerns and to conduct business. Rich Tidewater aristocrats who had townhouses in Jamestown rubbed elbows with the small freeholders in the Piedmont, the rolling country beyond the fall line of the rivers. Merchants and dockhands from the cape wharves mingled with settlers searching for pitch, tar, and turpentine in the Dismal Swamp. German ironworkers jostled with frontiersmen from deep in Indian territory, and the members of the Council of State mixed with planters who had lawsuits to plead in the General Court and with yeomen who had petitions to lay before the assembly.

Jack's passengers had boasted that the shops would be stocked with the latest goods imported from London as well as with the products of local craftsmen and that the town would hum with activity for the entire week. There would be horse races, fairs, and formal balls. Auctions would be held at various taverns and on Market Square.

Though he was relieved to see his charges melt into the crowds, he knew he would see them all again that evening at the opening ball at the State House. But Jack's real uneasiness came from being under Mad Dog's watchful eye. Just in case the perceptive planter might suspect something amiss, Jack felt compelled to put in an obligatory appearance for the sake of the man's mercantile interest.

His own mercantile interest lay elsewhere.

The caravel's rich cargo could find lucrative markets in the Far East with exotic names like Java, Macao, and Malaysia. Aye, the spice trade would be profitable—and would keep the *Maidenhead* far from the vengeful tentacles of the English high admiral who was Mad Dog's uncle.

In less than three days, Jack could vanish with the *Maidenhead* on the vast, trackless sea.

"These crude provincials dance as well as the best London society," the outgoing governor told Wyatt, the new one. The two men stood just inside the State House doorway.

Sitting nearby, Rose overheard the statement and had to smile. The "provincials" included ladies, knights, and younger sons of aristocrats who, prevented from inheriting by the law of entail came as adventurers to this promised land. Even a baron—Jack Morley, her rescuer.

She was one of those adventurers, wasn't she? Coming to the New World and leaving all that was familiar had taken a courage she hadn't know she had. At home, she had always been the biddable, submissive daughter. Here, in this wild Eden, she could sense herself gradually changing, growing stronger in spirit. No longer did she cry out inside, *Love me. Please someone love me.*

She curled between her fingers the downy, flaxen hair of her sleeping infant, whom she cradled in one arm. Strange, she could not remember the face of her son's father.

Instead, another face, Jack's, occasionally intruded on her thoughts. A gallant man, a gentleman, a handsome man. Not that looks were important to her. Dear Walter was certainly not handsome by any means.

It would have been wonderful had Walter loved her with the passion that Reverend Dartmouth loved Clarissa. It was so obvious in the minister's adoring eyes.

On the opposite side of the elongated room, sitting on a long bench with several other women, Clarissa tapped her foot impatiently to the lively music played by a backwoods fiddler and by old Clem on his flute. But the minister's puritan calling forbade him from asking his wife to dance. A shame, Rose thought.

A shame too that Walter was preoccupied in seeking out the German ironworkers to help him finish the remaining sections of his sawmill. Rose would have loved to dance—reels, jigs, hornpipes, contra dances—any and all of them.

Then again, how fortunate she was that she had a good husband, a man willing to work hard for her and the boys.

She sighed and turned her attention to her baby, who was trying to nuzzle her milk-engorged breast. She shifted him against her shoulder and began patting his back. "Go back to sleep, little one," she murmured along with the music. "Go back to—"

"He's so precious!" Annie cooed beside her. "Oh, let me hold him, Rose."

Feeling motherly pride, Rose passed her baby

to the big-boned young woman, who was now large with child herself. Coming to her feet, Rose smoothed out her crumpled apron. "'E's a handful. Bart and Isaac are tame compared to Jack."

"Where are the rascals?" Annie asked, then rubbed the baby's tiny nose with her own.

"Outside with their pa."

Annie raised her head and grinned. "Sampling the beer as me Jamie is no doubt doing."

But Rose wasn't listening. Her gaze locked on Jack Morley, who had just entered the room. He was dressed in a black velvet doublet and thigh-high leather boots fastened to his Venetian breeches by points. A short Spanish cape was draped from one shoulder so that the scarlet lining showed.

Her hands outstretched, she crossed toward him. "Jack! Jack Morley! I 'adn't thought ever to see 'oo again!"

Uneasiness flashed across his face and quickly disappeared. "Rose? I wasn't certain it was you." He gestured at her slim, corseted waistline. "You look so . . . slender."

Her laughter was light, airy. Like she felt at that moment. "I imagine I looked a bit bloated back then." She nodded toward the baby. "'Tis 'oor doing, if you remember that—"

She stopped and flushed, realizing what she had said. Later, she knew Annie would be all questions. "I mean, about 'elping bring the babe into the world and all."

He leaned over to view the object in question.

"Why, he has become a handsome lad! When first I saw the wee one, he was as ugly as a monkey."

Annie and she laughed, but her laughter ebbed when she saw that now the Earl of Monteagle was embarrassed. She knew why. They both were recalling that very intimate moment when he helped deliver her baby.

She lowered her voice. She knew Annie was eavesdropping over the music. "'Is name is Jack, you know."

He straightened, shook his head. "No. I did not." He seemed at a loss for words. Even anxious.

"I would like to introduce 'oo to me 'usband. If 'oo don't mind, 'e's outside—"

He glanced around the room nervously. "Would you care to dance, Rose?"

His request took her by surprise. Polly was dancing with her Duncan. John Rolfe and his wife, Joane, also shared the floor, as well as several other couples. "Well, I—I—"

"Go ahead," Annie said with a puckish grin. "I can manage little Jack just fine."

The dance was a round. She barely recognized these new colonial steps, but Jack's hands, lightly lifting her fingers at the appointed intervals, helped guide her through the set. At one close, lingering pass, he inclined his head and murmured, "You smell sweet. Of milk."

She thought he was belittling her. A hasty peek up into his sun-burnished face told her he meant no harm. Rather, she thought she detected a bemused expression. She felt herself blushing. This man knew her better than her husband. Incredible. "Little Jack has a mighty appetite for me milk," she mumbled.

At that moment, she spotted her husband standing in the doorway with Isaac and Bart. "Oh, my menfolk are here. I can introduce 'oo now. My husband Walter is the tall one there."

"Uhh—Rose." He still had her hand.

"Aye?"

"Rose—" His face flushed. "I am no earl."

Her brows furrowed. "Why did 'oo tell me 'oo were?"

He looked elsewhere, at the musicians, the governors, anywhere but at her. "'Tis a bad habit I have." He looked at her now. "One of many. Rose, I lie, I cheat, I steal, I—"

Her anger surprised herself, surprised even him. "All me life, I let people mistreat me because I didn't think I was good enough! But I had faith in 'oo. All the time, 'oo must 'ave been laughing at how gullible I was. Why, 'oo are no better than me. 'Oo are worse because *you* mistreat people!"

With a mocking curtsey, she detached herself and threaded her way through the dancers.

"Who was th—that?" Walter asked.

"Who?" she asked innocently. She could tell he was more puzzled than jealous. It never occurred to him that she was more than a mother to his two sons.

"The man you were da—dancing the reel with."

"Oh. Remember, I told you about 'im. 'E was the man who rescued me from the river."

"And de—delivered your ba—baby."

She held out her arms to Bart and Isaac. "Boys, would you care to dance?"

"Aye!" Bart said and grabbed her hand.

Isaac looked bashful but followed her back out onto the floor. If only their father would follow, too. If only their father could forget his first wife. If only Jack hadn't ruined her illusion.

So much unspent energy charged through Clarissa that she felt as if her shoes would dance off on their own. With a sigh of exasperation, she snapped shut her fan.

She glanced at Patrick. He stood in a corner, conversing with Modesty's husband. The man looked almost civilized. Almost. True, he was clad in deerhide trousers and moccasins, but he wore a fine lawn shirt with a frill down the front and an open buff coat with large turned-back cuffs. His tawny-brown lion's mane, seasoned with silver, flowed onto his shoulders.

"Your husband is a splendid man," Mistress Pierce said beside her. Her knitting needles clicked in time to the music. "Reminds me of me own dear departed man. When he had all his teeth, he was a good-looker, upon me word."

Clarissa's gaze switched back to Patrick, and she snapped open her fan. "Aye, my husband is a splendid man."

But where was his passion, his conviction? Alas, he was as colorless as his clothing.

For the ball, she had abandoned the somber clothing she had taken to wearing at Henrico. She had the rest of her life to wear brown homespuns. Tonight, she had chosen a gown of sapphire satin with silver ribbon bows lacing the bodice. The gown had a high-standing collar and drapings of lace that gave way to a decolletage so low that the brown rings of her nipples were almost visible.

When Patrick and Modesty's husband finished their discussion, which most likely was about politics, Patrick approached her and bowed low. "Mistress, the fiddler needs a rest, as do my ears. I fear tomorrow may come earlier than I like. Shall we retire?"

Her fan snapped shut again. "Oh? I thought you already had."

Her sarcasm passed over both him and Mistress Pierce. She rose, bid the woman good night, and, putting her hand in the crook of Patrick's arm, accompanied him from the State House.

Once outside, beneath the newly risen southern moon, her snippish mood subsided. "You know, I don't think the moon is as big in London."

Patrick smiled down at her. "Let's take a stroll across the green before returning to the Mercers'."

"Aye," she agreed readily. The local gunsmith and his wife had kindly offered a small room in their tiny house to accommodate her and Patrick for the duration of the General Assembly session, but the old couple were nosy. She felt they were always listening, always watching. She suspected that they judged her too worldly for her husband.

She spoke aloud her thoughts. "Tell me, Patrick, does there exist somewhere God's condemnation of the aristocracy?"

He peered down at her. "Whatever are you talking about?"

"That somehow 'tis wrong to have wide interests in the arts and literature, to see beauty in color and harmony in tradition?"

"But the tradition of your Old World," he said, strolling on beneath the white-flowered magnolias, "gave authority to only a few."

"That's just the problem with this wild land." she gestured vaguely toward the river with its fringe of riotous foliage. "For all its freedoms from authority, this New World had done away with the aristocracy of the past. I feel out of place here. In the Old World, gentry's coach gave way to a nobleman's, the yeoman tipped his hat to the gentry. Here there are no rules. No linkage between the conservatism of the Old World and the chaos of the New."

He turned to face her, taking both her hands in his. "There can be. You and I can create it."

The intensity in his eyes mirrored her emotions. "What do you mean?"

"We can build a bridge with our love."

She hardly dare to breathe. "How?"

"Through expressing our love for both the servant and the master, the red man and the white, the commoner and the aristocrat."

"Oh!" She felt like stamping her foot. "Your nobility is too much to suffer!"

"And between the puritan and the sophisticate," he continued, unperturbed, then lowered his head over hers and kissed the rounded **O** of her mouth.

When he released her, her fingertips flew to her lips. "You kissed me," she mumbled in astonishment.

His smile was gently mocking. "Aye. Even puritans are capable of expressing affection."

Affection? She wanted unbridled lovemaking, as wild as the new land itself.

Reluctantly, she let her footsteps follow along with his as he walked on to the gunsmith's house. Mistress Mercer greeted them at the door. She held an arthritic finger to her lips. "The husband is already asleep," she whispered.

Patrick nodded and led Clarissa on through the darkened house to the small anteroom where their bed was barely large enough for one.

In the dark, she and Patrick changed into shift and nightshirt, much as they did at home. But when they climbed into bed, there was no empty space as in their own bed.

Forced to lie on their sides, they faced the wall in the time-honored spoon fashion. His breath stirred the tendrils of hair that had escaped her nightcap. She was acutely aware of his larger thighs supporting her own, his left arm draped negligently across her waist, and, most of all, that fleshy scepter that proclaimed itself most prominently.

She had never seen a man naked, and her imagination dueled with her curiosity. "Patrick, I feel cramped. I need to turn over."

Wordlessly, he shifted, and she found herself facing his broad back. One bent arm cradling her head, she wrapped her other arm, almost carelessly, around his midsection. Her hand touched a long ridge just below.

He tensed.

She left her hand there.

His breathing quickened.

Slowly, gradually, her fingers closed over the ridge, measuring its thickness through his nightshirt. Marveling, she let her fingers follow its length.

She wasn't certain, but she thought that he made a low noise. It was a rusty sound like that of a gate hinge grating somewhere in the distance.

Her hand slipped beneath his nightshirt to encounter hard flesh.

This time, she was certain that the noise he made was a groan.

It didn't stop her. With excitement zephyring through her, she grasped his shaft which seemed to throb with a life of its own. From exploring, her fingers turned to caressing.

She took perverse pleasure in hearing his low, mumbled words. "Oh, God, Clarissa. Please.

Aye." She had finally made her mild husband lose control!

But her entertainment was short-lived when he rolled over suddenly, pinning her beneath him. "What—!"

His hand clapped over her mouth. "Sssh."

His hand still silencing her, he pushed her nightrail up to her waist. With great care, he placed himself at the entrance to her maiden-head. She gasped against his palm.

"Sssh," he said again. "The gunsmith's good wife will hear thee."

He hesitated, and she feared that his common sense would be restored. She goaded him further. As if by accident, her tongue stole out and licked the center of his palm.

"God help me!" He prodded that thin wall of resistance, saying, "I fear I am lost to the clamor of my senses!"

With that he thrust inside her. Whatever pain she felt was overcome by a great burst of plea-sure as he continued his long, rhythmic strokes. Later, when they both lay spent, he whispered, "Forgive me, Clarissa."

Her cheek upon his sleek chest, she smiled in the darkness. Until he muttered, "'Twill not happen again. I swear I'll abide by your decision if it means keeping you forever."

Why couldn't he fight for her love?

Mad Dog sprawled in the wainscot chair. A direct descendant of medieval thrones, it was made for dignity, not comfort. Everything was uncomfortable in the small house he rented from John Smith, who was presently mapping the Somers Islands that some were calling Bermuda. "You refused to go to the public ball last night, so why this?"

Modesty, still in her nightrail that early in the morning, ran a boar-bristle brush through her tousled hair that did not quite reach her shoulders. With her slender hips, she would have made an enchanting boy—were it not for her small, pert breasts. Neither they nor her stomach gave any indication that she was with child. He had taken himself a woman whose womb was as barren as his heart.

She peered at him from beneath her upraised arm. "Why would I want to mingle with the very people who wanted to burn me?"

"Yet you want to go to Market Square today."

Her bewitching eyes glanced to the window, where the shutters had been thrown back to let in the morning breeze off the river. "Aye. Polly, Rose, Annie, Clarissa—all the women transported with me will be there."

He watched her over his pyramided fingertips. "You wouldn't think of sailing with the *Maidenhead* on this evening's tide, would you now?" he drawled in an offhanded manner.

She turned wide eyes on him. "Why would I do that? We made a pact, didn't we?"

"You are an endless source of amusement, Modesty."

She eyed him through narrowed lids. "Wot do yew mean?"

"You could have gone to the trouble to unpack your valise. After all, we're going to be here a full week." He canted his head. "Unless you didn't plan on staying."

"I don't understand wot yew're talking about."

"Mayhaps you'll understand this—that the *Maidenhead* sailed this morning—on my instructions."

"Yew knew! Yew—" Beyond self-control, she hurled the brush at him.

He ducked. It glanced off the chair's paneled back, and he laughed at her furious expression.

She flung herself at him. "Yew scurvy clod-skulled arse! Yew bloody piss-bowl of an oaf! I could—!"

"Ought, ought, Modesty," he reproved, trying to subdue her flailing fists.

When that didn't work, he threw her across his knee and hitched up her nightrail. The magical half light of an August dawn lent a rosy tone to her buttocks that he couldn't resist. He slapped the delightfully curved bottom with the flat of his hand.

Her answering scream was more from rage than the pain left by his reddened handprint. "Yew bugger, yew—"

His hand clapped one rounded cheek and stayed there. "Is that what you prefer? To be buggered?"

She tried to wriggle free, and when he held her fast, she screeched, "Better that horror than the other—to conceive by yew!"

271

Abruptly, he stood, dumping her unceremoniously on the floor. "I am late for the assembly." He watched her scramble to her feet, her eyes flashing fury, then said, "Try to make yourself presentable by the time the courts adjourn for dinner."

Mad Dog forced himself to put aside his disgust with his marital situation and turned his attention to the General Assembly. For one purpose only, he sat through tedious debates concerning competition with the superior Spanish tobacco, the planters' resentment about marketing their tobacco through the Company when they might do better on the open market, and grumbling over the Indian menace.

Throughout the session that day, Mad Dog studied his formidable opponent, the burgess member sitting diagonally to his left.

The private plantations had presented a tricky problem to the Company. They represented the investment of influential men, the sort the Company wanted to attract to Virginia but also the sort who would bristle at interference in their affairs. To solve this, the plantations employing both bondservants and tenants were allowed their own representative in the House of Burgesses.

Richard Ratcliff was now by far the most influential planter in the colony. And a burgess member. At every turn, every discussion, every vote, the man sought to improve the status of Ratcliff Manor.

Mad Dog knew that he had guessed aright about the chink in Ratcliff's self-satisfied armor. And it was within Mad Dog's means, or would be when Holloway returned from England, to bring down Ratcliff's estate as easily as toppling a house of cards.

He wanted to see the man sweat blood, he wanted to see the man lose what he valued above all else—as he himself had.

Chapter Seventeen

Strange, Rose thought. Home was over two thousand miles away, more than a year and a half in the past. And yet, here she sat, once more carding wool.

She added another small bunch of wool between the thickly wired teeth of her two paddles and began rubbing them back and forth. These days the grinding noise set her own teeth on edge.

She glanced at Bart and Isaac, snuggled beneath the goosedown blanket. October's howling, freezing wind warranted a fire that evening, and Walter had stepped out to the woodshed to return with another armful of logs.

The door banged shut behind him. Chilly air slithered along the floor. "Gonna be sn—snow by morning. I should have kno—known to expect an early snowfall. The hornets built their nest higher than usual this year."

"And I was planning on making apple butter tomorrow." It was a chore better suited for out-doors.

"Lucky for us, some Powhattans st—stopped by to sell us the two turkeys they killed." He knelt to lay two logs on the andirons. "We won't have to lo—look to our larder."

"Aye, but I still feel uneasy around them, Wal-ter."

"'Tis just that ti—time of year again that makes you feel that way." He brushed the dirt and bits of bark from his spindly fingers. "But I te—tell you, Rose, those Indians who kid—kidnapped you at this time last year were just renegades."

"True," she conceded. "The Indians are be-ing unusually friendly." She paused in card-ing long enough to lean over the wicker cradle and tuck the blanket more securely around little Jack.

"Rose."

She glanced up at his thin, anxious face on a level with hers. "Aye?"

"I've never asked you about your pa—past, have I? About the child you carried when we mar—married."

"No, Walter." She leaned over and smoothed into place the thin wisps of hair across his smooth pate. He smelled of earth and sweat and new-sawn wood. "And I am verily grateful for that kindness. 'Oo are a good man."

She had been especially proud of him at the meeting of the burgesses two months earlier. With only a few stutters, he had argued persuasively against the Crown's right to end the Company's seven-year exemption from English import duties.

He looked down, as if concentrating on brushing the scattered wood chips toward the hearth, and mumbled, "The child, Jack, is it that man's you danced with at the Sta—State Hall?"

She set aside her carding panels and took his face between her two hands. "Dearest, I didn't know Jack until the day he . . . saved me life."

She could feel the tense muscles in his jaws relax. "I just wanted to know."

"I understand. There is something, too, I would like to know."

She hesitated, and he prompted her with an "Aye?"

"Are 'oo still in love with your first wife?" She was weary of being nice, of being patient. She couldn't carry on a one-sided marriage—no, *wouldn't*. It was up to Walter to take some initiative.

Blank astonishment yanked up his sparse brows. "Martha?"

She nodded solemnly. She had to know. She firmly believed that when one faced the worst, one could deal with it. It was the unknown that was so frightening.

He grinned. "Martha was a scold. I would have se—set her on the ducking stool had I the courage."

"But 'oo said . . . once 'oo told me that in bed were the times 'oo liked the best."

He flushed. "That's because in the dark I found it easier to ta-talk."

Of course, it made sense. She still had one more question. "We've been married over a year now. I'm no longer with child. Why haven't 'oo. . . . " Now it was her turn to blush.

He sifted dead ashes through his fingers. "I di-didn't know if you would welcome . . . if you would like . . . "

Her anger surprised her. "I think 'tis time 'oo found out." There, she felt better having challenged him. Anger didn't have to mean she didn't love him or that he wouldn't love her.

He came rapidly to his feet. He glanced around, took in the three sleeping boys.

She had been so intense, so intent on resolving her problem that she had all but forgotten the boys. "Where—where can we—?"

He grinned, then blushed from his prominent Adam's apple up past his cheekbones, all the way across his balding pate. "Ever made love in a wood—woodshed?"

"Large flakes at first, the storm will last; small flakes at first, it'll be over fast."

"When a dog howls at the moon in winter, it is a sign of snow."

At first, the folklore of the Henrico people had seemed ridiculous to Clarissa, but now she was learning to give some credit to local superstition. The snow was falling fast and thick, obliterating the parishioners' tracks before they even closed the door behind them. Appropriate for Christmas Day. Against the cold, she was wearing a red velvet cloak with fur lining and a beaver muff.

Despite the blustery weather, the pews were rapidly filling for the Christmas service. Though church attendance was compulsory, few people wanted to stay away. Quite aside from its spiritual purpose, the church was the community source of mental stimulus, of gossip, of news, and of drama.

Patrick mounted the small flight of steps to the pulpit. Above his head was a wooden canopy, for a sounding board. He began, as he always did, with a reading from the King James version of the Bible.

" 'Then Joseph being raised from sleep did as the angel of the Lord had bidden him, and took unto him his wife: And knew her not till she had brought forth her firstborn son.' "

He raised his eyes from the printed page, and his gaze impounded hers. She felt a rising heat that was quickly subdued by the sudden gust of frigid wind that entered the church.

All faces turned toward the double doors at the back of the room. A solitary soul stood framed against the dreary winter sunlight. Snow-flecked wind lashed his black hooded cape about his slender body. The man carried a gold-banded malacca cane, and he was dressed with a wonderful sense of grace, his style favoring softer materials such as satin, velvet, and silk.

"Nigel!" Clarissa gasped, rising from her pew. The room had grown fiercely hot. He had to be aware of the drama he was creating.

He strode down the aisle toward her in his indolent fashion. He was in fact languid by nature, though she knew that horse racing and cockfights could excite him. A single gold earring gleamed against his curling black locks. He took her numbed fingers in his gauntleted hands. "I promised you I would cross the world for you, my lady."

She had never lost her conviction that he would do so.

And yet . . . for so long, she had been awaiting a rescue. Expecting a magician to make everything right again, to restore the highborn heiress to her rightful place in society. She had known she was being extremely self-indulgent, but she had been brought up to believe firmly that she got everything she wanted, even compromises.

Not a person stirred in the tiny church. She glanced up at Patrick, then back at Nigel. "I have married," she whispered. "The Reverend Dartmouth."

For a fraction of a second, he looked

stricken. Yet his lordly confidence did not crumble. He was everything and more her memory had promised. Flamboyant. Vital. Virile. His features were beautifully chiseled, his skin ivory.

"I see." His gaze traveled to the pulpit, to the man also dressed in black. White deep cuffs and a white bibbed clerical collar contended with crimson sash and gloves. "An ocean could not stop me, my lady. Neither can a few words mumbled under pressure. Money can buy an annulment, especially considering the past circumstances."

Clarissa swallowed. Her gaze flew to Patrick. His features were unreadable.

She looked back at Nigel. His eyes were impassioned. "Choose," he told her.

"I . . . I . . . " She shook her head. "This is all too soon for me to think clearly, Nigel!"

He searched her face, trusting it to memory or looking for hope that her indecisiveness might be swayed in his favor. "In order to reach you, I obtained permission to represent the East India Company at the Virginia Company's quarter court session to be held in March in Jamestown." He bowed low. "Till then . . . enjoy the days full well, my lady."

Somehow she got through the Christmas services. After that, the winter days passed tediously. Patrick did not attempt to dissuade or persuade her, and for this she cursed him. He was so vacuous in his feelings.

And yet, she was vacillating in her own. To

remain in the colony was to give up hope of a life of refinement, of riches, of ease. Plantation life was so limited. Never would she have the opportunity to read daily gazettes; no operas or masquerades to look forward to.

What was there for her in this far-flung wilderness outpost?

Nigel loved her passionately.

Day after day, her mind waged both sides of the tortuous argument like some silent chess battle. Her emotions were a tiny boat on a storm-tossed ocean.

January gave way to February and the first signs that spring was not far off. Denuded trees sprouted tiny knobs that would soon unfurl. Shoots of green blades poked between the dead leaves of winter that speckled the ground.

One day late in February Clarissa sat outside, warming herself on the hickory bench secluded in the grape arbor.

The rustle of leaves underfoot announced a visitor, and she half turned her head to see Patrick. For six weeks now they had shared only the most superficial of conversations. "You have finished with writing Sunday's sermon?" she asked.

"Almost." He flipped out the skirt of his cassock-style coat and took a seat on the bench. "The time draws nigh."

"Aye. I know." They both knew of what he spoke. She waited.

* * *

At long last, was he going to discuss the plight of their marriage? Would he plead with her to stay? Or tell her he had decided to release her from her vows?

"I have not spoken to thee much of my family."

Her eyes widened. Surely he wasn't going to discuss genealogy at a time like this!

He gestured toward the sprigs of grass poking here and there through the dirt. "My mother loved to garden almost as much as she loved to read the Bible. I suppose that is why I love flowers.

"For the purpose of passing on wisdom, Mother often felt it necessary to construct a parable in plants. Once, when I was facing a difficult decision as a very young man, she laid down two paths. The first meandered aimlessly and was bordered by heavy-scented, almost decadent blooms. At the end was the plant, bleeding heart. The second, straight and narrow and hemmed in by primroses, led to a jack-in-the-pulpit. The message was not lost on me."

He rose. Could it be? His hazel eyes, were they actually brimming with compassion for her? *Her*, a highborn heiress? "Well, my writing awaits me. Fare thee well, mistress."

Early one morning in mid March, Mad Dog was splitting wood. The chore took him out of the cabin. He felt too large for it. He needed to work off his excess energy—and his concern.

Holloway should have been back soon after the first of year and here it was, the day before Good Friday.

With each swing of his axe, Mad Dog reviewed the facts. They were unpleasant. He had invested time, money, and faith in an enterprise that was not going to bring about its purpose—avenging Christopher's death. Mad Dog had to stare at his botched ambition. Ratcliff had evaded retribution. Meanwhile, Ant Hill, laboring under reduced funds, was teetering on the edge of bankruptcy.

At that moment, Modesty stepped barefoot from the cabin door. Arching her back, she curled her arms up and out and stretched languorously.

His axe, sharp enough to shave with, stopped in its upward path. To him, she looked like some satisfied feline. Sunlight filtered through her threadbare nightrail. All her feminine attributes were accentuated in gauzy relief.

Desire blazed through him like one of those fires that periodically ignited London—showers of burning sparks, molten lead running in scorching torrents, stones exploding from the intense heat and sounding like cannon fire.

"Put something on. You look like a strumpet."

"Well, well, another fine day."

His riven wood lay forgotten at his feet. "You let the fire go out last night," he growled.

She yawned, then said, "'Tis of little consequence."

"Oh?" He braced his hands on the axe handle.

The Savage

"Do you want to tell me why?"

She smiled cheerfully and ran her hands through her mass of hair to rustle loose its tangles. "We leave shortly for Henrico. We can start a new fire when we return."

He had forgotten that he had agreed to attend Dartmouth's Good Friday sermon. The last thing he wanted to hear was another sermon. He felt a meanness boiling in his brain. "What makes you think you will accompany me?"

Across the distance, she squinted at him askance. "Why wouldn't I? I am yewr wife."

"A fact I am well aware of. Which is why I want you here until you are with child. My son."

"Wot?"

His laugh was low and nasty. "After all, how can I trust a woman of your repute?"

Her hands curled into claws, she charged toward him. He dropped the axe handle and caught her wrists. He held her at a distance, rendering her blows ineffectual.

Suddenly she went stone still. "I don't want yewr seed ripening in me belly. I would rip it out first. Do yew understand me?" Her voice was harsh, defiant.

He stared at her, seeing, though, the pattern of his life. The shrews he had taken in marriage. He didn't know who was more accursed, himself or they. He released her with a shove. "What a disastrous choice I made in marrying you."

* * *

Modesty straightened and rubbed the small of her back. The sun was high, near the noon hour, and she still had the washed clothes to hang out to dry.

All morning she had bent over the scrub board at the river's edge, and her hands were reddened by the lye soap and her back ached. She had wrung water from Mad Dog's leather jerkin, wishing she had her husband's neck between her hands. Eventually her fury had subsided, leaving in its place a clamoring pain that felt as though it would burst her heart.

She cursed herself for staying with him—staying with him even when he left her so easily, as he had this morning. Taking the bay mare, he had ridden out like someone gone berserk on jimsonweed.

A rushing noise like a great storm caught her attention. Migrating geese rose off the sun-glazed water, and she stood in awe, watching as they temporarily blotted out the sun.

Then something else caught her attention— a solitary figure in a canoe, rowing rapidly toward her. Hitching up her skirts, Modesty waded calf deep into the chilly water to meet Juana. The sand clogged her footsteps, and the sturgeon were so thick with spring spawning that she had to be careful not to tread on them.

Closer now, she could see the panic in the Spanish woman's face. "Indians. Powhattan tribes. They come to kill. Jamestown people.

Surrey people. Henrico people. All white people."

She gripped the side of the canoe. "When, Juana?"

"Before day is out. Children—men—women—houses—animals—all white men's things to be"—she searched for the right English word—"gone." She snapped her fingers in imitation of Modesty. "Just like that. You tell Mad Dog."

"He's not here. He left early this morning. I don't know where he is."

The old woman paused, then said, "You come with me. We go to my place. Deep in the forest."

Just the image of her scalp hanging from Opechancanough's lance was enough to prompt Modesty to quick decision. Wrestling with her skirts, she settled into the canoe's prow. It rocked violently, then steadied, and Juana turned the canoe back upstream.

Her oar had cleaved the water no more than a dozen times when Modesty said, "Stop! Turn around."

The old woman ceased paddling and turned to stare at her with amazement.

Clarissa and her husband—Rose and Walter and the three boys—they needed to be warned! "We're going to Henrico."

Juana shook her head back and forth furiously and ran a finger across her throat. "Die quickly."

"We must warn them, Juana!"

Again Juana shook her head and resumed paddling.

Modesty grabbed up the canoe's extra oar and began back-paddling. The canoe wobbled treacherously. So there *was* a trick to keeping the canoe upright.

Seeing Modesty's determination, Juana gave up and paddled in unison with her.

Within the hour, they reached Henrico. The shoreline was empty of life, as were the wattle-and-daub houses strewn along the hill. Panic swept through her. Had the Powhattans already struck? But no smoke roiled from the homes.

Then she saw a slope-shouldered man with hat in hand hurrying from one of the houses. She recognized him from assembly time at Jamestown. From the canoe, she hailed him, calling out, "Master Rolfe, where is everyone?"

He stopped, looked toward the river, and spotted her and Juana. "They're at a barn-raising. I'm late."

"Tell them the Powhattan tribes are on the warpath. They must protect themselves at once."

"But the Powhattans have been friendly lately."

"Well, now they're unfriendly." She wasn't about to waste time arguing. She took up her oar again and began back-paddling.

"You have to warn Jamestown also!" he called back.

Was he crazy? At any moment howling Indians could pour forth from the forest.

With alacrity, she swung the oar first on one side of the canoe, then the other. Juana's strokes were just as rapid.

" . . . have to . . . warn . . . Jamestown!" she heard him shout after her.

Jamestown could go up in smoke for all she cared. Hadn't its good denizens been prepared to let her go up in smoke?

Annie's deep-chested laugh and Polly's good-natured ways haunted Modesty's mind.

Fie on Jamestown. She was just now getting her hair back. She didn't fancy losing it again.

She swung her oar even more vigorously.

But the demons of principles and ethics hounded her. "I must be a bloody fool," she muttered.

She hauled up on the oar, creating a back tide of water. Juana glanced around sharply at her. "We're going to Jamestown."

The old woman looked pop-eyed at her. But by this time she was apparently resigned to Modesty's unpredictable whims, because she offered no further protest but fell into synchronized strokes.

At every landing along the James River, Modesty gave out her warning. The sunlight grew fiercely hot. As the hours wore on, the current and a northwesterly breeze propelled the canoe more than their joint efforts at rowing.

Late afternoon overtook them—and a fleet of canoes. With horror chilling her blood, Modesty stared into the painted faces of scores of top-knotted warriors.

Mad Dog strode inside the Golden Parrot on Back Street, Jamestown's only hostelry. It was still under construction and, at the rate it was going up, would not likely be completed for another decade.

For the cost of an occasional pence for a pint of beer, a man might hear the latest news, listen in on the discussion of the best minds in the neighborhood, or play draughts or skittles.

Mad Dog recognized several of the men as burgesses he had met during the General Assembly. One man dressed in black velvet was new to him—and new to the country, because his face and hands were the pale shade of a man of the northern climes. A single gold earring gleamed at his left ear, and he carried a malacca cane. Mad Dog dismissed him as a man of affectation.

Ratcliff was there too, wagering at a game of piquet. He was not a creature with an inclination for socializing, and Mad Dog found his presence there curious.

The man's red eyes forsook the cards to cast an assessing glance at Mad Dog. A fleeting look of what Mad Dog could only identify as agitation crossed Ratcliff's raw features.

All the old fury boiled up in Mad Dog. Useless fury. It did nothing but consume the soul. He forced himself to turn away from his nemesis. He was fatigued after riding through the morn-

ing, afternoon, and into the evening. Furthermore, he was in a sour mood after his battle
with Modesty.

Ordering a tot of rum from the taproom
maid, he selected a pipe from the public rack,
broke off a portion of the fourteen-inch-long
clay stem for a fresh mouthpiece, and chose a
corner chair. He stretched his long legs and
smoked in reflective silence. Would he never
learn? Would he never learn to control that
wild, impulsive part of his nature? Did his reck-
lessness doom him to make disastrous choices
time after time?

He had fled his old life, had started over
anew. He was committed to living a life free of
the encumbrances of things and people. So
whatever had possessed him to deviate from
that choice which had come from the wisdom
of much experience—and marry Modesty?

The more he thought about her threat to kill
any child she would carry by him, the angrier
he became. Again and again he emptied his
glass. His pipe burnt out. His anger didn't.

He was only half observing the piquet game
and paid but little attention when young Duncan Kilbride rose from the gambling table, having lost a hogshead of tobacco. "'Tis time I
started home for dinner."

"Admit it, you are afraid the goodwife will
find that you closed shop early this afternoon
to gamble," John Rogers taunted.

"Me Polly obeys me as the master of me
household," the ruddy Scotsman blustered.

"But not master of the game," the fair-skinned man said. Mad Dog had heard him called Jarvis. Nigel Jarvis.

Ratcliff languidly plucked a bit of snuff from a lacquered box and sniffed it up one nostril. "We need a fearless player in your place, Kilbride."

Mad Dog accepted the bait and rose unsteadily. If his unrestrained nature had gotten him into this situation, then it would get him out. "Deal me a hand."

"And what is your wager?" Ratcliff asked, spreading his beringed hand to indicate the pile of pounds and notes he had amassed that afternoon.

Mad Dog tipped up his tankard, swallowed the last of the rum, and signaled the maidservant for more before replying. "My wife's marriage contract."

Around the table, the men's eyebrows raised. Kilbride, about to leave, spun around.

Nigel Jarvis cocked one black eyebrow. "Good God, old chap, you can't wager a wife!"

Mad Dog raked his gaze over the man. "Prithee, why not? I bought her contract. I can sell it if I so want."

Ratcliff shrugged. "A mere woman. They don't last long here in the colony. Surely you can do better than that."

"Then the marriage contract and this year's crop yield from my estates," Mad Dog said. "Against those of yours."

"Too high stakes for me," John Rogers mumbled, and Nigel Jarvis also bowed out.

A flicker of calculation shown in Ratcliff's eyes. "Let's make it interesting. Winner ends up with both estates. Loser gets the marriage contract."

The man must know he would win. He had to be cheating, had to have been all afternoon. "So done," Mad Dog agreed.

He summoned all his faculties, distorted though they were by his heavy drinking. He had been cursing his wife. Now he blessed her. She had at least taught him the rudiments of the sleight-of-hand. Her very chicanery would be the knife that cut her throat. Dry mirth at the symbolism carved his mouth into a smile. "I suggest we do away with the formalities of the game. Why not a simple turn of the card? High card takes the estates?"

Ratcliff's smile matched his own. "Why not? I'll shuffle, you cut. You do so well at that sort of thing."

He ignored the oblique reference to his past. "I'm saving my last cut for afterward, Ratcliff. I'll shuffle this one."

"Plan on cutting your wrists should you lose?" Ratcliff drawled.

He wasn't going to let the man goad him into unfocused anger. "King high, ace low?" He deftly riffled the deck of cards, watching for his favorite card.

Ratcliff shrugged. "Aye."

His fingers felt clumsy. Everything was at stake here. He either gained all—Ratcliff Manor and revenge—or lost all. Ant Hill, the sanctuary he had carved from the wilderness, would be Ratcliff's.

Mad Dog drew a fortifying breath. When he spotted the card, he dragged his left thumb across it and palmed it into his left hand, bringing the card to the bottom of the deck. One more time he shuffled. Feeling the sweat beading at his temples, he passed the shuffled deck to Ratcliff.

Wordlessly, Ratcliff completed the cut.

In perfect rhythm, Mad Dog spread the cards face down across the table with one smooth swoop so that they looked like a picket fence along a country road.

"Your draw," he told Ratcliff.

The man reached out a lace-ruffled wrist, his dexterous fingers slipping a card from the spread. He glanced at it, and a slow smile rifted his mouth. "Your turn."

Mad Dog realized that the ruffles worked to Ratcliff's advantage. And his own advantage? His wife's tutelage. Now if he could only pull off the illusion. His hand shaking, he drew a card.

With a self-satisfied smile, Ratcliff flipped over his card. Its jovial face was that of King Henry VIII. "That will be hard to trump."

He knew he had one chance to beat Ratcliff's king. He delayed the outcome. He lifted his refilled tankard in a toast of mockery to his opponent. "May the best man win."

Ratcliff nodded in acknowledgment.

He took a drink, then lifted his card's edge—he had managed to pull it off! He had manipulated the joker, the highest trump! No wonder the word *triumph* derived from it. The joker represented the court jester who could assume without rebuke any role he chose.

All Mad Dog had to do was lay down the card and Ratcliff Manor—and revenge—were at long last his.

And in that instant he knew. He saw it coming. Saw that he was being tricked into careless cruelty again. Only this time, it wasn't Ratcliff but he himself who was the trickster.

He shoved the winning card back into the spread with the others. "You win, Ratcliff."

Chapter Eighteen

Feeling thoroughly disgruntled, Jack strode away from the Jamestown custom house. It was Good Friday, the twenty-second of March, and everything was closed up tighter than a clam, including the partially completed Golden Parrot.

The afternoon sun was high and he was hot. Verily, he could use a draught of ale. No, what he really could use was a kick in the ass. He had to be crazy in the head coming back to this hellhole.

He steered his course for the *Maidenhead*. He got no farther than the wharves when a man's voice hailed him. "Sirrah, would your vessel be going upriver?"

He cocked a quizzical glance at the man, a coxcomb by dress. "If I am?"

"I desire to go as far as Henrico." He dug into his purse and held out a few Dutch guilders. "I would pay my fare. Allow me to introduce myself." He swept off his hat with a half bow. "I am Nigel Jarvis, late of His Majesty's prison, Marshalsea."

"Keep your coins, my friend. The ride is on me. I have had the pleasure of bed and board in one of Good King James's dungeons."

Once the seamen, well seasoned by now, unfurled the *Maidenhead*'s sails and she was underway, Jack invited Jarvis to the captain's chart room immediately below the poop deck. It was warm and very quiet except for the creaks of the rigging.

As there was no ale to be purchased ashore, he popped open one of the French wines ordered by a Bermuda City planter. With a mental shrug, he figured, so what if one bottle was broken in transportation?

He propped his jackboots on the desk cluttered with compass, astrolabe, sextant, hourglass, maps, and the scrolled deed placing a lien on Ratcliff's property. "Henrico is but a hamlet," he told the man across from him. He took a sip of the strong white wine, then asked, "What calls you there?"

"A beauteous maiden. The Lady Clarissa Lockridge. You know of her?"

"Beauteous indeed, but married, my good man."

"So I learned." With a shrug, Jarvis sipped wine from the leather noggin. "Her father is wealthy enough. An annulment can be bought. Anything can be bought."

The vessel's great rudder squeaked beneath them as the steersman veered his course again to follow the river around another bend. "I would have said so myself six months ago. However—" He broke off at the commotion coming from above deck. "By your leave," he said, setting down his noggin and rising to leave the room.

Jack took the companion ladder to the poop deck three rungs at a time and stepped out onto the deck just as the lookout in the bow blew a shrill horn. He crossed to the starboard rail. From the deck, he looked out upon a score of canoes and a nightmare of painted Indians. In one, a female stood braced, waving her hands for attention. Then he heard his name. He looked closer. By jove, the woman was Modesty. With her was the old witch of the woods, Juana.

"Drop the ladder," he told Elias.

Soon Modesty was scrambling up the swaying rope ladder. He helped her over the bulwark and said, "You look more frightful than Juana, if that is possible." The Indian woman still sat stolidly in the canoe.

Modesty was gasping, her coif had slipped off her head and was hanging by its ties around her throat, and her hands trembled as though every ounce of her energy had been expended. "Jack, there's going to be an—an attack on Jamestown!"

"Whoa." She wasn't making sense. "Those Indians in the canoes?" One of them he had thought looked like Arahathee. "Come on below out of the sunlight and have a drink to steady yourself, Modesty."

As if dazed, she allowed him to lead her to his cabin, where Jarvis was sampling another noggin of the wine. Jack introduced the two and seated Modesty in the window bay.

Her eyes closed, her body slumped, and utter weariness issued from her in a long, shaky sigh.

"Now tell me what's this all about," he said, pouring wine for her. "Didn't I see Arahathee out there?"

"Aye." She opened her eyes and accepted the noggin. "Juana and I were coming down river to warn Jamestown when—"

"A long haul to row," he said, taking a seat at his desk.

"—when we came upon Arahathee and his warriors." She took a deep swig and continued. "Listen to me, Jack! Juana . . . she learned of a planned attack. Every community . . . every house . . . every white person . . . man, woman, child . . . the Algonquin confederation plan to burn us all out. Today!"

He came to his feet. Fear, a kind of fear new to him, froze his blood. "Henrico! Have you alerted them?"

She gave a weary nod. "But I do not think me message was taken seriously."

"Juana can go on downriver to Jamestown and the surrounding plantations with the warning. We'll need Arahathee and his braves to help defend the upstream communities."

He came around his desk, heading for the door to give the orders, when she caught his full sleeve. Her strangely colored eyes were shadowed with anxiety. "Jack, Mad Dog rode out of Ant Hill yesterday. He was angry with me. I don't know where he is."

"He was at the Golden Parrot's gaming tables last night," Jarvis drawled from his corner chair.

"The gaming tables?" she repeated, just like a parrot.

Jarvis fingered his golden earring. "Aye . . . er, well, the truth be the man wagered you and Ant Hill against the chap Ratcliff's estate. Mad Dog . . . er, lost Ant Hill but got to keep you. I think he was riding back last night to collect you."

Now she jumped to her feet, splashing the wine over her dirty white apron. "Wagered me? How could he! I am his wife!"

Jarvis lifted his shoulders. "Well, he said that he had bought you, so he could sell—"

"Jarvis, you talk too much," Jack said, striding out the cabin door. Could he get to Henrico in time?

"I'll kill Mad Dog, Jack!" she screamed after him. "Do yew hear me, Jack? I'll kill the bloody varmint, then sell that lion's mane of his scalp to Opechancanough!"

* * *

Patrick was still at the church, talking with the last of his lingering parishioners while Clarissa had returned home to finishing preparing the Good Friday supper.

She frowned at the sound of gunfire as she worked in the kitchen. It would be extraordinary and profane for one of the villagers to be hunting on a holy day. Frying pan still in hand, she rose from the hearth and turned just in time to see the Indian enter. In his arm he held a flintlock musket. His dusky face was smeared with war paint. Coldly, he lifted the musket and trained its long barrel on her.

She never thought death would come for her in this manner. She had seen herself living to be one of those wealthy London doyennes, venerated by society. Odd, too, that in her imaginings she had never seen an elderly Nigel at her side.

The warrior took another step toward her, close enough for her to fling in his face the skillet's hot melted bear's fat she had intended to pour over a bowl of parched corn.

With a howl of pain, he dropped the musket. His hands flew to his scalded face. He was blinded, and the skin on his chest was already bubbling from the grease burns.

She grabbed up his musket and rushed past him out the door. Picking up her skirts in her free hand, she dashed toward the grape arbor. If she could shoulder her way through the brush and bramble without being seen, she could make her way downhill to the riverbank.

War whoops pierced the air. Indians were pouring out of the forest. They seemed more intent on plundering the houses first, which meant murdering anyone who got in their way. And she wasn't about to.

Oh, dear God, let there be a skiff, a canoe, even a barge, to take her away from this horror. She plunged into the ragged underbrush. Briers tore at her face and her sleeves and skirts.

She had gone no farther than half a dozen yards when the screams of a child reached her. She kept plowing ahead, slowed, paused, then whirled around and started back up the hill.

There in the grape arbor an Indian had a squirming, screaming Sally pinned beneath one knee. His hatchet was raised. He meant to deprive her of her auburn curls.

Clarissa raised the musket and squeezed the trigger. The musket misfired when the flint dropped out.

At that same moment, the warrior spotted her. A fiendish grin lit his copper face. Releasing Sally, he charged toward her.

She took the musket barrel between her hands and swung its iron-shod butt to bash him between his eyes. His head caved in like an eggshell. She thought she was going to retch.

In that instant, she understood and knew she

loved Patrick. She knew that nothing was as strong as real gentleness. Nothing so gentle as real strength.

Smoke and ashes billowed into the sky before the spire of Henrico's church even came into view. At least, it was still standing! Jack breathed a sigh of relief. Occasional musket fire punctuated the heavy summer air.

Elias piloted the caravel to the leeward side of the forested peninsula and moored it for boats to be sent ashore. Jack was in the foremost dinghy, Jarvis in another somewhere behind him, and Arahathee and his canoes of warriors followed.

Cutlass in hand, Jack waded through the sand-sucking river bottom and ran ashore. His worst fears were realized.

Every house had been torched. Close to a gutted storehouse lay the bloody body of a scalped man. Further on, at what had been the Company barn and was now a bonfire, corpses of both men and women, even children, were scattered. Some of them had been stripped of their clothing, others horribly mutilated. Near an overturned hogshead of pickled beef, a dog lay dead, its body pierced by an arrow. The acrid smell of gunpowder stung Jack's nostrils.

The muzzles of muskets poked from the church's sashes that had been slid open. Apparently, the survivors of the Indian raid were holed up in the church. Their attackers were concealed in the pines and brush beyond the green, but flaming paths through the sky marked their arrows' courses. The green was littered with the bodies of Indian warriors who had tried to creep closer to the defenders within the church.

Arahathee, his warriors, and a dozen of the *Maidenhead*'s corsairs fanned out at the water's edge of the embattled village. Jack sprinted across its common. His back felt broad, an easy target for an arrow or even an errant musketball.

He found cover behind a privy, miraculously untouched. A yeoman who shared the concealment with him had not been so fortunate. The man was propped against the privy's bloodsplattered planks.

When he noticed Jack, he beckoned him nearer. The man's eyes were glazed with horror, with pain. "Wouldn't happen to have a pipe on you, would you?"

"Sorry, your lordship. The best I can do is flint and tinder to light one." The man deserved at least a title of respect when dying.

A dark stain on the man's canvas tunic was slowly, steadily expanding. Powder burns around the wound indicated to Jack that the man had been shot at close range and nothing further could be done for him.

So the Powhattans were using firearms. He'd wager his last doubloon that Ratcliff had furnished the weapons. "What happened?"

"The Indians ... they came ... as friends

this . . . morning. Eating our proffered food. They . . . surprised us. Seized our own tools and weapons . . . and attacked."

Jack glanced back at the church. An indigo pall of mingled gunpowder and smoke enwreathed it. A single arrow protruded from the heavy door. Had she made it to the safety of the church? He weighed the time factor of making a dash for the church to ascertain his hope—or backtracking to her cabin to confront his dread.

The groan from the dying man beside him suggested a further possibility, that she might be there, still alive.

Jack spotted Jarvis crouched not far away behind a ox cart. "Take over here," he called. "Drive the red devils off."

Alarm glimmered in the man's eyes, and Jack assured him, "I am not turning coward, Jarvis. I'll be back."

He hoped.

He covered the mile-long path to the ironworkers' huts faster than the time he had outrun the bailiffs and monks who chased him through Whitefriars. The site of the smoking huts and the carnage made his stomach queasy.

Behind him, he heard running footsteps. He whirled around in time to spit a war-painted Indian on his cutlass. Bracing his boot on the ribs of the fallen Indian, he yanked out his cutlass's bloody blade.

Her cabin could be any one of the cluster of what had been homes and were now charred stubble of timbers. Then he saw the crumpled gangly body. Lying before a partial, still-smoldering doorframe, Walter Bannock had died defending his home and family.

Farther inside was another body. Nothing but ashes and unidentifiable. A sickening sorrow tore at Jack's lungs. Oh, God, was Rose among the rubble?

He stepped over Bannock's hacked corpse and prowled the ruins with a heavy heart and not much hope. Prying up still-smoking timbers, he burnt his hands. He found little—a pewter plate, a clay pitcher still intact, a pair of tongs, a small metal chest with brass handles.

Had she and the children been taken hostage? He doubted it. This was a full-scale massacre. So where could they be? And then he heard it— a faint bawling that could be a stray calf. Or a toddler.

He whirled, loped down the hill in the direction of the sawmill. The muted noise, more like coughing, came again, from there at the edge of the James, where a millrace channeled the water into a stream that poured over the mill wheel.

The smell of freshly sawn wood and sawdust flurried in his nostrils. He glanced around to see only boards and planks, ripsaws and sash saws, the mill wheel's water buckets. "Rose?" he called out with more hope in his voice than was in his heart.

A tow-headed tyke lifted his head from the wooden chute where water had run when the sluice gates were cranked open. Behind him, another boy's head popped up. "Mom! 'Tis all right! 'Tis that man that was at the dance in Jamestown."

Like a fairy, Rose, cradling her baby, fluttered up from the mound of sawdust in the saw pit. Or was it gold dust?

He scrambled down into the pit and grabbed her and the child tightly against him. Her clear eyes, their lashes tipped with sawdust, stared up at him, searching. For what? "Ye came back," she whispered.

"Aye. While I was gone I had time to think. I realized all my life I had been looking for something and I finally saw that I didn't have anything. Until you."

Her lower lip trembled. "There is not just only me. There are the three boys. Four of us."

Four! He rolled his eyes. Had he, Mad Dog, and everyone in this wilderness gone bloody crazy?

The wee one, little Jack, whimpered again. Jack shrugged and stared down into his madonna's lovely face. "Until you four."

Behind the church's altar, Clarissa gathered into the folds of her voluminous skirts five motherless children she had rounded up and herded inside the church. Rolfe's wife was dead. The same for the ironworkers' and the husbandmen's wives.

Two men grimly fired from the church's sliding wooden sashes that could be opened on warm summer days. Old Clem's antiquated harquebus wouldn't hit anything farther than ten yards. Rolfe had a flintlock pistol and a blunderbuss.

While the two men attempted to keep the Indians at bay, Patrick, his nightshirt only half tucked into his breeches, took turns loading the muzzles of their fowling pieces. He ramrodded round balls or buckshot, and, when required, a paper that held the explosive charge. Streaks of gunpowder painted his face like one of the Powhattan warriors.

Except they were determined to kill—and he refused to kill.

Did it have to come to this: kill or be killed? His faith in right and wrong was blending into a blurred gray line. Especially when he took time to glance back at Clarissa. Brave Clarissa, who had collected the frightened, abandoned children. She and the children were innocents. Why did they have to die?

His gaze ricocheted back to the window that faced the river. Beyond the straggling line of pines and just budding oaks, a dozen or so men off the *Maidenhead* were firing randomly at the all but invisible enemy. A dozen men against ten dozen or more Powhattans. The ship's crew were outnumbered, and the Powhattans had the patience to wait out the siege.

A well-placed arrow zinged through the window. Its fiery tip quickly set a pew cushion ablaze. He grabbed the cushion and beat out the flame.

Hardly had he finished when he looked up to see Rolfe take a shot in the arm. He crossed to him. "Here, good friend, let me see if I can bandage—"

Rolfe waved him away. "Listen, Reverend Dartmouth, the savages are going to overrun us. Clem and I'll create a diversion, while you take your wife and children and make a dash for the shoreline. If you can gain the ship—"

"A good idea, Rolfe, but I am staying here with you."

He began rolling back the man's bloodstained sleeve, but the patriarch jerked his arm away. "Don't you see, we're running out of munitions. There's nothing more you can do here. But you can help your wife shepherd the children to safety."

Rolfe made sense, yet to turn his back on the two men went against his grain.

As if to forestall further argument, Rolfe pressed his flintlock pistol into his hand. "Use it if you have to, Reverend." He nodded at Clarissa across the room. "You understand my meaning?"

Patrick swallowed hard. "God keep you and Clem in His hands, now and always."

He drew Clarissa aside and quietly explained the plan, all but the purpose of the pistol he now possessed.

Her violet eyes large, she only nodded. Then she assembled the children to her and said,

"We're going to play a game. A foot race from the side door to the ship there at the wharf. Master Rolfe and Clem are going to fire the starting shots, and then we see who can run the fastest. All right?"

Sally, her chin quivering, asked the logical question. "What about the Indians out there?"

Patrick stooped down level with her and took her small chin in his hand. "They may decide to run the race also. In that case, you must trick them. You go where they can't. Under the brush. But you always keep running. You want to get to the boat first."

That seemed to satisfy the redheaded youngster.

When Clem and Rolfe had loaded a final round, he nodded that he was ready.

The two men burst through the church's front door. They fired a volley toward the enemy-infested forest.

"Now!" Patrick said and herded his charges out through the side door.

Ahead of him, Clarissa ran with her skirt gathered in one hand and Rolfe's toddler in her arm. Her comb came loose and her yellow hair tumbled free. They got halfway across the green before the Powhattans realized the deception. Howls of rage went up, then arrows and lances zephyred around them.

Patrick risked a glance back and saw that Rolfe was on his knees, as if in prayer. He had been pierced by two arrows. Old Clem tried to get off a shot and couldn't. A hurled lance plowed into his back and emerged from his pot belly.

Three tomahawk-wielding savages darted from the forest to fall upon Clem and Rolfe. Four others, yelling bloodthirsty screams, charged on, their vicious gazes focused on their prey ahead of them.

The *Maidenhead*'s crew fired rounds of volleys at the pursuing Indians. And still they kept coming.

"Keep running!" he shouted at Clarissa and the children. Safety was only three score yards away.

Seemingly from out of nowhere, a war-painted buck lunged at Clarissa with a knife. At that same moment, Jarvis emerged from the tree line to intervene. So he had come to claim her. Patrick's heart took its own arrow of pain.

Jarvis bravely brandished his rapier at the Indian. Clarissa screamed. Jarvis's red-skinned opponent held the advantage. His knife could deal death without his ever coming within reach of the rapier.

"You cowardly bastard!" Jarvis hissed. "Fight me like a gentleman."

The Indian flashed a murderous grin. He raised his hand, knife poised, a deadly projectile.

The knife, instead of hurtling forward, thudded harmlessly to the ground in synchronization with the flintlock's ball that found its target. The startled warrior grabbed his chest.

Blood mingled with the black-powdered hole. His knees buckled. He toppled forward.

Clarissa's horrified gaze flew from the dead warrior to Patrick.

"Great shot, old chap!" Jarvis said.

Patrick ignored the remark. He threw down the evil weapon and scooped up one of the tots. Grabbing Clarissa's arm, he hurried her and the other two children on down the hill. Jarvis retreated with them, offering protection from the rear while at the tree-fringed shoreline a dozen armed crew members were providing protective cover with a barrage of grapeshot.

Once everyone had gained the shelter of the ship and the gangplank was raised, Elias felt it safe enough to order a cannon bombardment that sent the Powhattans fleeing.

Later, when Jack returned to take command, it was discovered that Modesty was gone, along with Arahathee and his braves—and the lien as well.

Relieved of his present responsibility, Patrick left Clarissa with Jarvis and sought out the ship's bowels. He felt like Jonah in the whale's belly. He couldn't escape his Creator. There in the dank dark, he had to review the enormity of his action, now more than an hour old: the taking of another's life.

Sitting on a coil of hemp amidst the ballast and cargo, he wrestled with his conscience. A brown rat served as an excellent companion, neither condemning nor offering empty words.

At last, Patrick realized what he must do.

He rose and made his way topdeck. Jarvis was alone at the railing, watching the shoreline slip by as the caravel made its way upriver to Ant Hill. "You're looking for your wife?"

"I expected to find her with you."

A curious look passed over the poet's face. "She's with the children in the first mate's quarters."

When he went to turn away, Jarvis stopped him. "Reverend Dartmouth, I owe you an apology. You saved my life."

He could only nod. He no longer had all the answers.

He found Clarissa just leaving the cabin. At the sight of him, she held her finger to her lips and quietly shut the door behind her. "The children are sleeping." She gave a wry smile. "At last."

The two of them stood alone in the dimly lit passageway. "Clarissa." As never before, he was overcome with shame. His pomposity. His judgment of her as a spoiled and selfish aristocrat. In truth, she had proven herself a noble lady.

He dropped to his knees and pressed his lips against her fingertips, then looked up into her luminous eyes. "I see now just how unfit I am for you."

Her brow knitted. "Because you have killed in the defense of others? Didn't David slay Goliath?"

"I have done that and more. Worse. I thought I deserved you . . . simply because I bought you for my wife. Jealousy, resentment, judgment—I entertained them all in my mind."

She sank to her knees, her skirts gently billowing around them like waves. She rested her hand on his chest. "But in your heart you nurtured only love. Don't you Puritans call marriage the Little Church within the Church? In marriage, every day you love, and every day you forgive. It is an ongoing sacrament—love and forgiveness."

He felt that until this moment he had been sleepwalking through life. "From the first moment I saw you, Clarissa, I wanted you. I laid eyes upon you and lusted after you."

She leaned into him and brushed her lips across his, then drew back with a soft smile curving her lips. "My dearest one, don't you know that the eyes are the scouts for the heart? Furthermore, I saw you at the marketplace long before you took note of me."

"You did?"

"Our home is a pile of ashes. We can rebuild it. But do you think you can plant that garden this time? One with primroses that border a path leading to a jack-in-the-pulpit. And mayhaps a fairy slipper too?"

He took her sweet, slender body in his arms. "About that night I took your maidenhead. . . . "

"Patrick, you great gawk, I gave it to you. As

you gave me your innocence."

He thought her eyes were far more beautiful than any violet flower. "We have some planting to do, my love."

Chapter Nineteen

Two predominant thoughts played ring-around-the-rosie in Modesty's mind while Arahathee's canoe rapidly carried him, her, and Juana upriver to Ant Hill:

I'll drive a stake through Mad Dog's heart while he sleeps!

He deserved no less. To have wagered her as if she were a pile of shillings—or a bondservant. All her life, she had been worth nothing to no one.

Until now. And then would come the second thought.

I've got the lien to Ratcliff Manor! Silver candlesticks, servants, soft beds, and sapphires! They're all me own for the having.

She bloody well deserved it all. Hadn't she

toiled like a workhorse all her life? And for what? Nothing.

Nothing, until she saw the rolled parchment with the king's seal in Jack's ship cabin—and Jack and that fellow Jarvis had left it for her to take.

For reassurance that she wasn't dreaming, her fingers constantly crept to her laced stomacher, beneath which the folded document was hidden.

When the bluff of Ant Hill at last came into view, she stared with rounded eyes, her mouth open. Nothing stood atop the bluff. Not the cabin, nor the barn, nor the outbuildings. Even the small shoots of cornstalks were missing.

In silence, Arahathee and his braves beached their canoes. Scanning the clearing, the charred peach orchard, and the encircling forest, they warily climbed the winding path to the top of the knoll. Destruction and desolation greeted them.

"Oh, my God," she whispered.

Arahathee knelt and ran exploring fingers through the smoldering debris. Only the two stone chimneys gave evidence that the fragments, burnt beyond recognition, had once been a home.

Watching, Modesty cut her fingernails into her palms. Her stomach knotted. Her lungs couldn't draw a breath. She had wanted to drive a stake through Mad Dog's heart, true. But she wanted to be the one to do it, not someone else.

She closed her eyes and silently prayed to that

God she had so long denied. All this time, she had thought she had been running from an indifferent, even a vengeful, God. It was the Church she had been running from—and had found God, instead.

She opened her eyes and asked the question she dreaded. "Is Mad Dog's . . . have you found his . . . his remains?"

Arahathee didn't answer. He rose and, with three of his braves, set off down the hill in measured paces.

She almost called out for them to wait. She didn't want to be left alone in the wilderness. Where would she go? What would she do? Without Mad Dog to bedevil, her life no longer had purpose.

Abruptly, Arahathee pivoted and returned to her. "Mad Dog has been taken captive."

She didn't realize she had been holding her breath. She expelled it in a little sob that was half relief, half fear. "By which of the Powhattan tribes?"

The Monacans' *werowance* held up the red feather. "Itopatin."

She understood. "Can you take me to his village?"

The Indian's eyes shuttered over. "*Werowances* do not treat with women."

"Itopatin will treat with me. I possess great magic that I can give him."

Skepticism mingled with disdain in his oblique eyes. His shrug was fatalistic. "Come then."

* * *

Modesty couldn't remember ever being so exhausted. Two days without sleep or food, constantly on the move, made her feel delirious. She tried to keep up with her guides, placing one foot in front of the other. Often she tripped. The Indians made no move to assist her to her feet. Even Juana seemed indefatigable.

Like a fool, a derisory court jester, Modesty kept following her guides—until the Monacan in front of her stopped stone still, as did the others of his clan.

Arahathee motioned for her to come forward to join him. "There," he said, pointing to a hilltop crowned by a few scraggly pines and houses that looked like oblong haystacks from her viewpoint.

Life seemed as if it would go on forever, she thought, then suddenly you find yourself standing on the edge of a precipice and know that it can all be over in one second. That all was for naught.

She nodded. "Let's go."

Juana folded her arms, signaling she would wait. Arahathee peeled off the beaded wampum belt that girded his loins, signaled to his braves, and set off.

The Powhattan houses were in the midst of gardens and fields. Closer up, the houses reminded her of arbors, with small young sprigs bowed and tied, and covered with tree bark. Smoke eddied from holes in the roofs' centers.

Quarrelsome and toothless old squaws and

bare-breasted women wearing beads and copper bracelets stopped in the act of weaving baskets or pounding corn to stare at the visitors. Children halted their games of tag to watch.

The men, their nostrils sporting small red feathers, deserted their fishing nets and their wrestling matches. They looked barbarous with their heads and shoulders painted red with the *pocone* root and some kind of animal oil.

Arahathee displayed to one of the Powhattan warriors his wampum belt that guaranteed safe conduct, and they were promptly led to a lodge larger than the others. An animal-skin flap was pulled back, and Modesty entered. Her eyes had to adjust to the darkness before she saw the fierce Indian sitting on a woven mat placed over a dais of logs.

Arahathee motioned for her to sit. Like the other three Indians, she sank to the ground, cross-legged. Arahathee began speaking. All this time, Itopatin never deigned to glance at her. But she watched him. About his thick neck, suspended by a leather cord, was a dried human hand.

A priest of some kind sat in the background, shaking a rattle, as if to ward off the evil spirits brought inside the lodge by the Powhattans' lifelong enemy, the white person.

At last, Arahathee finished his discourse. The old priest continued with his infernal music.

Then Itopatin spoke.

The smoke stung her eyes, but she sat immobile, waiting, listening to the strange, guttural words. Wasn't anyone but her hot? The lodge was like a sweathouse. She felt feverish. She tried to keep her mind from drifting.

When Itopatin stopped speaking, Arahathee turned to her and translated as best he could into English. "Itopatin has said he first wants to see this magic you would give him. Only then will he consider trading Mad Dog for the magic."

So he *was* here! "No. I first want to see Mad Dog. If he is alive, then I will consider trading my magic." She hoped the pulse pounding at her throat did not betray her fear.

Arahathee relayed her message, and when he finished, Itopatin motioned to one of the warriors, who left the lodge at once. Then the *werowance* turned his ferret eyes on her. The scorn was gone from his ferocious visage. The cunning in his gaze dueled with that in hers. She refused to lower her eyes.

The parting of the entrance flap released her from the battle of wills. Mad Dog was shoved forward. He stumbled, fell to his knees just short of the fire pit. His hands were lashed together behind his bare back. Crimson stripes welted it. The fire's red glow highlighted the knot at his temple and a swollen bottom lip crusted with dried blood.

He eyed Itopatin across the fire pit, then spat into it with contempt. The embers sizzled.

A muscle in Itopatin's rigid jaw flicked, but he snapped something to Mad Dog.

At once, her husband swiveled in the direction of Arahathee and herself. "You turn up in the strangest places, wench." His voice was a croak.

"I told yew I am a fairy."

Itopatin spoke up, and Arahathee said, "The chief wants to see your magic now."

She turned away from Mad Dog and said. "Tell Itopatin I will need a pot of their war paint—the *pocone* root and the oil they mix with it."

When the items were fetched, she fished the folded parchments from between her breasts.

Mad Dog eyed her with curiosity mingled with suspicion. "What in the bloody hell is that?"

One of Itopatin's braves backhanded him across the face for talking, and he reeled before he regained his balance.

Modesty smiled glumly at her husband. "The lien to Ratcliff's property. Jack returned with it this morning."

"Oh, my God," he groaned.

She spread out one of the parchments, printed side down, and anchored the curling ends of the clean side with four of the outer stones from the fire pit. When she plucked a feather from the oily braid of the nearest warrior, he rounded on her with his knife unsheathed. She stifled a scream.

Itopatin made a sign for the warrior to fall back.

She forced herself to relax, to steady her shaking hand. She dipped the feather's quill into the pot of paint and began to draw. Fairies. Trolls. Elves. Leprechauns. Even the likeness of Powhattan himself. All in crimson. Her hand flew over the parchment. She had to work quickly—she didn't want to stay in the village any longer than was necessary.

Itopatin watched intently. Everyone in the lodge did.

Finished with her drawings, she took the second parchment and laid its clean side face down on the just-painted parchment. Selecting a smaller stone from the pit, she began rubbing all over the top parchment.

The wet-ink racket was one she had observed at London Bridge, one of the principal literary streets of the city where several well-known publishing houses were. There, too, most pamphlets and gazettes were produced.

A successful demonstration of the swindle depended upon the inked drawing still being wet. The trickster usually selected a child for his mark. A clean sheet of paper was placed over a newspaper drawing, rubbed all over with the magic pebble, and when peeled off an exact reproduction of the drawing in the newspaper appeared.

The child seldom noticed that the drawing was in reverse. The magic pebble was then sold to the child for a price that depended upon what the greedy swindler felt the child could part with.

Modesty was hoping that Itopatin was both childlike enough not to notice the reversed drawings and that he was willing to part with her greedy price—Mad Dog.

With painful regret, she watched as the stone defaced the lien's printed text. Gone was her hope of silver candlesticks, servants, a life of comfort.

Her heart pounding, she peeled off the top parchment. She fought back the giddy laughter that bubbled inside her. Her trick had worked. Itopatin's ruthless effigy stared out of the parchment at its living image.

Words of amazement were muttered around the fire pit.

Mad Dog rolled his eyes. At the moment Modesty wanted nothing more than to box his ears.

Itopatin grunted, then asked a question, which Arahathee translated. "The *werowance* wants to know what can keep him from robbing you of your magic stone?"

She shrugged. "I give it the power. I can take it away. Tell him I want my man. I am leaving." She stood up to reinforce her statement, holding out the worthless stone. She could only hope her bravado was convincing.

Itopatin listened to Arahathee's explanation, stared at the drawings on the parchment, then at the stone. Finally he grunted his acquiescence.

Without looking back, she strode from the lodge. Surely Mad Dog and Arahathee and his warriors would have enough sense to follow her out. The sunlight blinded her. She risked a glance back. Yes, Mad Dog and the others were emerging from the lodge. Arahathee paused long enough to slice through the hemp cord that bound Mad Dog's wrists.

She didn't pause at all. She kept walking on down the hill, her legs as wobbly as a newborn's. Only when she and the men were deep within the surrounding forest within sight of Juana did she stop and round on her startled husband. "Yew foul-hearted swine! Yew scurvy, blood-sucking—"

And then like some lily-livered maiden, she fainted.

A ghostly image swirled in and out of Modesty's vision. A dark angel? She felt as if she were floating. Had she died?

She last remembered sinking into oblivion, Mad Dog's leonine head above her, his arms catching her. When the image coalesced into a solid form, her dark angel was her savage, her husband. "Where am I?"

"Sssh," Mad Dog murmured, with a tenderness she had never heard in his voice. "You're aboard the *Maidenhead*."

She grabbed his big hand with sudden anxiety. "The Indian massacre? The Reverend Dartmouth? Rose and the children? Walter? Jack? Clarissa?"

"They're all aboard and safe. Except for Walter. And many more, including Ratcliff. He burnt along with his estates. Apparently his business dealings with Opechancanough and Itopatin hadn't guaranteed protection of his personal life and assets."

She closed her eyes. "The others—they didn't stand a chance. It was so unexpected."

"I might have been one of them, but for you. You see, my first wife had been weak, whining, a clinging vine. She took the easy way out and committed suicide. I judged all women by her. Your indomitable spirit and your noble determination all this time at Ant Hill proved to me how badly I had erred."

She turned her face to the wall. "Where was yewr nobility when yew wagered me at the gaming tables and lost to Ratcliff?"

"I admit I was wrong to do so. I never claimed to be a saint. But I didn't lose at the gaming tables."

Her head swiveled back to him. "Nigel Jarvis was there. He said yew lost!"

"Jarvis heard me *say* I had lost. You see, I used what you taught me at cheating at cards. I managed to crimp the joker. When I realized that in winning Ratcliff Manor, I was losing you . . . I couldn't do it. I couldn't give up my fai— well, you know the word I am talking about. I don't want you to go disappearing on me by my saying that word. But you are one of those wee people who is as impulsive and reckless and unpredictable as her mortal husband. A fai—fey-like wife whom I have come to love."

She put her hand to her head. "'Tis the fever! It must be boiling me brain. By me faith, I'd swear I heard yew profess love!"

He smiled down at her with a tenderness that

choked her. "With bed rest you'll be all right. The last few days—the horror of the Indian massacre—they have taken their toll on your strength."

She knew her grin was cocky. "It ain't them that's done in me strength. 'Tis the wee one I carry. If he turns out as big as yew, 'twill be months afore I am able to leave me bed."

His eyes sparkled with a heat as pulsating as the southern stars on a summer night. He leaned over her, taking her face between his big hands. "If I have anything to say about it, you and I will spend very little time out of bed."

She had never felt such bliss. To be loved. She, a common alehouse maid and felon at that. "Oh, Inigo!"

"Mad Dog to you, you wench."

"Me name's Modesty, yew lout."

BIBLIOGRAPHY

Andrews, Charles M. *Our Earliest Colonial Settlements*. New York: New York University, 1933.

Bagust, Harold. *London Through the Ages*. Cheltenham, England: Thornhill Press, 1982.

Barbour, Philip L. *The Complete Works of Captain John Smith*. Chapel Hill: The University of North Carolina Press.

Breen, T.H. *Puritans and Adventurers*. New York: Oxford University Press, 1980.

Bridenbaugh, Carl. *Early Americans*. New York: Oxford University Press, 1981.

Bridenbaugh, Carl. *Jamestown, 1544-1699*. New York: Oxford University Press, 1980.

Callahan, Kevin. *Early American Furniture*. New York: Drake Publishers, Inc., 1975.

Colonial Williamsburg, Official Guidebook & Map. Williamsburg, VA: The Colonial Williamsburg Foundation, 1951.

Cucari, Attilio. *Sailing Ships*. New York: Rand McNally & Co., 1976.

Fulves, Karl. *More Self-Working Card Tricks*. Toronto: Dover Press, 1984.

David Freeman. *Everyday Life in Early America*. New York: Harper & Row, 1988.

Hayward, Charles. *English Period Furniture*. New York: Van Nostrand Reinhold Company, 1959.

Heaton, Vernon. *The Mayflower*. New York: Mayflower Books, 1980.

Hume, Ivor Noel. "New Clues to an Old Mystery." *National Geographic*. January, 1982. pp. 53-77.

Manarin, Louis H. *The History of Henrico County.* Virginia: The University Press of Virginia, 1984.

Morgan, Edmund S. *American Slavery-American Freedom, the Ordeal of Colonial Virginia.* New York: W.W. Norton & Co., Inc., 1975.

Patterson, James A.B., "My Father's Garden." *The Old Farmer's 1993 Almanac.* Dublin, NH: Yankee Publishing, Inc., 1992, pp. 222-225.

Riley, Edward Miles. *The Journal of John Harrower, an Indentured Servant in the Colony of Virginia.* Williamsburg, VA: Colonial Williamsburg, Inc., 1963.

Savelle, Max. *The Foundations of American Civilization— A History of Colonial America.* Westport, CT: Greenwood Press, Publishers, 1942.

Sichel, Marion. *The Costume Reference, Vol. II: Tudor and Elizabethan.* London: B.T. Batsford, 1977.

Smith, Jane Ockershausen. *One Day Trips Through History.* McLean, Virginia: EPM Publications, Inc., 1982.

Tunis, Edwin. *Colonial Living.* New York: Thomas Y. Crowell Company, 1957.

Warner, Pauline Pearce. *The County of Henrico, Virginia.* Virginia: County of Henrico, 1959.

Wertenbarker, Thomas Jefferson. *The Golden Age of Colonial Culture.* New York: New York University, 1949.

Williamsburg, Official Guidebook & Map. Williamsburg, VA: The Colonial Williamsburg Foundation, 1951.

Wise, Felicity. *A Williamsburg Hornbook.* Harrisburg: Stackpole Books, 1973.

SPECIAL SNEAK PREVIEW!

FANCY
Norah Hess

Young Fancy Cranson will do almost anything to keep her small family together. But the beautiful orphan will not sell her body to Chance Dawson or any other logger. Handsome, virile, and arrogant, Chance wants to claim Fancy for himself from the moment he lays eyes on her. The only obstacles standing in his way are her constant refusals to have anything to do with him. Yet amid the pristine forests of the Pacific Northwest, Fancy and Chance will discover a love that unites them in passionate splendor.

Don't miss *Fancy!*
Available now at
bookstores and newsstands everywhere!

Fancy

NORAH HESS

Chapter One

The tinny, raucous sound of the scarred and slightly out-of-tune piano ended with the last chords of "Camptown Races." For the next 15 minutes the dance hall girls could rest their tired and aching feet and have a respite from the heavy logger boots that had been tramping on their toes for the past 45 minutes.

Nineteen-year-old Fancy Cranson limped across the sagging wooden dance floor, her short red dress swishing around her knees as she made for the roughly constructed benches lined against one wall. She sat down and leaned her head against the rough, unpainted wall of Big Myrt's dance hall with a sigh of relief. Taking a small lace handkerchief from the low vee of her bodice, she dabbed at her damp forehead where short, pale blonde hair stuck to the smooth skin.

After a moment she leaned forward and kicked off her slippers, and after nudging them under the bench, safe from careless feet that might kick them across the floor, she began massaging her right foot through its black mesh stocking. Her arches ached from the height of her high-heeled slippers and her toes felt as if they were ready to drop off her feet from being tromped on by the heavy boots that laced to a man's knees that were worn by all the rowdy lumberjacks. She didn't know which hurt the most, her feet or her waist, where rough, callused hands had gripped tightly as she was hopped and swung around in a wild dance.

But there wasn't much Fancy could do about it. Any man who approached her with a ticket in his hand had bought the privilege of dancing with her for ten minutes, whether she wanted him for a partner or not. If she refused a dance, Big Myrt would show her the door.

And she needed this job, for a while at least. So she tolerated the drunks, the rough, bearded loggers who tried to look down the front of her dress, held her too tight, and made crude propositions to her.

Five weeks ago, when her father had been killed in a logjam, she had been devastated. To add to her overwhelming grief, when she counted the money they had kept in a cracked cookie jar she could have cried all over again had she had any tears left. The legacy left to her by big Buck Cranson was 21 dollars and 62 cents. That was not counting two horses, four rooms of furniture that had seen better days, and the care of her cousin Lenny, 21 years old.

All their logger friends had rallied around her, lending their support in whatever way they could, but Fancy knew she couldn't sponge off them the rest of her life. She had offers of marriage but turned them all down. Most of the men were as old as her father, and the others felt like family, she had known them so long. She couldn't feel romantic about them.

Her only hope was to somehow get together enough money for the fare to get Lenny and herself to San Francisco. Fancy's sister Mary lived there, along with her husband and young son. In Mary's letters, which arrived every month or so, she always urged Fancy to join her, writing that jobs were plentiful, and she would have no problem finding work in a restaurant or hiring on as a maid in a fancy house on Nob Hill. But city life didn't appeal to Fancy, and she hadn't given the idea any thought until now.

Fancy still wasn't enthusiastic about going to San Francisco, but it would be wonderful to see Mary after all these years. She knew life hadn't been easy for her sister; though she was loved dearly by her husband, Jason Landers was a drifter, moving from job to job. Fancy could always tell when things were tight with them: Young Tod would be put on a steamer and sent upriver to spend some time with Grandpa Buck and Aunt Fancy. After two or three months Mary would write that they should send her son home. She and her father would know then that the couple had managed to get back on their feet again.

It had been nice though, having Tod with them. Through the long visits they had gotten to know the little fellow, and they missed him greatly when he was gone. The last time he had been sent to them, around six months ago, he was a sturdy little fellow with a genial nature.

One thing had bothered Fancy a great deal: Why hadn't Mary come to their father's funeral? She had gotten a letter off to her sister immediately after the accident that should have arrived the same day. Mary would have had plenty of time to see her father one last time.

The only answer Fancy could come up with was that Jason had moved on to a different job, and the letter hadn't reached Mary. So what was Fancy to do now? she asked herself. She might not hear from her sister for months.

The answer came one day when she accidentally overheard a conversation between two loggers. "You ain't worth spit today, Sam," one of the men had complained. "I bet you was over at the Dawson camp dancin' last night."

"Yes, dammit, and I'm plumb tuckered out today."

"Used up a week's pay, didn't you?" the man said in disgust.

"Just about," Sam said with a sigh. "It don't

338

take long to do it. A man has to pay pretty good to dance with them girls."

"Yeah, and they probably make more money in a week than you do bustin' your ass gettin' the timber cut and hauled to the sawmill."

"They make the money all right," Sam agreed, "but it sure is nice dancin' with them."

The next day Fancy had packed and made arrangements to have her belongings hauled to the Dawson camp. Two days later she had moved into a small house and become one of Big Myrt's girls. She had been dancing for two weeks now.

Fancy came out of her preoccupation at the sound of shrill laughter. She wasn't surprised to see black-haired Pilar come strutting from her room, followed by a thick-set, red-bearded lumberjack. As the Mexican dancer shoved several bills down the front of her dress, Fancy couldn't blame the men who thought that for a price she would take them to one of the rooms leading off the big hall and entertain them during the 15-minute break.

The old adage about birds of a feather ran through Fancy's mind. The men had naturally thought she was like the other dancers, who made most of their money that way; it was the main reason they were there. Pilar liked bedding the men and took one to her room at every break.

On the dance floor Pilar was vivacious, ever smiling. But the women who worked with her knew it was all a facade. Beneath those sparkling black eyes and that wide smile was a spiteful and vengeful woman to be on guard against. None of the dancers liked her; most hated and feared her.

Fancy disliked the Mexican woman intensely. They had clashed over a man recently—Chance Dawson, the owner of the lumber camp. Fancy scanned the milling lumbermen who waited impatiently for Luther, the piano player, to start pounding the keys again. She didn't see the broad-shouldered, whip-lean body of the man who was the reason Pilar had come after her with a knife. If someone had told her that disappointment flared in her eyes, she would have told them angrily that it was all in their imagination.

Of course he could still come, Fancy reminded herself. It was still early, early for the dancers, at least. They didn't start working until midnight, and the clock on the wall said it was only a few minutes to two. He might be playing poker with some of the married men in camp now and perhaps he would come around later.

As Fancy massaged her other foot she recalled the first time she had seen Chance Dawson. She had been dancing here for exactly a week when the handsome, brown-eyed man had approached her with a strip of tickets in his hand and a devilish twinkle in his eyes. She felt her heart slam against her ribs when he handed her the tickets and swept her onto the dance floor. Never before had a man made such an impact on her. Living in a lumber camp ever since she could remember, Fancy had known scores of men, but none had ever stirred her interest.

When he asked, "Where did you come from, angel face?" as he smoothly swung her around the dance floor, his hand light on her waist, she couldn't make her tongue move to answer him immediately. Finally she was able to answer him breathlessly.

"I come from Tumwater, about ten miles down the river."

He had looked down at her with a quizzical smile. "What made you leave the camp and come here? Don't they pay the men good wages there?"

Fancy wasn't sure she heard mockery in his voice so she answered, "I'm sure they get the same wages as the men here do."

"Then you must have fallen in love with one of the lumberjacks and he went away and left you, so you decided to move on. Am I right?" The slim fingers tightened slightly on her waist.

"You're partially right." Fancy's lips curved in a wan little smile, remembering how she had adored her big lumberjack father.

"So, you're grieving a lost love." The tone said that was no big deal, that love was of no great importance. He stroked a finger down her cheek, then lifted her chin. Smiling wickedly, he said softly, "I can make you forget that man ever existed."

Fancy shook her head, a sadness coming over her face. "There's not a man alive who will ever make me forget him. He will always be in my heart."

Fancy felt the logger's displeasure at her words by the way he jerked her up against his hard body and said curtly, "We'll see."

They danced in silence then, but she was still held tighter than she allowed any of the other men to do. It felt good to be held against a hard chest. That was another thing she missed since losing her father: the way he held her close when she was hurting about something, like the time Mary had moved to California.

It was almost time for a rest period when he whispered huskily in her hair, "Do you want to show me your room, cuddle a bit?"

Fancy caught her breath and looked up at him, hurt and surprise in her eyes. He thought she was like most of the other dancers, that her main reason to be here was to make contact with men who would pay to go to bed with them. "I don't have a room here," she answered coldly. "I don't live on the premises. I have my own little house."

"Hey, that's better yet," he said smoothly. When the piano music stopped on a discordant note he ordered softly, "Get your wrap and let's get out of here."

"I can't leave here until the place closes at five o'clock," Fancy answered stiffly, pulling away from him. "Big Myrt would fire me."

"Let her fire you." The grip he had kept on her arm tightened. "I'll take care of you. All you'll have to do is be waiting for me with open arms

342

when I come in from the woods at the end of a hard-working day."

Anger gave Fancy the strength to jerk away from the possessive fingers. Glaring up into his warm brown eyes, she snapped, "I can take care of myself. I'll not be beholden to any man."

"The hell you say." The voice was harsh now. "You're beholden to every man you take home with you. You're depending on the money he'll put on your pillow before he leaves."

For a moment outrage nearly blinded Fancy. Then, hardly aware of her action, she felt the palm of her hand rocking with force as it connected with a lean cheek. As he stared at her, dumbfounded, she wheeled around and walked away.

The burly loggers stared after Fancy, hard put not to roar with laughter. They were wise enough, however, to bite their tongues and pretend not to have seen their boss get walloped by the new dancer that every man jack of them lusted after.

Chance Dawson—the owner of the lumber camp, Fancy later learned—started toward the door, his eyes black with anger and finger marks rising on his cheek, and was stopped by Pilar, her hand on his arm. "Didn't you offer her enough money, Chance?" she taunted him, loud enough for everyone to hear. "She's not called Fancy for nothin'. She comes high."

Chance shook her grip off his arm and made no reply to the catty remark as he strode out of the dance hall and into the night. It was then,

without warning, that Pilar had snatched a sti-
letto from beneath her garter and lunged at
Fancy, screaming that she had better keep away
from her man.

The raging dancer had been in for a surprise.
For all her delicate looks and her slender body,
Fancy was strong and just as swift as the
woman bent on stabbing her. Relying on tricks
learned from her dead father, Fancy grabbed
Pilar's wrist, jerked it behind her back, and
brought her arm up until the knife fell to the
floor. Then she brought the screeching dancer
to the floor, where she gave her a sound beating,
blackening Pilar's eyes and cutting her lips.

When the loggers, who had watched delight-
edly, thought Pilar had had enough they
dragged Fancy off her. The Mexican had given
Fancy a wide berth ever since. Nevertheless,
Fancy had been cautioned by the other dancers
to keep an eye on the dancer, and to be very
careful when she was alone; Pilar was sure to
seek revenge one way or the other.

Luther, rail thin and somewhere in his fifties,
came and sat down beside Fancy. Flexing his
long fingers, he said, "I'm afraid I'm getting
rheumatism, Fancy." Leaning his head back
against the wall, he added, "I can't pound the
keys like I used to."

Fancy liked the sad-eyed man very much and
suggested sympathetically, "Your fingers probably only need a rest. Can't you afford to take
some time away from the piano?"

Luther gave a short bark of laughter. "On

what Myrt pays me? I can't afford to take one day off, never mind a couple of weeks or so. Besides, she would soon replace me with some other piano pounder."

"Are you sure about that? I've seen a softness in her eyes when she looks at you."

"Girl, you've got to be blinder than a bat if you can see any kind of softness in that woman. Did you ever hear the way she talks to me? Just like I was some kind of useless old dog that got in her way."

Fancy grinned and asked, "You mean like the way she sees to it that you get a big, hearty meal every night while none of us dancers get so much as a cup of coffee? It doesn't look like table scraps that you wolf down."

"That's because she knows she's paying me starvation wages," Luther muttered, a flush coming over his pale face. "She probably figures it's to her benefit that I have a decent meal every day, that I can move my fingers with more energy."

"But maybe she's feeding you for a different reason," Fancy pointed out with a teasing grin. "Maybe she thinks that a good hot supper every night will keep you here where she can keep an eye on you."

Luther shook his head, amusement in his eyes. "You're quite a romantic, aren't you, Fancy?"

"No, I'm not; I just know what I see."

"Hah!" Luther snorted. "You can't see that Chance Dawson can't keep his eyes off you even when he's dancing with another woman."

"You're out of your head! He hasn't been near me since I slapped his face."

"That doesn't mean he wouldn't like to. It was his male pride you hurt, not the face you slapped."

When Fancy made no response Luther remarked, "None of those yahoos in here interest you romantically, do they?"

Fancy shook her head. "I'm afraid not. Anyhow, I'm not here to find a man to become interested in. I took this job to earn enough money to get me to California, where my sister lives. As soon as I've done that I'll be leaving."

"I'll be sad to see you go," Luther said sincerely. "You're the first lady I've been around in a long time. You don't see many of them in saloons and dance halls. You bring back memories of my youth."

"Thank you, Luther." Fancy patted Luther's hand, lying in his lap. "You're the only gentleman I've met since coming to this camp."

The loud clanging of a cowbell interrupted their conversation, signaling that the break was over. Luther gave Fancy a crooked smile, then stood up and made his way toward the piano. Fancy pushed her feet back into her slippers as a bearded logger rushed up and pressed a ticket into her hand. With a resigned sigh she allowed herself to be led in among the others, who were stomping and hopping to the tune pounded out by Luther.

She lost control of the many partners who

shoved and pulled her around the uneven floor, but the small leather pouch strapped around her waist bulged with tickets. When she turned them over to Big Myrt at closing time she would receive a good amount of money in exchange, to be added to the old cracked cookie jar hidden in her small house.

Hours later, as Fancy was whirled around the room by a man whose face she hadn't bothered to look at, she glanced out a grimy window. A sigh of relief feathered through her lips: The eastern sky was turning pink. The cowbell would be rung any minute now, announcing to the loggers that the dancers would be leaving.

She thought of Cousin Lenny, who would be waiting outside to walk her home. He would have their little house nice and warm, and there would be water heated for her in which to soak her aching feet.

Fancy's lips curved in a gentle smile as she thought of the child trapped in a man's body. When Lenny was eight years old he had become ill with a bad case of measles that almost snuffed out his young life. And though he had recovered, his mental growth had been retarded, and his genitals were also affected. Fancy thought the latter was a blessing: If he was always to be a child, it was good he would never desire a woman.

Now, at 21, he was big and strong, and yet very gentle. To look at his handsome face from a distance, one would never know of his handicap. Although his speech was fluent, he never spoke of things that would interest an adult. He was more apt to ask someone if he would like to play with him.

Lenny adored Fancy and would fight for her to the death. He was very affectionate, and some of the hugs he gave her when he was caught up in excitement almost broke her ribs.

Fancy remembered with sadness the day Lenny had come to live with her and Big Buck. He was sixteen, but his eight-year-old mind was filled with grief and bewilderment. His mother had run off and left her husband and son when Lenny was four years old, and now the father who had raised him had been crushed to death by a Douglas fir that hadn't fallen in the direction it was supposed to.

Fancy left off her unhappy reflections when, at last, Big Myrt rang the bell the dancer had been waiting to hear. Freeing herself from her partner, she got in line with the other girls to hand in her tickets.

Big-boned Myrt, with her painted face and red-dyed hair, was rough-spoken and rough-acting, but she was scrupulously honest with her dancers. She never tried to cheat them and didn't allow the loggers to paw them if the women were averse to it. She kept it strictly business between herself and the dancers, but she did have her likes and dislikes. She had liked and admired Fancy from the beginning. The young woman minded her own business, was a hard worker, and was dedicated to her simple-minded cousin.

Myrt disliked Pilar intensely. That one was a vicious troublemaker, man hungry and lazy. She intended to get rid of her before winter set in.

Fancy stood in the doorway for a moment before stepping outside, sniffing the odor of sawdust and pine bark drifting up from the mill yard, down by the river. She was reminded of her father and her eyes grew moist. She determinedly pushed the memory away and stepped outside. She looked toward the corner of the roughly built building, and as she had known he would be, she saw the shadowy figure of Lenny waiting for her. Fancy waved to him, and he came forward like a friendly puppy, asking her if her feet hurt as he put an arm across her shoulders.

"They're killing me, Lenny." She said what he wanted to hear. "Do you have warm water waiting for me to soak them in?"

"Oh, sure I do, Fancy," the big man assured her as they turned down the path that led to the small house tucked in among a stand of tall Douglas fir. "And I put salt in the water just like Uncle Buck used to put in his footbath. Remember how he'd always say that it drew the tiredness out of his feet? I sure miss him, Fancy."

Leaning on Lenny's strength as she limped along, Fancy said with a catch in her voice, "I know you do, honey. So do I."

"Don't cry, Fancy," Lenny coaxed anxiously, hating to see her cry. As though to console her, he added, "I've got a pot of coffee brewed and eggs and bacon laid out ready to fry as soon as we get home."

"You're a good fellow, Lenny Cranson." Fancy smiled up at him.

Lenny's pleased laughter rang out as he and Fancy entered the house and closed the door behind them.

Chance Dawson, on his way to the mill, had paused among the towering pines in the hope of catching a glimpse of Fancy as she left the dance hall. He despised himself for lurking around like a green boy wanting to approach a girl yet not doing it for fear of rejection.

Never before had he been so drawn to a woman, and he had known many in his 30 years. And he wasn't the only man in camp who practically drooled every time he saw her. Half his crew went around like lovesick puppies. Every time he saw one of his men dancing with her he wanted to smash the man in the face. He knew the thrill they were experiencing. He had known it, too, that one time he had danced with her. Her body had been so soft and supple, molding perfectly with his. She had smelled fresh and clean, with just a trace of rose scent in her hair; not like the heavy, cloying odor of cheap perfume the others wore, trying to cover up the odor of an unwashed body.

Chance realized now that he shouldn't have rushed the new dancer; had he given her time to get to know him she might be in his house—his bed—right now. But his rashness had been brought on by the unacceptable thought that one of the other men might find favor with her first.

Finally his long wait was rewarded. Fancy stood in the doorway. She stood there for a moment, and in that instant he made up his mind to approach her, to apologize for acting like an ass the first time they met, to ask her if they could start all over. When Fancy stepped outside he moved forward; then he came to an abrupt halt, a dark scowl coming over his face. A man had emerged from the shadows and was walking hurriedly toward her. The distance was too great for him to hear what was said between them when they came together, but he could clearly see the arm that came around Fancy's shoulders.

"So," he swore under his breath, "she doesn't want to be indebted to a man, does she? It sure as hell looks like she's depending on that one." And who was this man? Chance asked himself as the pair moved away, the man's arm still around Fancy's shoulders. Where did he work? He wasn't one of Chance's crew, and the next camp was nearly 20 miles away, down near Puget Sound.

A thought occurred to Chance that made him swear again. Maybe the man didn't work anywhere. Maybe slender, delicate Fancy supported him. There were women who loved their men so much they'd do that for them.

Chance's hands clenched into fists as he watched the pair move off through the pine,

Fancy leaning into the man, and him looking down at her, smiling and talking. When he threw back his head and laughed at something Fancy said before they entered her house and closed the door Chance wheeled around and strode away. He was torn between wanting to put his hands around Fancy's lovely throat and planting his fist in the handsome man's mouth.

An hour after returning home Fancy lay in bed, her stomach pleasantly filled and her feet aching a little less. She listened to the distant sound of a saw biting its way through a huge pine log. It was a sound she loved, a sound she had grown up with.

Did Mary miss all the racket that went on around a lumber camp? She wondered again why Mary hadn't attended their father's funeral.

Fancy's lids grew heavy and soon she was drifting off to sleep, lulled by Lenny softly singing "My Old Kentucky Home" as he cleaned up the kitchen.

Chapter Two

The morning was crisp and clear, and a sharp wind blew through his jacket as Chance looked down on a logjam in the river. Breaking up logjams was a dangerous business. He had lost his father to such an operation in '53.

He had buried the loved and respected man next to his second wife, who had passed away two years before from pneumonia; then, after staying on alone in Placer County for a year, Chance had moved on.

It had been such a day when he stocked a canoe with enough provisions for a few weeks and headed upriver, looking for a likely timber camp. After a week he had found this spot and sent for his ax men. Timber men, like cattlemen in the early 1800s, paid little attention to who might own the land on which the great trees grew. To those hardy men's way of thinking, whoever got to a place first owned it—or, at least, the timber. They weren't interested in the land.

Winter wasn't far off when Chance's four men arrived, and the first task he gave them was to build a shelter for the crew that would come later: teamsters, choppers, scalers, sawyers, and swampers. It took a week to put up the long building, and though there was nothing attractive about it, it was well built, with tight caulking between the logs and a roof that wouldn't leak.

In the center of the room the men had built a large fireplace that gave off heat in three directions, and above it they had cut a hole in the roof so the smoke could escape. Berths were built along two walls, and at the end of the long room they had knocked together three rough tables and benches to go with them. Later a grindstone would be placed in a corner. It would get a good workout once the choppers, with their double-bitted axes, began to fell the huge Douglas fir. Across from the emery wheel a water barrel and a bucket would be installed in which the men would wash up in the cold weather.

The day the loggers' quarters were finished the schooner that piled the river connecting the communities around Puget Sound delivered a load of heavy equipment, and a sawmill was set up. Arriving with the gigantic saw were teams of mules and oxen and Chance's stallion. And

354

some thoughtful person had added a cow to the lot. Many of his crew were married, most of them having children. The mothers would be thankful for the daily milk that would be provided for their children.

The axes were put to felling more trees, which were dragged by oxen to the sawmill. There the logs were sawed into lumber, one tree yielding enough boards to build a four-room house.

The cookhouse went up first, a building almost as large as the crew's quarters, for there had to be room for the cook's bedroom, not to mention a space for the big cookstove that would arrive with the cook, plus a worktable and shelves to hold plates, cups, and platters. All his cooking utensils would be hung on the wall next to the stove.

Chance's house went up next. It would be larger than the others that would be springing up among the tall pine for the married men. His place had to have office space where the men could come to express grievances—of which there were always many—settle arguments among themselves, and where they would receive their wages at the end of each month.

Before the men started on the small houses where the men with families would live, another large building was erected. This would be a dance hall, the domain of Big Myrt, a longtime friend of Chance's, and her dancers. This structure would contain Myrt's quarters and a series of small rooms for her girls, who would be arriving shortly after the crew did. The rest of the place would be the dance hall where, for a price, the loggers could be with the young women.

Now, a year later, as Chance let his gaze sweep over his camp, noting the smoke rising from the chimney of each building, he thought of his own cold quarters, where he hadn't bothered to light a fire to ward off the chill. He was seldom in it; mostly only to sleep. With the exception of old Zeb, his cook, and Big Myrt, he had no close friends. He got on well enough with his men during working hours, but other than that he seldom socialized with them. The emptiness of his life hit him. All he did was eat, sleep, and work.

But that wasn't the case with his men: They seemed to live full lives. This was a close-knit camp. Interposed with their hard work they found time to visit each other in the evenings, have gatherings on Sundays when the sawmill was shut down, picnics in the summer and small parties in the winter, when the winds blew out of the north and snow lay a foot deep on the ground.

Although he was never invited to any of their doings, Chance was proud of his men and their families. The wives were decent women, and most were hard-working. Some had found ways of earning money, an extra income for the family. Some washed the bachelors' clothes, Chance being one of the men to avail himself of the aid, while another wife who was handy with needle and thread mended the loggers' shirts and trousers, which were always being torn by brush or branches of fallen timber.

There was even a new bride among them who had been a schoolteacher before marrying a scaler. When the men went off to work each morning, leaving their quarters empty, she held classes for the eight school-age children. Her students would be coming along any minute now; the little girls with faces bright and eager would be hurrying, while the boys would be dragging their feet, their faces scowling.

Chance broke off his amused smile to give a wide yawn. He had stayed up late last night, playing cribbage with three loggers who were short of money until payday and couldn't afford the price of dancing with Myrt's girls. Those men who could buy tickets had napped from after supper until midnight, when the hall opened. They would have had sufficient rest then to put in a hard day's labor when the place closed at dawn. It was his habit, also, when he knew he was going to dance a few times with the girls, to take one of them to her room during a rest period.

But he hadn't gone there often lately. He knew with certainty that he should stay away from the place. He doubted if he could stay away from Fancy Cranson even if it meant taking a chance of getting his face slapped again. She entered his mind a dozen times a day, and his nights were filled with dreams of her, dreams that were so erotic, he would awaken with a hard arousal in his hand.

Also bothering Chance, Fancy reminded him

of someone; a woman he knew, or had known. Maybe a girl from his youth, maybe the first one he had ever slept with. They said a man never forgot that first one, but he was pretty sure his had been a whore, and a man never remembered them.

"Hey, Chance, how long are you gonna stand there starin' at them logs?" a cracked voice asked from the doorway of the cookhouse. "I can't keep your breakfast hot all day."

Chance turned around and looked at the wizened face of his cook, affection in his eyes. Old Zeb was more than a cook to him. He had been doctor, nurse, adviser, and countless other things over the years. He couldn't remember a time when the ex-sawyer hadn't been a part of his life.

Ten years ago, when the dreaded cry, "Whip the saw!" rang out everyone knew that a tree trunk was splitting. Men dropped axes and ran. The tree might not fall in the direction in which the sawyers had intended. And that had been the case then. On its way down the tree had hit another one, and the large trunk had whipped around as though it was a young sapling. When it finally lay still, the earth shuddering beneath it, Zeb lay on the ground, his legs pinned beneath one of the huge branches. When the men rushed forward, three of them lifting the tree limb off Jeb and two dragging him free of it, his left leg had been broken in two places. The nearest doctor was 50 miles away, and Chance's father had set the breaks the best way he could.

The leg had mended, but Zeb was left with a decided limp. His days of working timber were over. Seth Dawson had persuaded his longtime friend to become the camp cook.

When Chance walked into the cookhouse Zeb placed a plate of ham and eggs and fried potatoes on the table before him. "Looks like we're gonna have a nice clear day for a change," he said as he poured coffee into the cup at Chance's elbow.

"About time," Chance answered; then he dug into the plate of steaming food. It had rained off and on for the past three days.

Chance pushed his empty plate away, drank the last of his coffee, and stood up. "I'd better go check on the men down at the river. There was quite a logjam there earlier."

"I expect it's been broken up by now. You've got an experienced crew workin' for you."

Chance mumbled a reply. His attention had been caught by the man who had just walked out of Fancy's house. He recognized the big handsome fellow, carrying a basket, as the same one who had met and walked home with her a week before. His eyes widened in a stare when the man placed the wicker on the ground, pulled a wet dress from it, and carefully spread it over a rope that had been stretched between two trees.

As he watched, disbelieving, two more dresses followed, then a pair of men's drawers. A dark scowl came over Chance's face when delicate ladies' underwear was hung alongside them. As shirts and trousers joined the other articles of clothing, he looked at Zeb, a question in his eyes.

Zeb shrugged his shoulders. "I don't know who he is. All I know is that he came here with that pretty little Fancy girl. Keeps to himself, always stays around the house."

"He doesn't look sick or crippled. I wonder why he hasn't asked me for a job."

"Maybe he's just downright lazy. It don't seem to bother him that a woman is supportin' him. He sure is a handsome feller, ain't he?"

"Well, handsome or not, he's got no pride, that's for sure." Chance snorted his indignation. "You'd think he could see how beat Fancy is when she leaves that dance hall."

Zeb slid Chance an amused look from the corner of his eye. He'd never seen his young friend so riled up over a woman before. He turned his head away from Chance so the irate man wouldn't see the wide grin that tugged at his lips. It appeared that Chance Dawson had finally fallen for a woman—and had fallen hard.

Zeb managed to pull a semblance of sobriety to his face before responding to the muttered remark. "I agree," he said, "it ain't easy bein' a dancer, havin' your toes stepped on, makin' men keep their hands where they belong. But I reckon Fancy loves her man enough to do it. They seem awful fond of each other," he continued to jab at Chance. "He waits for her at the dance hall every mornin' and walks her home. They hug, and he keeps his arm around her as they walk along, with him talkin' forty to the hour."

"There's no figuring women," Chance said, disgruntled. "She's such a fiery little piece, I'd never in the world think that she would work so hard to support a big, strong, healthy man."

"I guess when the love bug hits a person it makes him do a lot of crazy things," Zeb said, sliding Chance another amused glance.

Chance gave a disgusted snort. "I doubt if love has anything to do with it." He stepped outside and started to walk away, then paused when he saw a horse and rider coming up the trail from the river. The stranger reined in beside the cookhouse and said to Zeb, "I'm lookin' for Chance Dawson."

"I'm Chance Dawson." Chance stepped forward. "What can I do for you?"

"Are you kin to Jason Landers?" the man asked.

Chance nodded, apprehension gripping him. What had Jason done now? he wondered before answering. "He's my stepbrother. Why do you ask?"

"I'm afraid I have some bad news for you."

Chance waited, his body tense.

"Landers and his wife drowned this morning, trying to cross flood waters down by Puget Sound."

The blood left Chance's face and his stomach clenched. He felt Zeb's supporting hand on his upper arm as he choked back the denial that sprang to his lips. It was impossible to believe that Jason's laughing and carefree face was stilled forever in death . . . and Mary, too, with her gentle ways.

He choked back the lump in his throat and managed to say, "They had a young son; is he gone also?"

The stranger shook his head. "He's all right. The way he tells it, the mare he was riding refused to go into the water, which was lucky for him. His ma and pa's mounts were caught in an undertow and were swept downstream. I'm sorry to tell you this, but it's doubtful their bodies will ever be found."

"How'd you know where to find Chance?" Zeb asked.

"One of the loggers in Al Bonner's camp recognized the Landers name and said he thought you were related to him." The man looked at Chance.

Chance pulled himself together and said, "I'll go get my nephew just as soon as I can saddle up."

"You'll find him at Al Bonner's camp, down near Puget Sound. Do you know where it is?"

Chance nodded and struck off running toward the shed where he kept his stallion.

The stranger turned to Zeb and asked, "Do you know where Fancy Cranson lives? The boy said she was his aunt, and that she was living in Dawson Camp."

"Yeah, she lives here." Zeb stared goggle-eyed at the stranger. "You say she's kin to the boy too?"

"Yes. The boy is all broken up about his parents and keeps crying for her."

"Fancy lives right over there in that little house." Zeb pointed to the one with the red curtains.